monsoonbooks

TWILIGHT IN KUTA

T0169095

David Nesbit settled insurance claims in the City before seeing the light and embarking on a year-long trip around Asia that changed his life, mostly for the better. Now, having lived in Indonesia for more than twenty years, Nesbit divides his time between educating the nation's youth as a teacher and writing Asia-based fiction and opinion pieces. *Twilight in Kuta* is his first novel.

TWILIGHT

IN KUTA

DAVID NESBIT

monsoon

monsoonbooks

Published in 2018
by Monsoon Books Ltd
www.monsoonbooks.co.uk

No.1 Duke of Windsor Suite, Burrough Court,
Burrough on the Hill, Leicestershire LE14 2QS, UK

ISBN (paperback): 978-1-912049-28-8
ISBN (ebook): 978-1-912049-29-5

Cover design by Cover Kitchen.

A Cataloguing-in-Publication data record is available from the British
Library.

Printed in Great Britain by Clays Ltd, St Ives plc
20 19 18   1 2 3 4 5

Prologue

Coffee Plus Café, Plaza Indonesia, Jakarta, 2006

We click the moment we meet. Of course, we've already been chatting for weeks online but this is our first date. I spot her as soon as I enter the café in Jakarta's Plaza Indonesia shopping mall. Her beaming smile ensures she will always stand out in a crowd.

Having lived in Indonesia for fifteen years, I am used to the kindly disposition of Indonesian girls but something about this particular girl has piqued my interest online. She wants to delve deeper than the others. She wants to know why a foreigner has been living in her country for so long. She can sense I am holding back in my answers to her questions and she is determined to get to the bottom of it.

She reaches across the table and takes my hands, right there in the café.

'Come on. Tell me. I can see it in your eyes,' she says kindly.

I try to stall her. 'Tell you what? What do you think you can see?'

She isn't to be deterred. 'I don't know exactly, but I can see something there. Some kind of pain. So, come on. What is it?'

Over the years I often wondered at what point *it* all began. Was it the day I left Europe for a round-the-world trip? Or was it when I found *her* in bed with the local *dukun* or 'medicine man'? Perhaps it was my fateful decision all those years ago to turn left rather than right upon entering the beach in Kuta, Bali? More pertinent and even more difficult to answer, what did '*it*' even refer to?

* * *

It was on Kuta Beach, Bali, in July 1990 that the very seeds of my life in Indonesia were planted.

People of a certain age and inclination will remember where they were and what they were doing at this time. No? Let me remind you. It was the height of the 1990 FIFA World Cup. Remember now? Italia '90, Gazza's tears, penalty shoot-outs, fat men singing opera.

I spent the majority of this tournament watching England manager Bobby Robson and his boys stumble their way to the semi-finals while I was travelling around Southeast Asia and, come the big day — the day of the World Cup final itself — I was to be found traipsing down to the beach in Kuta, which was then, as it is now, a big draw for tourists visiting the Indonesian island of Bali.

I had been on Bali for about a week and, apart from a couple of half-hearted day trips to slightly more salubrious locations, I had spent almost all that time either in cafés or on the aforementioned stretch of golden sand, spreading myself horizontally and taking in life on the beach. Hordes of visitors from Indonesia and overseas visit the three-mile-long stretch of sand on the southern tip of the island, making it an ideal place to doze away the hot afternoon hours whilst indulging in a spot of people-watching. And it was often me who was the object of interest. Countless Indonesians took it in turns to approach and wile away the time in conversation with me. Some wanted nothing more than to share a few words and have a photo taken with the strange looking *bule*, or white guy, while others would try to sell me something: clothes or souvenirs, occasionally girls.

It was following one such conversation that I became aware of a gaggle of local girls walking along the beach. They were grouped closely together and were wearing normal street clothes: t-shirts and jeans, rather than swimming attire. Students on a school trip, I imagined. They meandered past me a few times, with a couple of them glancing in my direction and whispering to each other before giggling and pointing me out to others in the group, who then repeated the process.

Amid plenty of pushing, nudging and elbowing, the group began to walk in my direction. I decided to continue to keep up my pretence of playing it cool until the gang was ten meters or so away. After all, I reasoned, it was better to make sure it was me they were actually coming over to.

Anyway, approach me they did, and we enjoyed an amiable, if limited, chat for a few minutes. Once I had posed for the obligatory pictures, the group began to wander off up the beach in search of further examples of this strange *bule* tribe.

All except her, that is. She stayed.

She told me her name was Yossy and that she was twenty years old, two years younger than me, and that she was at university studying English literature. She was indeed, she explained, on a school break with her friends and the next day would be heading back to a city called Surabaya on the neighbouring island of Java.

She was not especially sexy, but she had a certain something about her, physically. Although not a giant, I still towered over Yossy, who was tiny in comparison and couldn't have been as tall as five foot. In addition, she probably weighed no more than a hundred pounds soaking wet and yet still she couldn't exactly be described as petite.

As she spoke, I was taken in by her manner. It was bewitching in a way I hadn't encountered before. She had a way of speaking through her eyelashes whereby she would tilt her head slightly downwards while glancing up through her long lashes, as if gauging my response. She spoke softly in good, yet not perfect, English with a rising intonation, which made each sentence sound like a question, and weirdly I found myself feeling drawn in by this funny, articulate and friendly young lady.

She asked me what I thought of her country, and rather than reply in the glib non-committal manner I had employed with most others who'd asked me that, I actually told her what I really thought.

'It seems nice, but I don't really understand the people,' I said.

'How so?' she enquired.

I told her that although everybody seemed to be forever smiling, it was hard to know if they were being genuine or if they just wanted something from me.

She smiled and said: 'Most of them probably do want

something, you know.'

Yossy then explained how her country was still very poor and a lot of people just lived day-to-day if not quite hand-to-mouth.

'We see someone and we make friends easily, then we move on easily too,' she explained. 'We are friendly but we don't let anyone too close to us, and when we meet new people, especially *bule*, we kind of see if there is any benefit or advantage we can get from them.'

'That's awful,' I countered. Yossy looked up through her eyelashes at me and continued.

'No, not really. We don't try and rob or steal or cheat, we just believe that people come into our lives for a purpose. There is a reason for everything that happens.'

Whilst I was not exactly convinced of her philosophy, I found it to be an interesting one; the concept that we go through life taking what we can from each person and then moving on to the next one as if we are nothing more than glorified worker bees perhaps sounds a bit cynical, but probably does contain more than a grain of truth.

We were so engrossed in our conversation we almost missed the world-famous Kuta Beach sunset. It really is a sight to behold with a glorious array of colours producing both a hue and shifting shadows that transports you into Beatles' *Yellow Submarine* animation. In fact, Yossy told me the whole purpose of her group's afternoon excursion to the beach was to experience the sunset and instead she had 'wasted her time' talking to me.

Charming, I thought.

Then I saw her grinning through her eyelashes again, and I

realized she'd been having me on.

'Ha, I think you are a mysterious boy,' she mocked.

'Mysterious? In what way?' I queried.

'Ah, I dunno, kok. Just mysterious. Come on, we have to go back to our hotel now. You can walk back with us if you like.'

As twilight fell on Kuta Beach, Yossy and I rejoined her friends, who were hovering at the entrance to the beach waiting for us, and who subjected Yossy to some good-natured teasing. Yossy affected to be faux-angry at something one of her friends said to her and pretended to storm off for a minute or two before coming back to the group.

We stopped at the small place she and her friends were staying at. I remarked that it didn't look much like a hotel to me and she explained it was a *kost*, or boarding house. As her friends finished saying their goodbyes to me and drifted inside, Yossy and I continued to chat outside.

I knew the time for us to part was fast approaching, and I actually found myself starting to develop a bit of a lump in the throat. I had found this small, friendly girl very beguiling and I didn't want to say goodbye just yet. We stood there and kind of looked at each other and although it would have sounded crazy had either one of us said it out loud, I think we both knew that this was the start of something and not the end.

As I walked back to my own hotel a few minutes later, all thoughts of watching the FIFA World Cup final had evaporated. I dug my fingers into my pocket and wrapped them round the piece of paper on which Yossy had written her name and address. This was all I could think about now.

*   *   *

Jakarta, 2006

Back in the café my new date listens to me, never interrupting, never judging, just listening. I unburden myself and for the first time in many years I begin to feel liberated: I begin to believe I am alive again. I speak honestly and openly and without embarrassment. When, after two hours, I finally come to the end of the story of my life in Indonesia, she leans over to me.

'Until now? That's how things are at present?' she asks.

'Yes,' I reply. 'Pretty much. But I don't care anymore.'

She takes my hands again and looks directly into my eyes. Her stare penetrates deep into my soul and she waits for an age before saying, 'Yes, you do. You do care, but don't worry.'

'Why not?' I say, almost in a whisper, my voice choking and tears not far away.

She holds my hands, eyes and heart all at the same time.

'Because I will save you.'

And I believe her.

My name is Neil and this is my story.

Neil's Story

Surabaya, 1995

Those were the happiest days of my life, and, what's more, I knew it at the time.

Usually people look back on certain periods in their life and think, yep, those were the best days of my life. Not me. I was aware that I was living them right there and then.

The year was 1995 and I was living in Surabaya, on the island of Java in Indonesia. Yossy and I had been married for a couple of years and I was madly, swimmingly, incredibly and, no doubt very annoyingly, happy.

Oh sure, I could have had more. We all could, right? We could all have more money or more friends or more fun or more something.

But more happiness, more contentment, more feeling of being alive?

Nope, not I. I was living the dream. I had it all.

I was on top of the world.

Yossy and I had started corresponding a few months after I returned to England in 1990. The letters started off friendly enough but rather inconsequentially, rather inconsistent too, in the beginning, maybe once every couple of months. (No email or Internet then, remember.)

As time went by, slowly the letters seemed to have more meaning for both of us. I started to reply to ones from her a bit quicker and I started to look out for hers. Photos were exchanged, and the letters became more personal, less 'how are you and what are you doing?' and more intimate. We shared problems, ideas, hopes and feelings.

We became closer. We became friends.

Finally, in 1992, two years after my first visit to Bali, two years after the World Cup, I decided to make a second tip to Indonesia, this time specifically to visit Yossy in Surabaya.

Our three weeks spent in east Java together were blissful, full of long walks and talks, romantic star-gazing and declarations of undying love and commitment, and we made the decision to permanently seal the deal, as it were, in a further twelve months or so.

When I returned to England I expected to encounter at least some resistance from friends and family when I told them what I was planning. I thought someone would call me crazy and try and talk me out of giving up my life in England and moving to the other side of the world, seemingly at a whim, yet nobody did. I like to tell myself it was because everyone could see the determination in my eyes and that they knew my mind was made up. However, a small part of me fears they were probably just glad to see the back of me.

The months apart dragged on and were the most miserable of my life. We kept in touch by snail mail, of course, and by twice-monthly phone calls, but those were dark and desperate times all right. I missed Yossy so much and although I knew it was only a matter of months until we would be together again, that winter was bleak, to say the least.

I became a bit of a hermit, and although I didn't totally cut myself off from my friends and family, I found myself spending more and more time on my own. This was partly because I didn't much feel like going out, but mostly because I was trying to save money.

One thing I did do during those cold and dark months, though, was to make a serious commitment to learn Indonesian.

Although a variety of teachers at secondary school had spent five years trying to beat into me the vocabulary necessary to be able to ask for directions to the supermarket in French, I had never been particularly gifted at learning languages. In the typically arrogant British manner, I had always assumed if any of these funny-foreigner-types wanted to speak to me, well, they'd just have to learn English, wouldn't they? Now however, I broke the habit of a lifetime and spent many a long and lonely night with my head stuck in Linguaphone correspondence learning coursebooks.

To my surprise, I actually didn't find it too difficult to learn the basics. Compared to English, Indonesian is a reasonably straightforward language. Verbs do not change their form to signify the different tenses as they do in English, and there is also considerably less vocabulary in general. The whole language seems structured on the principle that 'less is more' and that people can work out from context the timeframe of events without having to change everything around all the time.

For example, the word for 'eat' in Indonesian is *makan*, and this one word is used in pretty much all contexts. Whereas in English we might say: *I eat, ate, have eaten, will eat, had eaten, am eating, will be eating, was eating, had been eating* and so on and so forth, in Indonesian '*Saya makan*' (I eat) covers it all.

Anyway, time rolled on, albeit slower and more miserably than I ever thought possible, and eventually the time came for me to depart the UK for Indonesia. If I thought the weeks and months apart from Yossy had been upsetting, they weren't a patch on my final weeks in England. Talk about mixed feelings! I had so many goodbyes and farewell parties to get through I thought I was going to explode: work colleagues, friends, neighbours, Saturday football club teammates, Sunday football club teammates, more friends, and finally, most heartbreakingly, my family.

Saying goodbye to my mum, brother and sister at Heathrow Airport and not knowing when, or even if, I would see them again nearly finished me off. All of us hugged each other. Trying to be brave and not be the one to break down was just so unbearably sad.

All I could do was hang onto my mum and whisper how much I loved her.

'I am so sorry to leave you, Mum,' I said, choking back the tears. 'But I have to go, Mum, I have to. I just can't live without Yossy. I'm so very, very sorry.'

My mum just held me. She couldn't speak. When, after an

age, she finally did, she said, 'I know, son. I know. Just make sure you always love her right.'

As we broke apart the last words she said to me were, 'Son, be happy always. I love you.'

So, by 1995, I *was* happy. Just as I promised my mum I would do, I loved Yossy right, and we were enjoying life together. I loved life in Indonesia and I seemed to settle really quickly. Of course, things were different and I had to get used to a different culture and ways of doing things, but I seemed to fit right in with no problems, and whenever something did crop up that threatened to vex me a little, I had Yoss there by my side to support me.

Surabaya is a coastal city on the east side of Java. It is the second biggest city in Indonesia after the capital, Jakarta, and has a population of approximately four million in its provinces. Unlike Jakarta, there is still a heavy reminder of the Dutch colonial period in certain parts of the city and many town houses in the Jembatan Merah area of the city built by the Dutch masters date back to the mid nineteenth century.

Jembatan Merah translates as Red Bridge and it is named so in order to commemorate those who fell in the 1945 Battle of Surabaya. The British army really did a number on the indigenous population of Surabaya over a period of three days and bombed them to the edge of oblivion. This was in retaliation for the murder of Brigadier Mallaby, who had been in Surabaya at the time allegedly trying to broker a peace agreement between the locals and the Dutch army.

Up until 1942, when they were pushed out by the invading

Japanese, the Dutch had colonized Indonesia for more than three hundred and fifty years, and in 1945, at the end of the war following Japan's recapitulation and retreat, the locals wanted independence.

The British came from Singapore in order to try and facilitate a handover of power to the indigenous people, but for some unknown reason someone killed the brigadier in charge. The British were not amused and gave the locals twenty-four hours in which to give up those responsible or else the whole city would pay the consequences.

Twenty-four hours later, with nobody coming forward or being given up by others, that is exactly what happened. The British went a tad over the top, it must be said, and proceeded to bomb the hell out of the city, killing tens of thousands of people. A particularly brutal battle took place on a bridge over the city's river and was fought with such ferocity that it was said blood could be seen dripping into the river from the bridge for days afterwards: hence the rechristening of the bridge 'Jembatan Merah'.

Surabaya is hardly a cosmopolitan city now, and back in 1993 when I came to live there it was even less of one. It was relatively strange to see an expatriate in the city's malls or cinemas, and so whenever Yossy and I ventured out at the weekend we would be accosted by groups of people staring at us. This didn't really bother me much, in fact I found the novelty of it slightly amusing if anything. Yossy, however, was usually far from amused!

We spoke about this phenomenon on occasion and Yoss told me that the reasons people paid us so much attention when we were out together were mixed. Some, she said, were genuinely interested because they had not seen a real-life westerner; others were jealous because for some a 'white boyfriend' was a status symbol; while yet more were judging us.

Yossy reckoned that some people, especially older ones, were probably thinking that I was just like those mean white guys on TV shows like 'Beverly Hills 90210' and was almost certainly a playboy, while others would be judging her as a *'gadis nakal'*, a naughty or promiscuous girl.

I told her to just ignore the stares and the whispers, as it wasn't worth getting upset by them. In return she told me that I might enjoy all the attention now but I had to be careful because not only would being stared at and being talked about get old quickly, but it also had the potential to cause problems further down the line.

'You'll see, Neil,' she told me. 'Everyone is talking about you now and you're their favourite, but just wait and see how quickly people here can turn on you if you give them the slightest chance.'

I worked as an English teacher in a small institution of further education in the west of Surabaya. It was ostensibly a secretarial academy, whereby young ladies who'd just left school would come and spend six months training to be secretaries, but in reality it was little more than a 'time-fill' course which did little if anything to educate or prepare them for any possible employment. The students were taught typing as well as basic computer skills and other bits and bobs that were supposedly going to help them get jobs in offices, and it was my job to 'teach' them English.

You will note the usage of inverted commas there as in

actuality my teaching comprised of little more than providing bits and pieces of English vocabulary and then encouraging discussions or role-plays in English. Although the job itself paid peanuts, the school provided me with a work visa and other related documents, and didn't take up too much of my time, so I was able to supplement my meagre income by offering private English lessons to individuals and, more lucratively, to companies and businesses.

This private work, although technically illegal by the terms of my work visa, necessitated I travel around the city going from place to place. As money was tight, the preferred mode of travel was almost always public transportation, and, boy, this was an eye-opener for someone used to a provincial British transport system.

Buses were antiquated converted trucks. If you were ever unfortunate enough to go to a First Division football match in England in the 1970s you'll be familiar with the experience. These buses were full to overflowing. People were squashed into every available cavity and if you had to stand you would often find your feet would be off the ground. There were no timetables or schedules, and a bus would simply leave the terminal when it was full to the rafters and not before. This meant if you wanted to get on the bus en-route it was almost impossible and so the only bearable way of travelling by bus was to go to the terminal first. People would actually choose to travel ten miles in the opposite direction so they could arrive at the terminal and at least try and start the journey in some semblance of comfort.

The bus would then leave the terminal at a healthy lick, and gradually get faster and faster throughout the journey. The doors would be wedged open, meaning those standing at the front and back of the vehicle would be holding on for dear life. (I'm not joking either, as on more than one occasion I saw people lose their grip and go flying off the bus as it rounded a corner too fast.) On every journey, approximately ten minutes after leaving the terminal, a conductor would come round to take the fare. How, you might wonder, could anyone possibly make their way through such a solid mass of humanity and collect money. Well, amazingly, it somehow proved possible each time. The conductor was usually a small and lithe guy who would slide between passengers, past them, by them, over them, under them and seemingly through them and manage to collect his fares before the bus reached the city and passengers started to disembark.

Back to my job, and even in the private sector, teaching was really pretty simple and straightforward as long as adequate preparation was done, although the hours were long. I usually left home early in the morning and didn't get back until late at night. This meant I was usually in a state of permanent exhaustion, and to tell the truth I soon found I could lie down and go to sleep at any point of the day, given the chance. That couldn't have been too good for my health.

Still, no major problem there. I was still young, just turned twenty-seven, and together Yossy and I were busy saving like crazy. Our immediate plan was to have enough money to buy a car to help with the tiredness factor so I wouldn't need to travel everywhere by public transport.

We lived in Sidoarjo, a small hamlet about fifteen miles

or so outside of Surabaya city. Our home was a simple three-bedroomed, one-storey place that we were renting while we tried to save up for a mortgage. It was in a clean and tidy housing complex, and although most of the neighbours couldn't speak English, I was welcomed into the neighbourhood.

Although the norm in Indonesia is for even the most average of middle-class families to hire a full-time maid, or housekeeper, Yossy and I didn't bother. We were both out working most of the day and so the house didn't really get untidy, and we would send our clothes to the laundry and do any cleaning at the weekend.

All of this enabled us to live very self-contained lives together and some people might have ventured that we lived too much in each other's pockets. Neither one of us really had any close friends, although I was probably guiltier of this than she was. Neither Sidoarjo nor even Surabaya had anything of an expatriate community to speak of, and so the only people I came into contact with were those I met through my work. I didn't mind, though, as most of the time I was working, travelling to work or trying to get what rest I could.

We would normally try and leave the house together at around 6 am and travel into work in Surabaya by public transport. Now, as I said, this was not an experience for the faint-hearted, but once we had negotiated it our day would begin in earnest. Yossy would disembark from the bus on the slip road that led to the airport, and I would continue on into Surabaya proper, arriving at the so-called Secretary Academy in time for a 7:30 start. The early morning starts were no real issue for me as I'd been used to waking up early back in the dark days of working in England, but what I never really got used to was the heat. Even that early in the day I found myself sweating profusely after the slightest exertion, and so I learnt to wear light clothes to work and to change into more formal teaching attire once I arrived.

At the academy – I use that word loosely – I would invariably only have a couple of lessons in the morning and then I would be free to go off chasing the big(ger) bucks. I would normally hang around at the school for a while and take advantage of the air-conditioning for as long as possible (not to mention the photocopying facilities for the materials I needed for my private lessons) and then head out into the midday sun for the journey to the first in a succession of short hops around the city. I mainly taught in offices, but also had some work to do in people's houses and even in other schools. This last scenario was a bit risky, as I was only supposed to teach in one school as per immigration rules and regulations, so I didn't make a habit of it.

After work I would normally leave Surabaya around 9pm and make my way back to Sidoarjo, arriving home around an hour or so later. Sometimes, though, and these really were the best of times, Yossy would come to wherever my final lesson of the day was and pick me up when I finished.

Typically on days such as these I'd be teaching after hours in an office and when I'd finished I would find Yossy in the reception waiting for me. On those days I was so proud of her, and so proud to introduce her to people as my wife. I was always delighted to see her and to be given the chance to show her off to my students. Although not conventionally beautiful, Yoss had a way about her, you see. She had a lovely radiant smile and a charming manner

– sweet and welcoming, always friendly, and yet a tiny bit naïve also. She made friends easily and got on well with everyone she met, and yet at times I still couldn't really reconcile how or why she would want to be with me. This wasn't me being falsely modest or self-depreciating, it really was something that kept me pondering. I mean, as well as being my wife, soulmate and best friend, Yossy was also the smartest person I knew.

On nights such as these we'd normally head to the cinema or for a simple dinner somewhere and unwind. Despite the hour or so it had taken Yossy to travel into town to meet me on top of a full day's work, she never once complained of being tired. As for me, well my tiredness would always just melt away upon seeing her and, anyway, a little tiredness was a small price to pay for what I had.

I just couldn't believe my luck and good fortune with the way things worked out. I knew I was taking a bit of a risk when I came out here to live in May of 1993, and things for the first few months weren't exactly plain sailing, but after two years or so I really did feel blessed at how life was panning out.

We all have our little foibles and worries, don't we? And for a long time my fear, if you can call it that, was that I was destined to be a 'nice guy who'll make someone a good boyfriend or husband one day' without ever actually managing to do so. Oh, don't get me wrong, I wasn't unhappy when I lived in England or a loner, or anything. I just had an unexplainable feeling that for some reason I was never going to really fall in love, and in all probability would be one of these unlucky sods that never really ends up with anyone.

Yossy changed all that. She was my world and all I ever dreamt of and certainly far more than I ever dared to hope for. Every minute I was at work and away from her I was thinking of her, or talking about her to someone (usually my long-suffering students or colleagues in the school).

Looking back now, I just can't really reconcile the person I was then with the man I am today. I can't believe that I am the same person, or, more importantly, that Yossy is the same woman. Looking back now it seems like those days were all a dream or a film and they bear no similarity to the reality of life. In comparison to what things were to become and are now, I can see that back then we were just playing at life and that everything was just an illusion.

When things first went wrong, and for a long time afterwards, I would look back on this period of my life and feel immense pain, regret and heartbreak. I felt a pining and a yearning for what I had lost: for what I'd had in my hands and allowed to slip through my fingers. Soon I realized, though, that I had never really had what I thought I had, and that nothing back then was real.

Now I am older, whenever I find my mind drifting back to this stage in my life, I'm able to hold myself in check and pull myself out of my reverie before things get too maudlin.

Now, all these years later, I can honestly say I feel nothing at all one way or another concerning those years – apart from a tinge of sadness because I don't feel anything, that is.

However, back then Yossy was always there for me.

In the summer of 1995 we took a short holiday to Bali together. This was the first time we'd been back to Bali since we met there five years earlier and in a nod to the past, we decided to stay at the hotel I had stayed in back in 1990 – a place called the Melasti.

Many years later this hotel was to gain notoriety for its role in the story of the 'Bali Nine' – a gang of nine young Australians who got involved in a drug smuggling ring. Evidently the Bali police, acting on a tip-off from the Australian Federal Police, became aware of a plot to smuggle heroin through Bali and onto Sydney. As a result the Bali police staked out the Melasti where some of 'The Nine' were staying and then arrested the entire gang at the airport as they attempted to depart to Australia with the drugs strapped to their bodies. Ultimately, charges were brought, sentences were handed down and two of the nine were finally executed with the rest being sentenced to between twenty years and life in jail.

However, back on that summer holiday of ours in 1995 drugs were the furthest thing from our minds and Yossy and I were still every bit as much in love as we'd ever been. We woke early most days and then walked around the open-air clothes markets where Yossy would engage in friendly haggling with the proprietors. Whilst I would either pay whatever exorbitant price I was first quoted, or haggle perhaps a five percent discount, Yossy had the ability (and the guile) to be able to secure absolute bargains at rock-bottom prices. She would charm, joke and smile her way into the hearts of the sellers so much that by the time a deal was finally struck she had them practically giving her their goods, and happy to do so to boot. I would be worrying that her stringent haggling was going to end up causing bad feeling, but I needn't have worried because she had such a way about her back then that all and sundry in her presence couldn't help but be charmed and feel that they were the most important person in her orbit.

Following breakfast, we would head back to the hotel for a while before setting out on a day-trip somewhere. Unlike my first visit to Bali, this wasn't a holiday spent lying on the beach. Amongst the places we visited was Ubud, where we went to see the Puri Sareng Agung, a large palace used and owned by the last monarch of Ubud. Ubud itself is the creative and artistic hub of Bali. Previously a totally remote and undiscovered location, it first became popular in the 1930s due to its seclusion and breathtaking beauty. Early visitors to Ubud included such luminaries as Rudolf Bonnet, Noël Coward, Charlie Chaplain and H.G. Wells. Nowadays it is still a relatively quiet and peaceful place, with only a few cafés and simple boarding houses. It is still considered somewhat of a retreat for artists and those wishing to spend time away and rediscover themselves. Indeed, it provided the backdrop for the Balinese section of the book *Eat, Pray, Love* and the film of the same name.

Well, although I probably didn't do as much praying as I should have, Yossy and I certainly did our fair share of eating and loving during that week. We spent time cycling in the mountains during the day, and making love during the evenings.

They were the purest, simplest, sweetest, happiest of days.

We were blessed.

When we first got married, Yossy worked at the airport for Mandala Airlines, a local company. It was a good job and rather a prestigious one in local circles. To be accepted one had to undergo a rigorous selection process and then a lengthy training programme. She was often as tired as I was, but still she found time for me.

She worked in the office and at the check-in counter and it was a job she did for about three years and, although she seemed to enjoy it, she began to get a small case of itchy feet. Although I was no doubt somewhat biased, I did believe Yossy had the intelligence and work ethic to do pretty much whatever she wanted in life, and the world of Mandala Airlines didn't really seem to offer up that much in the way of long-term possibilities.

After applying for several new jobs, she procured an interview at a company called PT. Bali Party.

Yossy's interview went well and she was offered the position of trainee sales executive at PT. Bali Party. She started work there and, following a week's training in Jakarta, spent some time finding her feet in the regional office in Surabaya.

As far as I could tell, it was a kind of timeshare company, selling holidays to customers for a fixed period of time each year. As the name of the business suggested, the properties being rented out were all in Bali, and so having fallen in love with the island, it seemed natural for her to want to have some sort of connection with the place. An additional attraction was the fact that amongst the perks of the job was the opportunity to have an annual, all-expenses paid stay at one of the company's properties in Bali

It was, of course, somewhat different from her job at the airlines, but she soon got into the swing of things and started enjoying it. It was good to see her full of life again after having become a bit down in her last few months at Mandala Airlines. The colour was back in her cheeks once more, and she was soon bubbling away and in a state of seemingly permanent hyperactivity.

I remember one slight worry I had about her taking on a new job was the selfish one that it might take up more of her time and she might start to leave me behind in life, so to speak. However, I needn't have worried as if anything her new job and her new zest for life brought us even closer together.

Barely an hour went by without her calling me wherever I happened to be teaching so she could give me an update on what she was up to and what was happening in the intricate world of timeshare selling. It was great to see her so happy and that happiness just rubbed off on me and the two of us as a couple.

I remember after a month or so of working at Bali Party she phoned me at work one day and asked for my permission to go out with her friends that night. How about that? *Asked for my permission*. Although times are changing, in Indonesia the woman still somewhat defers to the man in a marriage and 'permission' has to be sought for pretty much even the slightest deviance from the daily routine.

Needless to say, permission was duly granted.

That night, as it happened, I managed to finish work at a reasonable hour and I called Yossy. She was, as usual, delighted at this turn of events and asked me to accompany her and her new friends. Not being the most naturally gregarious of people, I was a bit reluctant at first but she soon talked me round and so I reluctantly agreed to tag along.

As things turned out it was quite an enjoyable evening in the end. We all met up at Yossy's office and I found myself being subjected to a long round of introductions to her friends; a group of perhaps ten or so people, all in their early to mid twenties, and evenly split gender wise. They all seemed genuinely pleased to meet me and the look in Yossy's eye told me she was more than happy at this coming together. That was the wonderful thing about her: she always seemed to really be proud of me and to want to 'show me off' to people. At first I found it all a bit disconcerting and even a bit patronizing at times to tell the truth, as being an insecure sort I used to suspect ulterior motives of some kind. Quite what I was worried about, I am not sure, but in the beginning being paraded around, as I called it, felt uncomfortable to say the least. However, after a while I realized that this was just Yossy's way and she really did merely wish for me to be happy and by her side always.

It was humbling to feel so loved.

Back to the night in question, and I was struck by how well-spoken and sophisticated all her friends seemed to be. They were all immaculately dressed, spoke fluent English and carried themselves in the way that successful, confident young professionals do.

The only slightly confusing part of this initial meeting was the way they all individually either asked permission to accompany Yossy and I, or else thanked me for inviting them. One by one they took the opportunity to sidle up to me and uttered a version of the following, 'Hey, Neil. Thanks for inviting me. Are you sure it's OK if I join you guys tonight? Yes? Well, thanks a lot, then.'

I was a bit perplexed to tell the truth, because as far as I knew we hadn't actually invited anyone and it was nothing more than a night out together, so when we were together in the cab heading up to a small club in the south of the city I took the opportunity to ask her about this.

'Don't worry, hon,' she said, 'they are just being polite.'

When we reached the club it was pretty dark and there was a live band gently playing melodic rock. Finding some tables a little way back from the stage, and slightly tucked away, totally suited me because one thing that living in Indonesia had taught me was that a lone *bule* in the audience at an event, or amongst the guests at a gathering, would often be picked on by the MC or whoever was performing. This would lead to the poor sap either being asked to come on stage to introduce himself or else to sit and suffer while the guy entertained himself and everyone else present at his expense. With this in mind, a place in the shadows suited me just fine, thanks.

We all ordered some food and watched the group strutting their stuff. I don't know what I was expecting from either the group or the evening in general, but both were really not bad actually and I found myself relaxing and having a thoroughly pleasant time. After a couple of hours I realized I had to be up early the next day and so I suggested to Yossy it was time to start thinking about making a move.

As the bill was being prepared, I started to get my wallet out to pay for my and Yossy's share, but she stopped me, saying she would take care of it.

'We all pooled our money in the office before we left.' she told me, 'I'll use that.'

Who was I to argue, thought I, and finished up my drink.

On the pavement outside the club a discussion took place about whether or not to go onto a 'real' club or else call it a night. It turned out that the club in question was a place called Limelights. Evidently it was notorious for being a sort of rave club.

At the somewhat ancient age of 27, I felt that was the sort of place that deserved to stay in the darkest recesses of my memory and be left there. I could see Yossy wanted to tag along, though, and, after a bit of persuasion from me, she headed off into the night with her friends while I took a cab home.

Looking back, that night may well have been the catalyst for what was to follow, but for now I had to negotiate my way home in a taxi. Taking a taxi in Indonesia was a whole new ball game to anything I'd ever experienced back home. The roads were absolutely flooded with them, for a start, and everywhere you looked dozens would be out on the street at any one time. If I happened to walk any distance further than a hundred metres or so, I could be sure I would be accosted by up to half a dozen drivers of the blessed things, all beeping their horns and competing for my patronage.

The thing is, though, that practically every taxi company was nothing more than a bucket shop. Almost all the companies were the same in that their fleet of vehicles were totally decrepit and barely moved over twenty miles an hour; any AC the contraption ever possessed had long given up the ghost; there were no seat belts; the windows wouldn't wind down, and ultimately the drivers were incompetent at best and downright crooked at worst.

It was impossible to take a simple journey without having to play the 'taxi game' described thus: firstly the passenger would hail a taxi, climb in and tell the driver where he or she wished to be taken. The driver would then state a price – usually exorbitant and three times what the meter would read if used for such a journey – and the passenger would then invariably either try to haggle the price down or try to insist the driver use the meter. A request for the latter would now be countered by the taxi driver informing the hapless passenger that said item was *'rusak'* or broken. At which point any passenger with the slightest nous about them would make to get out of the taxi only for the 'taxi-pixies' to magically fix the meter just in time to prevent this being necessary.

So, after one fairly transparent effort to defraud or extort the passenger had failed, the sap would embark on his journey. What would follow would invariably be the world famous trick of taking the longest route possible due to *'macet'* or 'bad traffic' or even *'maaf, aku hilang'*. Sorry, I'm lost. This particular rouse of course, is in no way unique to Indonesia.

However, the intrepid Indonesian taxi driver does indeed carry a few more original tricks up his sleeve. One is to switch the meter off a hundred meters or so before the destination is reached in the hope that the passenger hasn't been paying attention and he can then overcharge him exorbitantly upon arrival, while another trick is to absolutely totally never have any change whatsoever. This is done in the hope that a passenger will simply hand over a large denomination note and tell him to keep the change. If the passenger does not do this then the driver will, very reluctantly, take the note and walk as slowly as is humanely possible around the immediate vicinity 'trying' to find a roadside kiosk or small shop that can provide the necessary *'uang kecil'* small money. Invariably, though, the driver will eventually report back to the passenger, who has been waiting in the vehicle all this time, that he has been unable to find anyone to break the large note, and so the game continues.

Surabaya, November 1995

Months rolled by and Yossy became busier with her job. She worked almost as many hours as I did and when she arrived home she was often exhausted and out on her feet. She still loved Bali Party and her friends there and seemed to be developing quite a tight group with half a dozen or so of the more outgoing and flamboyant set. I am not sure if I have got all their names correct here, but from memory there was a guy called Ari, his girlfriend, Yuni, another girl called Reina, a chap whose name escapes me, and finally a bloke called Satria. Evidently they all worked in the same department and formed a kind of 'Dream Team' designed to chase new clients. It all seemed a bit complicated and, although interested, I found it all a bit difficult to follow at times.

Yossy certainly seemed to be cut out for the job though. She had patience and an inherent kindness, which meant she was willing and able to assist her less able friends and colleagues with help and advice, if necessary even by telephone after she had finally returned home late into the night.

For my part I was still working hard doing what I did. Business was good and I was earning considerably more money than before. I had started doing a lot of private teaching and so was spending most of my days running around the city from place to place wherever there was a job on.

As a result, we were able to start saving quite a lot of money and earmarked the New Year as the time to buy a car, and after that the plan was to crack on and save for the deposit on a house. That, as I told Yossy, was an investment for the future and was better than renting, which we had been doing since we got married and which, although cheap, I considered to be lost money.

Although I did have my own bank account and Yossy and I had a joint one, she was the one who handled all the money. That's the way we both decided we wanted it from the beginning as she could deal with all the bureaucratic nonsense while I played the dumb foreigner. A role I came to play all too well.

I must admit it was a role I enjoyed playing back then, though. Although able to speak basic Indonesian, having studied it fairly intensively in the year before I came out here, it sometimes played well to not let on I could understand much of what was going on and so be able to eavesdrop on what people were saying. It also enabled me to have a ready-made excuse for not doing the awkward and annoying little things I didn't want to do.

Anyway, Yossy was happy to look after the finances. She paid all the bills and sorted out all the things such as savings, payments, utility bills and the like. I really couldn't be bothered with all of that sort of stuff.

Then one day, all of a sudden, Yossy left Bali Party.

It all went wrong in a blink of an eye and I felt so sorry for her when it did. She was simply devastated and couldn't stop crying. It broke my heart to see her so down and I wished there was something I could do to put things right. I was just grateful that she had such good friends helping her so much and being so supportive.

In a way, I guess it could be said that my insistence she look after our money was to blame for what happened. In January of 1996 we finally decided to splash out and buy a car. We went to the local Toyota dealer who gave us a good deal on a Kijang. Cars in Indonesia are very expensive in real terms and ours was no exception, with a ten million rupiah down payment and monthly instalments of about a million and a half rupiah for three years. So, all told it made a bit of a dent in our savings and there was a small monthly burden to consider too, but taking into consideration the amount we were both earning, it was nothing for us to worry about.

As it happened, a couple of days before the end of the month I gave Yossy the money as normal to go and pay the monthly instalment wherever she made it (I really should have known where this was, but I didn't) and arranged to come to her office to pick her up at around 10pm as normal. When I got there, instead of the receptionist asking me to take a seat while she called Yossy, as was normal practice, she ushered me straight through. I thought this was a bit weird but didn't really think too much of it until I caught sight of Yoss.

She was in floods of tears and was being comforted by Satria.

I took her in my arms and slowly, through her sobs, the story unfolded. It seems she put the money in her handbag which she left under her chair at some point in the day, and then when she went back to it later ... well, I think you are ahead of me here.

There was no other possibility than the fact that one of her colleagues had stolen the money. She was, understandably, devastated to think that one of her so-called friends could do that to her and so was I.

We decided there and then that she couldn't work there anymore and she quit on the spot. I personally phoned her manager in Jakarta and explained what had happened and why Yoss would be leaving with immediate effect.

Following that, my poor wife spent the next two months staying at home moping. I suggested that we should use the break to visit my family in England, as it had been almost three years since I was last there and they were yet to meet Yoss, but she seemed too despondent to think about anything other than the fact that one of her friends was a thief.

While I continued working all over the city, she spent her days at home consoling herself with phone calls and visits from her friends. She explained to me many times that she felt too heartbroken to trust anyone again for a long time and all she wanted to do was to try and forget the whole experience of Bali Party. Whilst I sympathized with her and the pain she was quite evidently going through, I couldn't help but feel she would be able to put things behind her a bit quicker and truly move on if she didn't spend so much time talking to her former colleagues on the phone or meeting up with them for lunch. After all, I reasoned, one of them had stolen her money and as the thief had never been caught, and certainly had never owned up to it, for all she knew she could have been talking to him or her every day.

Throughout this painful time I remained there for her always. I did my best to get home quicker than I had previously, and I made a point of calling her from wherever I happened to be working at least two or three times a day. It helped that I was now mostly teaching English in offices in the business sector of Surabaya as it meant I could avail myself of telephone facilities a bit easier and so call Yoss at set times each day.

Yossy's spell on the sidelines dragged on for another couple of months and then something happened, or rather, I discovered something that had been happening for months, and I was cut to the very quick. In a blink of an eye the very soul and essence of my existence and being was dragged kicking and screaming out of me, leaving me an incomprehensible mess and a mere shadow of the man I had always considered myself to be.

When I first discovered what had been going on it felt every bit as painful as if she'd been having an affair. The betrayal and hurt was such that at times I truly thought I would die and on many occasions I just couldn't breathe, I really couldn't, and I would go into this kind of hyperventilating state of flux doubled over with my hands on my hips and my cheeks puffing out in the manner of an exhausted marathon runner.

It was not so much what had happened that was having this affect on me, more the realisation of what was *not* happening; namely, my life was not what I thought it was.

The sense of wellness and peaceful existence I was feeling previously was been shown up for what it was in reality all along: self-congratulatory, naive, stupid smugness.

Even now I can't believe I was so ridiculously, gormlessly, half-wittedly trusting and blind. Well, never again, that's all I can say. Never again am I going to be taken for a fool in that way. Never again am I just going to believe what she, or anyone else for that matter, says to me.

God, how could I have been so stupid?

There I was doe-eyeingly accepting everything she told me, never once questioning her, never once asking anything or raising any point, just wilfully accepting the *fact* that she was paying all our money into the bank, had been paying into the bank steadily over the past three years, when all the time she was doing nothing of the sort.

Actually, I have no idea, and no way of knowing now as I am sure she won't ever tell me now, if she ever put any of our money in the bank in those three years, or if she had originally done so and then simply used it up over the few months she was at Bali Party and the immediate aftermath.

All I know is instead of the supposed 30 million rupiah, or almost ten grand, she told me was in our account we actually had precisely bugger-all.

Not a brass farthing. Nothing. Nix. Nada.

What hurt more than being completely skint, at least what I think hurt more – it's difficult to tell- was the three years of lies. Where was the truth, the honesty, the trust, and the love I thought we had? Where was the marriage?

All of a sudden I knew why she didn't want to go to England when I suggested it back then; she knew we had no money to pay for it

All of a sudden I also knew who it was who paid for our nights out with her friends.

How could I have been so stupid???????

I only found out by accident. If I hadn't found the last month's phone bill I would still, even now, probably be in the dark and as blissfully ignorant and slow, as she obviously had me marked down as.

After becoming unemployed, she continued to go out to meet her ex-Bali Party friends, usually at lunchtimes or at the weekends. And all the time she was spinning me the line that they were paying for it. Well, I didn't really pay it much heed at first but when these lunches started happening with more and more frequency I did start to wonder a bit.

Anyway, her mate, Satria, lost his job a short while after Yossy quit — for reasons I was never really sure of - and the two of them remained good buddies. Now, I never suspected the pair of them of getting up to anything, and I still don't, simply because the guy is almost certainly gay.

I knew they were in constant daily contact by phone, commiserating with each other over their bad luck, and I said to Yoss a few times that I hoped she wasn't always the one to call him as I knew he lived in a boarding house and had no landline phone there. I knew he only had a mobile phone, and if Yoss was calling him then it was bound to be very expensive.

No, she assured me, that wasn't the case. He was calling her.

Was he ever!

On coming home particularly late after work one night, I was feeling pretty tired and not on top form and so I just wanted some food and then to get to bed. I got home to find Yoss on the phone to our mate Satria, but rather than finish up the phone call (quickly) to him, she simply smiled a greeting at me and proceeded to carry on yapping for another forty minutes or so.

By the time she finally got off the phone I was not best pleased, to put it mildly, and even less so when she informed me that there was nothing in the house for me to eat. This really did put me in an uncharacteristically bad mood and it prompted me to let loose a bit on my feelings regarding her excessive phone chats with Satria.

She was a bit dismissive of my complaints and said, once again, that as he was calling her there was no problem. This really wasn't the crux of the matter as far as I was concerned, but I did sort of use it as a stick to attack her with.

I told her I didn't believe her (even though I did) and I wanted to see the phone bill. I didn't wait for her to find it or, more likely, to tell me she didn't know where it was, and started rummaging around for it in the dressing room table's drawers.

When I found it I immediately wished I hadn't, as I almost did myself an injury upon seeing the amount.

'250,000 rupiah!!!!!' I screamed: 'How the hell could it cost this much?' That is over eighty quid! I then yanked out all the phone bills going back six months or so and found them all to be much the same, except for one month which was double that!

Yossy had been telling me our average monthly phone bill was a princely 50,000 rupiah at most.

Unbelievable!!!!

I set off on a tirade at her. For the first time in the six years we had known each other I really lost my temper because even with my still somewhat less than perfect Indonesian language proficiency I could understand the statement showed that calls to a certain mobile phone number accounted for the vast majority of the amount.

I was ranting and she was silent. She didn't say a word, and the only reason I can give for this unprecedented muteness was she must have been in shock at the extent of my anger.

I was shaking with fury and then it occurred to me to ask her something. No, not ask, but demand. I demanded to know there and then exactly how much money we had saved in the bank, to the penny with no fudging, or maybes, or don't knows.

The look on her face told me what I needed to know.

We had nothing. Not a pot to spit in!

Surabaya, August 1996

We moved on.

As I said, it hurt as much as if she had had an affair, but we moved on. We had to. It was either that or give up on our marriage, and I didn't want to do that.

Everyone makes mistakes sometimes, and perhaps it's true that everyone makes one almighty humdinger of a mistake in their life; a mistake so big, bold and bad that there can be no possible explanation for it and all that can be hoped for is that no irretrievable lasting damage is caused and that anyone in a position to grant forgiveness does so.

I told Yoss that this was her humdinger, there could be no

repeat and now we would move on.

I still kept up my work here, there, and everywhere and slowly I started getting my groove back. I went through a relatively short period where I wondered what it was all for and whether or not I simply could be bothered or motivated to keep going, but gradually I got rolling back into the swing of things.

Then, a few weeks on and more drama. I was in my office at the institute planning my lessons as normal and the phone rang.

'Hello, Mr. Avery?' asked a pleasant-sounding female voice.

'Yep, can I help you?'

'Yes, this is Clarrisa at MasterCard,' she said. I was momentarily caught in a flux between slight annoyance and confusion. I had no credit card nor wished to have one and felt marginally vexed that I should be disturbed by what was obviously a cold selling call.

'Mr. Avery,' said Miss Pleasant Voice, 'The reason I'm calling is …'

She ended the conversation and hung up. I held the receiver in my hand and stared at it. The room had gone mute. I began to shake. I wanted to vomit. I wanted to scream. I wanted to run and escape.

I did none of those things and instead I just quietly put the phone down and walked out into the car park.

There, heartbroken once again, I broke down and lost it, big time.

Later, when we were in the car together and without saying a word, I handed her a piece of paper with the figures written down on it She looked at them blankly. Is it a mask, I asked myself, or did she really not know what they related to?

Evidently not.

'What is this?' she asked in all innocence.

'What do you think it is?'

'No idea. You tell me. I don't have time for your games.' This is Yossy on the attack. A fearsome sight at the best of times.

'Got a phone call this morning,' I told her. 'Those figures there are the amounts you have run up on your credit cards. I didn't even know you had *one* card until this morning and now I find you have *two* and owe more than eight million rupiah!!!!! That's almost three grand!!!! Not only are we skint, but we owe fucking millions!!!'

'Neil,' she started.

'Fuck off,' I finished.

Three months of not talking followed. Not much anyway.

To give her some due, she actually had the grace to appear contrite and, dare I say, even ashamed of what had happened.

I, on the other hand, just had no idea what I was supposed to say or do from there on in. I knew from watching films and reading books containing plotlines such as the one I found myself in, I was supposed to be feeling a moral outrage and throwing things while ranting and raving.

I should have been packing my bag, or hers, or at least threatening to do so.

Yet, I didn't. I couldn't.

It's not that I didn't feel anything at all or that I was numb, it was just that I seemed to have lost the power of speech or movement. Now I can relate to how some people experience something so harrowing or jolting that they go into a kind of shock and, although remaining perfectly mentally stable, are unable able to ever speak or relate to anyone or anything in the same way ever again.

Not that I am comparing what I went through to that experienced by those poor souls, I'm just saying I can understand that kind of catatonic state.

Yoss tried to engage me a few times over the days and weeks that followed but I would always just shake my head and wander away from her. I knew at some stage we would have to sit down and have this out and see whether or not we could sort this one out, or if we even wanted to try to do so, but I just couldn't face it and so I put it off more and more. I just didn't know what would happen.

The one thing I knew I wanted was to never feel like that again the rest of my life.

Time is a great healer, so I'm told anyway.

I guess things *did start* healing in the sense that I eventually started getting used to the idea of having no money, of not being able to afford to go anywhere or do anything, of having no sense that my life was any sort of a success, of knowing the marriage and life I thought I had was nothing more than a bucket of spit.

Through this, though, the real pain, the real kick in the nuts, came from the realisation that Yossy wasn't, *had never been*, happy. I thought we had it all, I really did. I really thought we were *both* so happy and that pain, the pain of knowing that I wasn't making the person I loved, *love*, happy is the one that cut me most.

Even now, all these years later, I find myself thinking, wishing, if only I could turn back the clock and make Yossy happy again, make her love me again as she used to. If only I could get her to look at me as she used to do, to be the centre of her world as she was mine. That yearning will never diminish, no matter where I am or what I do in life.

In the misery of the weeks and months that followed all of this, however, I would sit up late at night with my thoughts after Yossy had gone to bed alone. Full of regret and self-pity, I'd think to myself, *if only I could go back in time and make sure we'd never met then I would not know this bloody pain.*

These were the saddest of thoughts. The crushing of dreams, the realization that things had changed and forever, and that the life I had was gone.

I felt so alone. Living in a foreign country with hardly a friend in the world, or so it seemed, these were once more desperate days. I had never found it particularly easy to make friends when I lived in England, and so now thousands of miles from home I felt truly isolated. Every day was groundhog day: drag myself up, stagger out the door, take public transport to work as we could no longer afford to run a car, race around the city looking for work, take public transport home again fourteen hours later, and stagger into bed. Next day, wake up and do it all again.

And all the time Yossy and I were at best being cordial, at worst ignoring one another.

What was there anymore?

Awwww ... this is just not fair, I'd think to myself late at night. This is not what I signed up for and I just don't think I deserve this. I mean, what did I do wrong, what happened? All I ever did was love her, right?

Come on, I don't act like a knob head, do I? I don't go out drinking or chasing other women, or spending all our money. I don't abuse her or be mean to her in any way or do anything a million other useless husbands do.

So why-oh-bloody-why??????

I guess this sounds like the pathetic whinging of a sap; a sap that like millions of other saps before him sapped himself into sapdom, if there is such a place for us losers.

Bollocks!

I tried. I really did. I was not going to be beaten by this. I had worked too hard and sacrificed too much to just walk away from Yossy, our marriage, and our happiness and so I made a conscious effort to really try and get things back to the way they were before.

I let go of the resentment I had been feeling and I resolved to work even harder in an effort to get back the life we had before. Rather, the life I thought we had had before. However, it wasn't easy, and sometimes I felt that she was being deliberately obtrusive, as if she was trying to push me away; trying to get me to be the one to call time on our marriage.

Her whole demeanour told me she was still nowhere near happy and she seemed to blame me for this. In fact, she seemed to hold me singly responsible for every slight misfortune or setback we experienced. Every time things didn't run quite to plan or as smoothly as she would have liked that was the sign for another tirade of how all it was all my fault, of how I had brought misfortune and bad luck into her life, of how stupid and thoughtless I was.

An example: it seemed Yossy had transgressed in age by about fifteen years and all of a sudden become extremely childish. I'm not exaggerating when I say she would blame me if the weather was bad. Really. If it rained she would use her womanly logic to conclude it was my fault for being such a miserable person and so God was acting accordingly in sending mood-appropriate weather.

Another example: If we went shopping I would often find myself cast in the role of a parent trying to deal with an errant child. She would walk the aisles of the supermarket picking up superfluous items and putting them in the basket even though she knew we had barely any money for true necessities let alone nonsense like ornaments for the house or boxes of chocolates 'in case we get visitors'.

It was so soul destroying to see her so unhappy and to think, if even for just a minute, that I was to blame for her unhappiness. Every day was just a haze of unpleasantness, indifference or inherent sadness for the pair of us and I really didn't know why.

It got to the point I was scared to look at her, let alone talk to her. I could see the resentment coming off her in waves, and I just knew she was spoiling for a fight: an excuse to let rip at me again.

I really didn't know what I could have done to shatter her so. I could only hope and pray that all of this passed and one day we could get back to being how we were before. We were happy back then; really happy. I would have done anything to go back to how things had been.

As much as I fought for it, though, I didn't hold out much hope. I truly believed, and spent many a tearful night trying to accept, that my marriage was over in all but name. I knew she wanted to be free of me but there was no way she would say as much. To ask for a divorce would result in massive loss of face for her in front of her family, and there was no way she would go through that, so to try to push me into leaving of my own violation seemed her only way out.

Oh, what a nightmare!

I was devastated, absolutely heartbroken. You see and hear other people talking about their failed marriages and they seem to just brush it off as 'one of those things' or a 'tough break' and they get on with their lives.

Not me. I was in despair and literally didn't know what to do with myself at times. I never knew pain like that and I hope I never do again.

Three years later – Surabaya, 2000

I watched as Tessy burst into tears for what was already the fourth time that morning and it was still only 6.30 and I couldn't help but smile. Not that I took any pleasure in her distress, I hasten to add. It's just that the simple act of watching her in action, any action, has always been capable of filling me with pure joy and happiness.

Since her birth, she has been my light, my love, my feelings, my heart, my hope, my happiness and my life. I have loved every hair, muscle and sinew of her being with an intensity that at times has threatened to have me self-combust at any given moment. When she was little, especially, I couldn't bear to be out of her presence or sight for even a second and goodness only knows how I ever got any work done in those days.

What's more, what was even better, was I knew the feeling was mutual. That was one little girl who loved her daddy with a passion.

She always wanted to be with me, to sit with me, to have me hold her or feed her or talk to her. No one seemed to be able to calm her when she got one of her little tantrums like she was having now, but just the sight of me always seemed to do the trick and once she spotted me and opened up her arms with tears rolling down her little face and she implored me, 'DADDY ...' the deed was done.

I was hers and she was mine and all was well in the world for us both again.

Tessy came along as a surprise, to say the least. Without going too much into detail, at the time of Tessy's conception there wasn't a lot of detail to go into, if you get my drift. Yossy and I had not exactly been enjoying an all-thrusting, rip-roaring time of things in that department during that particular period in our lives, and added to the fact that during the first few years of marriage when we were, uh, more regularly intimate, nothing had happened on the reproduction front, it was all the more a wee shock when Yossy fell pregnant.

It shames me (almost) to confess when I first heard the news I was minutely tempted to stop and ponder the child's paternity for half a millisecond. After all, Yossy didn't exactly have an unbeaten batting average when it comes to the honesty and truth stakes, but after the aforementioned period of contemplation I realised what I was suggesting and the remoteness of its possibility even after all the problems we had experienced.

There was also the matter of Yossy's reaction when she found out she was pregnant. Nobody can feign the happiness and delight she displayed then. It's just not possible. If she'd had anything to hide or anything to feel guilty about then it would have shown then.

Anyway, who cares? I was as delighted as her.

Tessy really brought us back together and gave us happiness and hope again. The dark days of those bleak years or so ago seemed to belong to another lifetime. Little Tess was such a funny, sweet, happy, inquisitive, lovely little girl and gave us so much joy, fun and happiness.

Hark at me, the first man to ever become a father, going on like this. Well, I tell you what, no man has ever loved his kids more, that's for sure.

Everyday I would take her to her playschool or else try and pick her up and always make sure there was another period of what our American friends would term *quality time* in the afternoon or evening with her.

We had a full time maid, or *pembantu*, who helped take care of Tess, but Yoss was a good mother and also liked nothing more than being with Tess. She really was a little ray of sunshine.

Yoss became happy in her work now, too. We opened a small English language school when she was pregnant and that developed and expanded in the first two and a half years or so after Tess was born.

We started by simply renovating the garage in our house and turning that into a single classroom. We soon had so many students sign up that we ended up renovating the whole house into a small school with three or four classrooms and having to rent somewhere else to live.

The school continued to grow and in no time we had two schools and plans for a third. As good as it was, I didn't really have too much to do with the business side of the school, leaving most of that to Yoss, and I just taught there a couple of hours a day if I could as I was still spending most of my time running (well, driving actually) around Surabaya chasing the big bucks teaching in companies.

We seemed to have finally sorted out our finances and even started the process of buying our own house. We actually started saving quite regularly and were able to afford to finally go to England the year Tess turned two.

It was my first time back since I came out here in '93 and, obviously, Yoss and Tess' first ever experience of Blighty. I think they both enjoyed themselves, although they found it rather cold and the food a bit strange.

I must confess that although I also enjoyed the trip, it felt very much like what it was: a holiday. It didn't feel in any way that I was coming home, as it were, and I actually felt a bit of a stranger in my own country.

Everything just felt a bit different, you see. Things seemed to be cleaner and more well-organised than I remembered when living there; people appeared to be more professional in their jobs but not as happy or friendly; as I just said, the weather was colder than I remembered. Another thing was the TV and entertainment world had moved on so I no longer recognised or knew most of the presenters on TV or many of the programmes or pop stars or other people in the public eye.

Yep, it was a bit of a strange feeling. Rather a case of feeling like a fish out of water, I fear.

Still, all in all it was fun and my family certainly enjoyed meeting Yoss and Tess.

'So? That's good, isn't it?' I hear you, dear reader, say. 'Seems you finally had your life sorted out.'

'Nope,' reply I. 'That was just the calm before the storm.'

By the end of the year it had all gone wrong again. Well, I say it had 'gone' wrong. It hadn't, really. In fact, nothing had actually happened as such, things had just drifted into mutual antipathy. Time waits for no man and the year was once more coming to a close. Tess was now a couple of months past her fourth birthday and had become a lovely, well-behaved, well-adjusted little kid. All the more surprising seeing that her parents barely bothered communicating any more.

Oh, I don't know. I just seemed to give up on Yossy. Yeah, yeah, I know this sounds like 'poor little me' again, but I'd just had enough of trying to reason with her, of trying to find out why she was permanently unhappy or angry, of being blamed for the aforementioned anger or unhappiness or anything remotely resulting in the slightest problem or deviation from the day's norm.

God, I was sick of it.

Yossy seemed to be happy for a while with the onset of motherhood and the opening of our businesses, but I can see now it was just a case of the cracks being papered over and she was still in fact deeply rooted in misery. She was back to her snidey, surly 'woe-is-me' worst, and I had no inkling of why or how to fix things so I didn't bother and simply gave up.

Initially, as she started withdrawing back into her shell, I would try and bring her out of her flux by asking her what was wrong, why she never smiled, why she never seemed to take any happiness from life or from people and the things around her but I would be met by a wall of silence. All I could ever get from her was the bland acknowledgement that she was 'not happy'.

She would, at best, sit in silence if I happened to be in the same room as her, or at worst try and pick an argument so she would at least have an outlet for her frustrations. On occasion I could actually see her brain whirring as I walked into the room. It would be as if she was pondering: 'How can I have a go at him now? What thing can I pick up on and turn round and make his fault so I can fly at him and then feel a bit better about myself?'

A typical conversation as I walk into the house following a full day at work might go as follows:

Me: 'Hi dear.'

Silence and pouting.

Me: 'Had a good day?'

More silence and pouting – her brain whirs into action.

Me: 'What's for dinner?'

Her: 'Humphh.'

Me (getting exasperated): 'What's wrong?'

Her: 'Nothing.'

Me: 'So, what's up?'

Her: 'Why didn't you cut the grass this morning?'

Me: 'Eh?'

Her: 'Why didn't you cut the grass before going to work this morning?'

Me: 'You what? I never cut the grass. We don't have any grass. We don't have a lawn.'

Her: 'Well, we should do. We should have a lawn. Why didn't you buy a house with a lawn?'

Me: 'Eh?'

Her: 'Oh, I hate you. You're useless!'

I went past the hurting stage, hurtled beyond the trying to fix it stage, and bypassed the even pretending to show concern stage altogether.

I just couldn't be bothered with it all anymore, and I finally did what Yossy had been accusing me of doing since really rather quite early in our marriage: I changed.

I decided then that I was just going to live for me and for what I wanted to do in life. That sounds very selfish, but it's not quite as bad as all that. I didn't mean I was just going to do whatever

I wanted to do without any care or thought of anyone else. No, I know that such a lifestyle could only lead to more misery and unhappiness. What I mean is, I was going to try and lead a life whereby I didn't allow her, or anyone else, to upset or worry me anymore.

I simply didn't want to know anymore. All I cared about was spending time with Tess and trying to live out my days in relative peace and anonymity.

That was the reasoning behind things anyway, and I realise that the ripe old age of 33 could be said to be a tad premature to be settling for such an existence, but I was exhausted. I felt twice my age and I truly believed the only way to be around to see old age and thus Tess grow up was to switch off totally.

So I made a decision that Yossy could do whatever she wanted to as long as she did it quietly without involving me.

So she did. In both her private and her business life she started to get up to all sorts. She developed a multitude of 'business partners', and almost immediately three new schools popped up. I wasn't privy to any of the details of these business arrangements and I couldn't see how they all expected to see any return on their investments, and, to be frank, I couldn't have cared less.

I simply told her not to involve me and if it all came crashing down around her ears, which I was sure it would, then she was on her own.

As for her private life; well, I don't know … where to start? She had all manner of men around her for one reason or another, and someone who actually cared a bit would, I suppose, would have wanted to know who they all were and what their relationships to her were.

Everything now supposedly cantered on her school and her business. She brought in some sort of local *dukun*, or witchdoctor, to ensure the business had the necessary good vibes and was protected from evil spirits. Before undertaking any decision, big or small, she had to ask this *dukun* for guidance and if he agreed with whatever she was proposing then she went with it, if not, well, she just left it. I am not sure Steve Jobs ever worked on such business principles, but still.

Part of this spiritual guidance, it seemed, was to provide, ahem, 'therapeutic' massages. I arrived home unexpectedly early one day and rolled into the house from the garage as usual, and as I came in I thought I saw the servant, the *pembantu*, give me a strange look; almost as if she was surprised and a wee bit frightened to see me.

Now, perhaps I should elaborate a little on the topic of domestic help in Indonesia before I go any further with this particular yarn. Whilst in the west it is uncommon to have hired-help, so to speak, it is the norm in Indonesia. The very vast majority of households from the lower-middle classes upwards will employ at least one full-time helper. These people are invariably, but not exclusively, female and are known as *pembantus*, which literally translates as 'helpers'. Now, the vast majority are employed on a live-in basis and so will find themselves being on call to do household chores for anything up to eighteen hours a day for the equivalent of around fifty quid a month.

Wow, I hear you say, talk about exploitation, and I must admit that seeing that description written down before me I can see how people might think that way. However, when taken in context the situation is a little different. Wealth distribution amongst the population in Indonesia is amongst the most uneven in the world with something like the richest 2% of the country owning up to 90% of the country's wealth. Rural areas are particularly poor and educational opportunities, when they exist at all, are basic with a very high percentage of children not finishing elementary school. This is especially so in the case of girls, who are still seen as inferior to boys.

This means every year there is an influx of young women moving from the country to the cities and towns in an effort to find work. With only the most rudimentary educational backgrounds, their employment opportunities are somewhat limited and so they tend to become domestic workers or else gravitate to industrial work in factories – sweat shops – where they will usually be expected to work the same hours as domestic workers for about the same pay.

As *pembantus* they will usually live with a family and be expected to cook, clean and do the laundry. They will be on call all day, it's true, but will rarely actually work much more than a few hours a day. They will be treated as a member of the family, have their own room, eat the same food as the family, watch TV together and generally be cared for and looked after. The salary they receive will be low by western standards but will normally remain almost untouched in an average month as all the *pembantu's* living needs and expenses will be provided by the family she is employed by.

Anyway, I always had a reasonably good relationship with our *pembantu* and we got along fairly well with my pidgin Indonesian and her non-existent English, but, as I say, on this day in question she looked rather concerned to see me.

I proceeded on my merry way into the bedroom and upon opening the door saw the reason for the *pembantu*'s apprehension. Yossy, bless her little cotton socks, was lying on her stomach on the bed covered by the quilt, while Johnny, the *dukun*, was straddling her. He, at least, appeared to be fully clothed while I couldn't see whether or not she was.

She didn't miss a beat and smiled up at me as if a guy coming home to find his wife in bed with another man was the most common and normal thing in the world.

'Hi, honey,' she droned: 'I feel so tired. Mr. Johnny has agreed to give me a massage. Good, ya?'

Mr. Johnny for his part at least had the grace to look if not guilty, then certainly a tad embarrassed and worried, as I guess is probably par for the course in such circumstances.

'Ok, deh' said I, and went back out into the living room to watch telly.

I think a slight diversion with regards to the general topic of *dukuns* in general is also called for. They are supposedly magical entities, who have the power to ensure all types of desired events or happenings occur (or don't, as the case may be) and they are also alleged to have healing qualities applicable for the most intricate and diverse of ailments. Now, needless to say I was always somewhat sceptical of these gentlemen (they are always men) and tended to give them a wide berth at the best of times.

Having had a western upbringing, I found the whole concept

of *dukuns* and black magic far fetched, but although I would sometimes share my doubts regarding the whole concept, in the main I kept my own counsel regarding such matters. However, one event that occurred shortly after Tess was born did cause me to slightly revisit my way of thinking.

When we took baby Tess home from the hospital after she was born, we were naturally delighted. She was everything we'd been hoping and praying for but there was one slight problem. No matter what we did or tried we couldn't get Tess to settle down in the room we'd allocated her.

Every time Tess was led into the room she would scream and scream as loud as her little lungs would allow and just would not stop. Nothing Yossy or I did seemed to calm her down and no amount of soothing or cuddling seemed to make any difference whatsoever. Yet as soon as either of us wandered into another room with Tess in our arms, the wailing would cease instantly.

'Neil. We have to face it. There is something in the room that is disturbing her. Even a noodle-brain like you can see that, surely?' Yossy started for the umpteenth time. 'We have to get a dukun in to see what the problem is.'

I was aghast. 'No way! I'm not having some quack coming here and poking around my house. No, there has to be some logical explanation as to why Tess can't settle in this room.'

Yossy eyed me scornfully. 'Like what, Mr Logic? Come on, I'm all ears. Let's hear it.'

Sometimes I really did regret teaching Yossy English to the level I had. However, that was the nature of the beast.

'I don't know, do I?' was my rather weak response: 'Maybe

this room has recently been painted and the smell is still lingering to her sensitive nose. Or perhaps there is a draft in here that is making her uncomfortable, or maybe …'

Yoss cut me off. 'Maybe … maybe … maybe,' she mimicked: 'Maybe I married a clown. I'm calling the *dukun*, and that's that.'

That was indeed that, and an hour or so later said *dukun* was at our door. I didn't need to be told to stay out of the gentleman's way (Yossy's evil eye in my direction did that trick) and I had no desire to get involved anyway. Instead, I busied myself with making a cup of coffee in the parlour kitchen at the back of the small dwelling.

From my vantage point, I could hear the guy making some kind of weird incantation and I could just make out a lantern of some kind being waved around. I thought I could also hear Yossy joining in on the chorus but wouldn't have liked to bet money on that one. It would be a braver man than me to get that confirmed either way.

Finally the chanting stopped and, miraculously, so did Tess's cries. That was strange, but still not enough to entice me from my place of sanctuary and my coffee.

When I finally did venture out of my hiding place, Yossy brazenly informed me she had taken two hundred thousand rupiah out of my wallet to pay the man. This less than shame-faced admission was met with another snort of derision from me and I was just about to remark that was nice work if you could get it, when Yossy cut me off by putting a finger to her lips in a shushing manner and nodding in the direction of Tess's room.

There was a sound coming from there: the sound of a little girl snoring.

In addition to coercing *dukuns* into compromising positions, Yossy seemed to be going through a stage of experiencing some kind of predilection for young men barely into their twenties. She appointed four or five of them to work as teachers in her school and she then took a shine to one guy in particular. His name was Arin and he was promptly installed as her 'school manager'.

Goodness only knows what his actual job description or responsibilities were, but all I knew was he seemed to spend an inordinate amount of time in the presence of my wife. They were together all the time, morning, noon and night. When not in the schools there they were in our house having 'meetings' or forever setting off somewhere together, both within Surabaya and outside.

One of their most favoured spots in those days was Malang. This is a resort a couple of hours drive to the south of Surabaya and is a kind of weekend retreat where you can go and rent a villa for the night or weekend. The weather there is a bit cooler and it is actually quite a pleasant place to stay. Although it was a basically a weekend-retreat sort of place, they didn't ever stay there overnight, not in the early days of their, ah, partnership, anyway – instead they travelled up and back on the same day. In their rare communications with me I gathered they were ostensibly looking at properties in which to open a new school, but I had my doubts.

After they'd made a few journeys there and back, I found myself actually being invited to join them for the weekend. We all went there and stayed one gloriously sunny weekend. By 'all' I mean Yossy, Arin, Tess, and a load of other teachers from her school and it really was the weirdest thing.

As soon as we got there Yoss practically dragged me into the bedroom and insisted I give her a royal rodgering. Now, considering we hadn't exactly 'known each other' in the Old Testament way on a regular basis for some time, I was somewhat taken aback by her rather uncharacteristic enthusiasm, Nevertheless, I made little headway when I brought the matter up and was practically called a wuss and told to put up and shut up.

Indeed.

Three weeks later. We went to the doctor's. The test was negative.

Hmmmmm. What was all that about, I wondered.

Anyway, I was soon to find myself in a position of no longer being able to take the moral high ground, even if I could be bothered to do so. Yep, you see, muggins just had to go and do it again. Without sense or sensibility, and when I least expected or indeed wanted to, I fell in love with someone else. You would think that with everything else that was happening in my life at that point in time, combined with my age and my experiences, I would know better, but there you are.

Her name was Jolie and I met her through my teaching a few months after Yossy started disappearing up to the mountains of Malang on a regular basis. I guess the normal thing to say in circumstances like this is that at first I didn't plan on anything occurring between us, that she was purely my student and that things just started happening without either of us realising our planning it.

That would be wrong, though. Right from the outset I felt something click and I just had a weird and wonderful feeling about things. She was blessed with the appearance of an angel and the only truly fitting adjective for her was *lovely*.

Right from the word go I felt something for her, and not just lust or desire or any other yucky emotion. On the contrary, I felt something warm and right and nice and good stirring inside me.

I knew it was early days yet and there was no way of being able to tell how things would pan out but for the first time in many years I felt excited and nervous.

And alive.

And not the slightest bit guilty.

In fact, she would be the one often asking me if we were doing the right thing, if we should be feeling guiltier than we were, and if there was any future in it all. I did my best to reassure her, of course, but it was all somewhat unchartered territory for me too, and I'm afraid I wasn't always able to assuage her fears, but I did my best to encourage and support her and let her know how serious I was about her and how much she had done, and was doing, for me.

Six months later, though, I was back living in England.

London, November 2002

I don't want to go back to Indonesia. I am happy.

There was no one calling me 'stupid' (if they were talking to

66

me at all, that was). There was no one calling me in the middle of the night demanding I be responsible for repayment of my wife's debts. No problems with immigration coming to my door looking for a payoff all hours of the day (and night). No *dukuns* or young men with designs on my wife within eyesight.

Just calmness and a realisation that the life I was leading in Indonesia really wasn't normal. This new life in England defined normality. This was the sort of life most people lead. They get up, go to work, come home, relax and then go to bed. That's it. No fuss, no drama.

Simplicity is genius, as someone much smarter than me once said.

I was very lonely that winter, but also was very happy. I missed Tess so much it was physically painful, but on the other hand I was able to see things clearly and after such a long time away from England, I was enjoying everyday life again.

For example, I was enjoying simple things like walking down the street and not being stared at (way back Yossy had warned me that that would get old quickly — I hadn't taken much notice at the time, but she had been right) and I enjoyed simple things I had taken for granted before but had missed in the time I'd been away. Things such as the long summer evenings, for instance, contrasted with Indonesia as well as the changing of the seasons. With Indonesia being very near the equator I was used to almost exactly twelve hours of sunshine and twelve hours of darkness every single day three hundred and sixty five days of the year and totally constant (hot) weather.

I was constantly working, and so always tired, but it was

all coming together, or so it seemed. I got back into the habit of watching English TV shows again, got up to speed on local and national news, got back in touch with old friends, started reading my old favourite newspapers and magazines again, and generally began to settle down.

The only real blot on the landscape was how much I missed my darling Tess. I knew it was going to be hard living without her but I didn't realise just how hard. I truly think if it wasn't for her I would never have returned to Indonesia and I would definitely have ended the thing known as my marriage then and there.

I would speak with Tess a couple of times a week and tell her all about what was happening in England and what her aunts, uncles and cousins were up to. She always sounded so cheerful and happy on the phone, and I thank God that throughout everything that's happened in her life she seems so well adjusted. On the phone there was never any crying or asking me to come home or why I had to work away right now. I am blessed to have her, and I love her so much.

As for Yoss, though, well, I can't really say I missed her at all. Sometimes back then, and even now if I'm totally honest, I used to think of how things were in the early years and I missed them. I missed the way we were and the love we had, or appeared to have, for each other back then. Then just as I would get all misty eyed and start convincing myself there was something there worth fighting for and trying to save, I'd focus on the way things really were. I remembered the unpleasantness, the fighting and, worst of all, the indifference, and I'd wonder, 'Is it all worth it?'

I came to England in June ostensibly to work on a summer

school for foreign students wanting to learn English while experiencing the country and its people, with the supposed aim of evaluating the state of the work market in order to be able to make an informed decision on whether or not the three of us should settle there.

I was under no illusions of Yossy actually wanting to be with me, rather it was probably a case of her having burnt all her other boats back in Indoland and so she now saw Blighty as a last-chance-escape-valve. Maybe I'm being a bit cynical here, but I know she had many creditors chasing her, and probably many other people besides.

I had no choice but to go back to living at home with my mum while trying to save some money for a deposit on a place of my (our?) own. I found it a bit embarrassing being back at home at my age even if it was just in the short term, but needs must, eh?

2am Sunday morning

I'd just finished an extra shift and was on my way home. Yoss sent me a text requesting I call her urgently. I replied telling her I would do so in a few minutes when I got home and that when I did she should get to the point, whatever it was, quickly and not indulge in ten minutes of waffle as was her wont.

I got home, sorted myself out and sat down with the phone. As usual I had the stopwatch going with the intention not to exceed five minutes. Pretty expensive, these transcontinental phone calls, and this, added to the fact I just wanted my bed, meant I was not really in the mood for a long talk about nonsense.

Me: Hi, Yoss. What's up?

Her: Hi. What time is it there?

Me: Late. What's the matter?

Her: Errrr …

Me: Just tell me.

Her: I'm not well.

Me: What's wrong?

Her: Something wrong with my stomach.

Me: What?

Her: I don't know.

Me: Have you been to the doctor?

Her: Yes.

Me: What did he say?

Her: He said it's either a tumour or …

Me: Yes?

Her: I'm pregnant.

Me: Huh?

Her: It's either a …

Me: Yes, I heard. Which is it?

Her: What?

Me: Which is it? Are you pregnant or is it a tumour?

Her: The doctor says I'm pregnant. That's what he thinks.

Me: Is that possible?

Her: No!

Me: So, you have a tumour?

Her: Yes … Or I'm pregnant.

Me: You said that's not possible.

Her: It isn't. But the doctor says I am.

Me: Have you had sex with anybody else?

Her: No.

Me: But the doctor says you're pregnant?

Her: Yes.

Me: Have you had a test?

Her: Yes.

Me: And?

Her: It's positive.

Me: So, you're pregnant.

Her: No. It's impossible.

Me: It's late. I'm going to bed. Goodnight.

Click

So, there I was in England, living with my mum, in love with one woman thousands of miles away (Jolie) while unable to escape the clutches of misery another one (Yossy), also thousands of miles away, was causing me, and on top of all that I was missing little Tess so much it was physically hurting.

What a mess.

In the words of the late, great Dusty, I just didn't know what to do with myself. Every which way I looked I couldn't see a way out of my troubles. If I did what I believed 99.99% of other men would do, then I would walk away from the marriage with Yoss and never look back, and I knew that was what anyone I asked would advise me to do. Perhaps it was for that reason, that of not wanting to hear the truth, that I never did ask anyone for advice. I never once let on to my family or friends, whether in Indonesia or England, exactly what was happening back in Indonesia. Nobody was any the wiser about how bad things had become between Yossy and I, or of her medical condition or even the very existence of either Arin or Jolie.

Thinking about the three women in my life: Jolie, Yossy and Tess, brought about a whole range of emotions. I loved Jolie and wanted to be with her, but I didn't know if that was practical or even if that was what she wanted anymore. When we'd been together in Surabaya we'd loved each other. Really properly loved each other, I mean, not just uttered the platitudes. Back then she'd listened to me, held me, advised me, loved me and then loved me some more. Now though, we were half a world apart and had been for some time, and time and distance can do things to the strongest of relationships in the best of circumstances.

Jolie was sweet and innocent in a way that took me back years to the way Yossy had been when we first met but she was also different to Yoss in many ways. She had more of an easy-going personality for a start, and seemed to be someone who could quite possibly go through her entire life without ever once really getting angry or saying anything mean to anyone. At 23 she was still young and hopeful for what the future might hold in store, whilst I was already feeling my age and in danger of becoming jaded and an old man before my time. Despite my rather jaundiced outlook on life, however, Jolie did love me. She'd told me that often when I was living in Surabaya, and again now over the phone while I was in England. She was a candle of hope for me in what was becoming a rather bleak winter of discontent.

Tess was breaking my heart. Breaking it in a way neither Yossy nor Jolie, or any other woman come to that, could ever do. She'd always been a 'daddy's girl' and the miles and months apart couldn't change that. I carried her pictures around with me everywhere I went and I never passed up an opportunity to show them to anyone and everyone I came into contact with at the flimsiest of an excuse. Many was the bemused taxi passenger or English-language student who, upon making the most innocuous of remarks, found themselves practically being forced to wade through a collection of snapshots of my five-year-old princess while being regaled with anecdotes of her amazing talents, skills and abilities.

Yes, I guess I was kind of boring at times.

Yossy, though, that was different. I felt so many conflicting emotions regarding her. I worried about how she was looking after Tess, I worried that people were taking advantage of her naivety and bad business sense. I was also disappointed in her, in what and who she had become, and how she, I felt, used people up. I often remembered our very first conversation a dozen years earlier on Kuta Beach when she blithely informed me that she subscribed to the viewpoint that some people were just out for themselves and to see what they could get from others before moving on to someone else, and it pained me. I knew that there was a part of me that still did, and always would, love her, but did I miss her? No, not at all. I really didn't, and that was what was saddest of all.

I guess I had been hoping that going to England would somehow make things clearer and lift the fog a bit, and in a way it did. The phone call from Yossy certainly had the effect of bringing things to a head, if nothing else, and I realized I couldn't let things go on the way they were: I would have to go back to Indonesia, even if temporarily, and sort things out once and for all.

So I booked the cheapest flight I could and headed back to Indonesia. On the plane I went over my plan again: I would fly into Jakarta and then on to Surabaya where I would accompany Yoss to the doctor, get a proper scan and find out just what the heck was going on. Then, depending on what the scan showed up, I would make my decisions and take back my life. I had it all worked out. I really truly loved two girls and I wanted them both. I was, I decided, going to do anything necessary to get them both.

Needless to say, it all went tits up. Again

First, I stopped off in Jakarta on the way to Surabaya to see if we could sort out what was up with Tess. I was due to arrive in Jakarta in the early hours of the morning and leave for Surabaya the following afternoon, but first I had a sort of job interview. When I knew I was going to come back and try and sort out this mess, I had a bit of a hunt around on the internet and managed to line up a couple of interviews, one in Jakarta and another in Surabaya.

After thinking things through, although I knew I didn't want to come back here to stay, I had to concede it might be for the best. So the following lunchtime I had my 'sort of' interview with a guy I used to know vaguely years back in Surabaya. He had opened an English school in Jakarta in the mid 90s and had tried to persuade me to move with him then, but stupidly at the time I thought Yoss and I were happy where we were and so I turned him down.

Anyhooo ... we met up and had a nice lunch and chat together and he offered me a job teaching with him and talked vaguely about also needing a manager for a new school he was opening. I told him I was very interested in the teaching position, but didn't push myself forward too much regarding the management job. An hour or two later and I was on the plane heading to Surabaya to see Yoss and Tess for the first time in eight months.

Finally I arrived, got my bags and made it out of the terminal. I was feeling hot, tired, none too happy to be back and generally a bit miserable.

That all changed the moment I saw Tess.

She's sitting on a steel barrier as I come out the terminal and immediately she starts yelling my name and tries to jump down.

'Daddy, Daddy, Daddy,' with her little hands waving twenty to the dozen.

She jumps down and runs to me. I sweep her up in my arms and just hold her.

She's mine. I love her. She's my girl and I need her, love her, and can't be without her.

No matter what.

So, with a weariness and a sense of dread we made an appointment and went to the doctor. The same one we'd visited six years previously almost to the day under much happier circumstances and, as I expected but hoped against hope, got the news confirmed. There it was on the little telly. Look, the doctor pointed out to us, there's the little dot that is to be sprog number two chez Neil.

Oh dear, oh dear.

I arched an eyebrow at Yoss. It was about all I was capable of right then. She looked devoid of any emotion whatsoever, while I couldn't wait to see how she was going to tap-dance her way out of this one and lay this particular conundrum at my feet.

That's the magic of the girl: you just really never knew what she was going to come up with next.

After a day's silence, she had the answer. A good night's sleep was all she needed to come up with a thorough explanation for the growth inside of her. Panic over, everyone, all has been explained.

A miracle conception.

She had, she explained with the straightest of straight faces, no idea how she had managed to reach her current state of having a six-week-old foetus growing inside of her, and so, she informed me, it is clear that the Almighty chose her to deliver a, presumably, pure and heavenly child into the world for some divine, if as yet unspecified, purpose.

Hey-ho.

I went to sleep. I had nothing to say to Yossy, so I simply went to the spare bedroom, the one I had spent most of the last two years I'd been in Indonesia sleeping in, and curled up and went to sleep.

The next day I woke up and played with Tess and helped her with her breakfast, and then without saying a word to Yossy, we left for her school. On the journey to school Tess chattered away incessantly about this, that, and the other. She asked me a million questions about England, her cousins there, the weather, when I would be going back, did I have any presents for her, her school, her friends, and … Mummy's new friends.

Tess told me innocently how her mum was very busy now and

in fact often so busy that she didn't have time to even come home at night. 'But it was ok, Daddy, because Mummy's new friends always look after her and take her everywhere she wants to go.' I just listened without interrupting and let little Tess babble on. She babbled all right. She babbled about the man who let Mummy come with him to Singapore and to Bali a few weeks ago. She babbled about the phone calls Mummy often got late at night and the she babbled about the people who came to the house looking for Mummy when she was not there. Mummy was very lucky to have so many friends, Tess told me gravely, because she, Tess, only had a few friends at her school. I just listened.

After I dropped Tess off at her school I went to see Jolie.

I tell Jolie I'm leaving Yoss. I lay it out there, convinced she is going to fall into my arms, kiss me, and start planning our life together.

She doesn't.

'Things have changed,' she mumbles.

'How? What's changed?' I ask.

'Well … I can't do this anymore. I feel so guilty.' Dead eyes stare at the floor.

'Guilty to who? To my wife? Why? She doesn't love me. She will be glad to see the back of me.' I'm gushing now, near to pleading.

'No. Not to her. To you, to Tess, to me … ah, it's difficult to explain.'

So she doesn't, and I go.

Heartbroken.

Again.

I just didn't know what to think anymore. I mean, I know it must sound ridiculous, but I actually got to thinking maybe it was true; that it really was some kind of unexplainable miracle conception. Living with her I thought I had become immune to her lies and her performances, but this was something else again. Here she was, caught red-handed in adultery and yet still displaying the uncanny ability to twist things around so I actually found myself beginning to apologise for doubting her. I started to think she was either telling the truth or else she should be on the stage, her performance was that good.

She swore over and over again that she had not had sex with anyone else, not once, not ever since we were married, and do you know what? I felt myself wavering.

Yeah, yeah, I know what I'm saying. I know how absurd and unbelievable, in fact downright impossible the very notion of this miracle conception is, but in the light of her adamant stand and determination of denial, in my addled brain I felt confused as to what choice I had other than to accept her at her word.

She stood there and swore to God, to her dead father's soul, to me, that she had not been unfaithful. Her eyes shining brightly, she looked directly into mine and promised with all her heart that she still loved me, wanted me, and needed me. I can feel her now as she held me and told me how much I meant to her, how she had never stopped loving me and how this child could be a new start for us.

I so wanted to believe her. I really did, because I knew that if I didn't then I had nothing, and I couldn't bear that.

Oh, I was not completely deluded. I knew something must

have happened, but I also knew I was very unlikely to ever find out what exactly. I gave her every chance to tell me and I told her that if something had happened when I was away in England, whether it was one-off thing, a regular 'sex-buddy' thing, or a full-blown affair, then she should tell me and we could sort it out together. She vehemently denied any of these took place and she just stated she had no idea how she came to fall pregnant and that it must have been a gift from God.

Although neither of us mentioned it, there was one other avenue potentially open to us. It was not really a real option, however, and that is why it was never mentioned.

So, I accepted the job with my old friend and started work in Jakarta in March of 2003. I ended up being sort of railroaded into taking the management position but actually soon found myself enjoying it and the job was not difficult at all. I felt I had landed on my feet despite being under-qualified for my new position as the Director of Studies at an English Language School.

Although I had sufficient experience in teaching, I still didn't have any formal teaching qualifications at this point and I knew that I would be coming into contact with those that did, so I would definitely be needing to up my game. This in itself didn't really worry me and I was looking forward to the challenge. I had managed to save and salt away some money whilst working in England, and I was now in a position to start studying again and finally get some qualifications. I knew I couldn't keep 'winging it' so I enrolled online and got cracking on a degree in education.

At the same time, I started to get used to my new surroundings.

Although I had visited Jakarta a number of times when I lived in Surabaya, I'd never stayed long and wasn't particularly a fan of the city known locally as 'The Big Durian'. I'd always considered it to be too noisy, crowded, polluted and, to be honest, too much. Previously, I'd always maintained I could never see myself living in Jakarta, yet, with necessity being the mother of invention, or something, here I now was having to get to grips with the place.

To be fair, I found my prejudices and fears regarding the city to be both outdated and unwarranted, and I quickly discovered that Jakarta had a charm all of it's own. Although bigger, busier and noisier than anywhere I'd ever encountered before, it was never boring and it really did offer up opportunities for all tastes. For example, I found a much larger expatriate society than in Surabaya and I was able to start playing proper organised football again. After such a long time of 'going native' I now found myself making expatriate friends and as a result experiencing more of what the city had to offer.

I visited museums and art galleries for the first time in my life, and also enjoyed the experience of becoming a semi-regular visitor to the theatre too. I was introduced to a new cosmopolitan way of life and in no time at all, it seemed, I became acclimatised to my new surroundings.

I fell into a new routine whereby I would wake up early and go for a run before breakfast. Then I would settle down for a couple of hours studying before heading to the office to start work at around 11. As lessons at the school didn't normally commence until mid-afternoon, I would then have a while in order to deal with administrative issues and plan my own lessons. Reasonably late finishes of around 8 or 9pm would usually prevent too much socializing during the week, but weekends would be spent following leisure activities, both old and new, and making new friends.

Jakarta's malls are legendary and the metropolis is probably second only to Singapore in Southeast Asia in that respect. Never really having been one for spending days on end traipsing around such places, they held little personal interest for me but even I had to admit they were a haven for when I wanted to visit good eateries, bookshops or cinemas.

The traffic jams were, and are, legendary of course, but steps are constantly being taken by the city's municipal government to try and alleviate this. My arrival in Jakarta more or less coincided with the inauguration of the city's bus-route programme. This is a system of bus routes around the city designed to reduce private vehicle use. One lane of the main thoroughfares in Jakarta is totally cut off to general traffic and only buses can plough these routes. The bus lanes are raised to prevent normal traffic entering them. The upshot of this innovative programme is that the pedestrian travelling around Jakarta now finds it much easier to get around.

Another less successful innovation by the city's governor was the introduction of a 3-in-1 traffic system. This was a system in which certain designated areas of the city were no-go-zones at certain times of the day to private vehicles with less than three occupants. The idea was to try and encourage car-pooling, and so policemen were stationed along these routes checking that each private car did indeed contain the minimum number of people. However, this 'solution' proved to be unworkable and thus short-lived due to the almost immediate appearance of 'street jockeys' – a name given to the number of intrepid people who quickly figured that standing along the routes leading into the 3-in-1 areas offering themselves up as extra 'passengers' was as good a way as any of earning a few rupiah.

Although I was a bit disappointed that my return to England hadn't quite turned out the way I hoped, and also that Jolie had knocked me back, I still felt I had been lucky and come up trumps with this deal and the way things had worked out in general. The school was, of course, sponsoring me with regards to my work permit and visa, and also agreed to sponsor Tess, who under Indonesian law was automatically deemed British and so needed relevant immigration documents, never mind the fact she had an Indonesian mother, and was born and had spent her entire life here. The school also provided me with a partially furnished house and transport to and from the school, so things were finally beginning to look up.

Initially, Yossy was staying in Surabaya while Tess finished kindergarten and the plan was for them to join me at the end of the school year.

And yet, Yossy continued to insist she had not been unfaithful. I knew that it was lies, of course, and my moment of wavering and actually beginning to believe her had passed, but I did now think she had a point when she said that all of this could be a blessing in disguise and we could at least try and start again away from everyone and everything else back in Surabaya.

As the pregnancy progressed, I preferred not to think about it too much and I just concentrated on establishing myself in my job and preparing for their imminent arrival.

As I said, I was living in a school house not far from my job and relished the experience of living completely alone for the first time in my life. I lived a simple but enjoyable life then, and it was great to just kick back and relax after all the stresses and strains of the last few years. I managed the art of rudimentary cooking and so knocked myself up something simple like egg, sausage and chip sandwiches most evenings. I hardly ever went out anywhere, and I just stayed home enjoying my culinary delights in front of a 20p knock-off DVD most evenings.

I was beginning to get my mojo back and, as much as I had enjoyed my time in England, was actually quite happy to be back in Indonesia.

The one frustration I was consistently feeling then, though, and it really was quite a big niggle at times, believe me, was my almost constant inability to be able to contact Yoss. She had at least three mobile phones which were seemingly permanently switched off, the house phone at our place just rang and rang, which indicated it'd been unplugged, and whenever I called one of the schools in Sidoarjo looking for her, her staff informed me she was not there and they had no idea where she was.

Frustrating, as I say.

She arrived at my house out of the blue. It threw me off kilter a bit, to be honest, this just turning up. I wasn't expecting her and I thought she would at least give me a bit of notice.

However, that's not what flummoxed me the most. Nope, somewhat more perplexing was the fact that she was quite obviously around six or seven months gone and in addition to Tess and the servant, she had someone else in tow. A male someone at that and, so she informed me, he would be staying with us.

With that she went to what she described as 'her' bedroom to unpack, followed by Tess, the servant and this guy. I was left alone in the living room and, with nothing better to do, I went off to what was obviously now 'my' room and went to sleep.

It seemed that this chap was one of her workers from the schools in Sidoarjo. His name was Ritchie and he had, in Yossy's words, 'helped' her a lot.

It was a bit of a brow-frowner as to what exactly Ritchie intended doing now he was in Jakarta or, indeed, why Yoss would think we should be putting him up, presumably free of charge.

The cause of even more scalp-scratching was why exactly the four of them set up in 'her' room while I continued to sleep alone.

Very perplexing.

So, anyway, the next few months progressed and events unfurled. The child, a boy, was born in September that year and a DNA test to determine the little lad's paternity wasn't exactly a nailed on requirement as anyone giving the fella and Ritchie the most cursory of glances could be in no doubt whatsoever.

Yossy, upon realising the 'miracle conception' story was out of legs, came up with another, equally fantastic, explanation for little William's coming into being. This tale involved black magic, white magic and the necessity to be with child in order to ward off evil spirits attempting to attack her.

As I was otherwise detained in England, she related, she needed to find somebody to impregnate her, and so Ritchie was her man of choice. Now, evidently she didn't think he would be up (in a manner of speaking) for this, and so she gave him a 'magic potion' which made him act in the, er, required manner.

Anyway, conception was achieved (although whether this was at the first try or not is sadly unrecorded) and William was the result of it all.

And yet … it still wasn't the end. So, why? Why and how could someone, anyone, put up with such behaviour, such blatant disrespect and downright absurdity? I wish I could answer that. I wish I knew.

Oh yes, I tried to leave her on a number of occasions or else tried to persuade her to go, but it never worked. Either she bluntly refused to go, or else I had a change of heart and decided that I did love her still and I did want things to be ok again.

My problem was I couldn't let go. I couldn't let go of either my love for her or of the memory of the times we shared together. I suppose I also couldn't let go from hoping that somehow, someday we would have that back again.

I guess this is what having Alzheimer's disease must be like. I mean, I spent most of my time in a fog-like trance with short spells of clarity and lucidity when I was able to see things as they really were and as other people surely did. In short, I could see her lies for what they were and the fool that I was.

They never lasted long though, these spells. All too soon I was once again lost in a fog of confusion and self-delusion where I convinced myself that everything was fine and she was telling me the truth and that we had a marriage in more than just name alone.

I would go from day to day coping with other aspects of my life – my work, fitness, etc. – and nobody except those closest to me ever suspected anything out of the ordinary. Most people never began to imagine my situation.

Yet even the very small number of people who did know what was going on, those who were the closest to me in Jakarta and to whom I told some, if not everything, of what'd been going on, were unable to assist or advise me in any meaningful way. Nobody could get through to me. Nobody could truly understand what was happening or, more pertinently, why I was allowing these things to happen.

The only explanation I can give to this day is that I felt like this was it. This was my life; the cards I had been dealt with were these and nothing was ever going to change.

Coffee Plus Café, Plaza Indonesia, Jakarta, 2006

Back in the café, on my first date, I was approaching the end of my tale of woe.

I told her how Ritchie was no longer here on a permanent basis. He had a job the other side of Jakarta and rented a room, or *kost*, closer to his office, only returning sporadically. Yossy still slept in the other room together with the maid and the two children, while I continued to sleep alone in 'my room'. This arrangement suited us both for now, and I no longer asked her to spend any time with me in that way.

I hadn't been living the life of a monk, though, and I believed the only way I might ever be in a position to alter my life was by meeting someone through these illicit trysts who I could care for. It didn't exactly fill me with pride, being unfaithful in this way, but I rationalised it on the basis of 'needs must'. After all, Yoss and I had not had any sort of physical relationship pretty much since Tess was born.

I had had a few relationships with other girls over the previous few months, and some had meant more than others to me. Some had been brief liaisons, unsavoury and unsatisfactory, but one had left an indelible mark on me, as I explained now in the café.

A short-lived affair with one particular young lady knocked me sideways, as what started as just another roll in the hay got a bit out of hand when I developed feelings for her. It all ended up a bit messy and bounced me off-kilter, to tell the truth.

But back to Yossy: I wished she would just go. I wished she would be strong and make a decision to leave me and to be with Ritchie or to live her life alone, or whatever, but she wouldn't. She wouldn't go even if I tried to kick her out. She said she had no money to go anywhere else and if I insisted on her leaving she would take Tess and go and live in a village somewhere and my daughter would suffer as a result.

She knew I couldn't accept that and so on it went.

Sari's Story

She called me a *bule-mania*. I am not a *bule-mania*, am I? I don't think I am. I just like *bules*, that's all. I think she was cruel to say that. It is the same as calling me a bad girl, and I am not a bad girl, I think.

Do you know what a *bule-mania* is? Do you know what a *bule* is? I will tell you. *Bule* is the name people here in Indonesia give to white men or ladies, expatriates. We call them *bule* because this word is similar to albino and we think their white skin makes them look like albinos. Some of them don't like to be called *bule* and they say it is not a nice word. They say it is the same as calling a black man a nasty name, but I don't think it is. We don't mean it as a bad name. It is just a word we use. Do you think it's a bad name? Am I bad if I call a white man a *bule*? I don't think I am.

Anyway, a *bule-mania* is the name for an Indonesian girl who likes *bules* very much. Usually a *bule-mania* will always want a *bule* boyfriend or to be near *bules* and sometimes people think she is a bad girl. I am not a bad girl, I think.

There are many reasons why someone might like a *bule*. Some people, but not me, think they are very handsome; some think they have a sophistication or 'coolness' about them; others think they must have a lot of money if they come from somewhere like America or Europe; while others think if they marry a *bule* their kids will be adorably cute!

Me? I like them because I think they are different, special, and mysterious. I think they are well mannered and well educated and know how to treat people nicely. That's all.

Maybe I should tell you about myself. My name is Sari. Actually, Sari is my nickname. My real name is Ratnasari Dwi Pramiati, but everybody calls me Sari or just Ri. I prefer to be called Sari. In my country everybody has a nickname and everybody's name means something. My name means *the girl full of love and wisdom*. I don't think I am wise, but I know now I can be full of love in the right condition.

Actually, *she* said I fall in love too easily.

She was my best friend in the office and her name was Selvey. She was older than me and married with a baby boy. His name is Eric and he is very funny. She had a picture of him on her desk. Selvey was very nice to me but she didn't like it if I always talked about *bules*. I don't know why, but I don't think Selvey liked *bules* very much and she didn't agree that they are handsome at all. Selvey sometimes used to call me a 'mummy's girl' because I didn't have a boyfriend for so long, but I know she always cared for me and she just wanted me to be happy.

Selvey said that I liked *bules* too much because I was always talking about them or else reading about them in magazines and books. I said that I was just interested in different people from different cultures but not crazy about them. I think she believed me sometimes and was just kidding with me, but other times I think she was serious.

Sometimes it was hard to understand Selvey, because often she was quiet and fierce looking. She didn't talk much to me sometimes, and that made me feel like I had done something wrong and so I felt sad or worried, but then she would change suddenly and be very friendly again and spend ages just chatting away to me. Selvey never wanted to talk to me in English, though. She said we are Indonesian and so we should speak to each other in Indonesian. I know she can speak English very well, better than me for sure, because I often heard her talking with our clients on the phone, but she always refused to talk to me in English. I don't know why.

I guess sometimes older people can be hard to understand, right? Not that Selvey is that old, really. I think she is maybe 35 or something like that.

We worked together for more than three years after I joined the company straight from university, and in that time you'd think I would understand more about her, wouldn't you? Well, as my story unfolds you'll learn that she is full of surprises.

Well, my story really begins a while back. I worked in an office in Jakarta for a finance company. It was easy work but sometimes a bit boring. I had lots of free time and so usually spent it reading on the internet or talking with my friends. I had many friends in the office, but most of them were a bit older than me and they were married or had serious boyfriends. At that time I didn't have a boyfriend yet, but I used to think I would like one soon.

Whenever I was not busy in my office, I had plenty of time to browse the internet. I liked to read the news and see what was happening here in Jakarta and Indonesia, and also in other places in the world. I always tried to read everything in English because I have always wanted to learn more. I think if a person just reads things in their own language then they don't learn so much.

Whenever there was nothing very interesting to read on the internet, I would have a look on some of the expat chat sites. There were two sites I particularly liked to look at. They were called *Jakchat* and *Expat*. They were websites set up for expatriates, *bules*, living here. They gave much advice to the *bules* about how to live here, find a job, make friends, etc., and they also had forums where people could write with questions and sometimes opinions about life here.

I liked to read the forums because I think it helped me to understand more about the *bules* and their lives. I sometimes used to try to read what they said to Selvey but not usually, because I knew she didn't like *bules*. Sometimes the forums could be very busy with many people posting news and questions and stories, and sometimes they were very quiet.

Actually, anybody could join the forums. You didn't have to be a *bule*; you just chose a nickname and became a member. I became a member, but Selvey didn't. My nickname on both websites was SariGal80. I think it was a good name for me because my real name is Sari and I was born in 1980. Back in the beginning I didn't often post on the forums. I usually liked to just read what other people posted.

Selvey often used to say I shouldn't write on the forums at all and if I did then one day I would have a problem with a *bule*. I didn't know why Selvey said that at the time and I just thought she worried too much.

One day I logged on to the internet and saw there were lots of people writing on the forums. Some people were writing on the personals forum and other people were replying to them. There was a discussion about mixed relationships between *bule* and Indonesian people. Somebody wanted to know if the forum thought a relationship between people of different countries could be a success or if there would be too many differences.

Some people wrote that they thought there would be no problems, but others wrote and said there would be some. I remember thinking at the time: love is blind and if two people love each other then they can overcome their problems. I also remember telling Selvey this but she didn't look very interested. She said I was naïve and I should go back to work. I don't think I was naïve. I think I was just romantic.

I read all the forum's posts on the topic but I didn't post anything myself. I don't know why. I read about one girl's experience with her *bule* boyfriend. She said she was with him for six months but he was never faithful to her. She said he had many other Indonesian girlfriends at the same time as her even though he was quite old and not very handsome. I felt sorry for her, but other people on the forum said that is normal for *bule*. They said that *bules* always have many girlfriends and they like to have fun only. I don't think that is true. I think *bules* are good people, usually.

There was another new thread on the forum that day. This

one was started by an expatriate, a *bule*. He said his name was Charlie and he was from England. He said he had been in Jakarta for just a couple of weeks but he would stay for one year while he worked at a company here. He sounded interesting, but also a bit lonely and so I started to feel sorry for him. He said he had no friends here and he was looking to find some people to maybe meet for a coffee or something.

Reading down, I saw a few people had replied and welcomed him to Jakarta. One or two gave him some advice about places to go if he wanted to meet people but nobody suggested meeting him. I wondered why not.

I had a thought: Do you think he would want to talk to me or to meet me?

I felt I would like to help him to feel happy in Jakarta. He must have been feeling sad to be away from his family and friends and in a strange country where he didn't know anybody, I reasoned. I wanted to help Charlie. Was that wrong, do you think? I think he sounded like a nice man.

I didn't want to ask Selvey if she thought I should write to him because I knew she would be angry and call me a mummy's girl again, so I just looked at Charlie's profile on the website and I saw he had given his email address. Maybe I would send him an email introducing myself and welcoming him to my country. I don't think there is anything wrong with that, right? I don't think that would make me a bad girl, do you?

Yes, I decided, I would write to him later but I wouldn't tell Selvey, and I may tell Ari or I may not. We'd see.

Ah! Who is Ari???

Didn't I tell you? Ooops! Ok, well, although Selvey was my best friend in the office, Ari was my best friend outside it. In fact, I think he is probably my best friend overall, even better than Selvey.

His name is Ari (short for Ariansa Wiboso) and he has been my friend since we were together in the third grade of elementary school. He is a funny boy and my good friend and always helps me and supports me and never makes me angry or sad, unless he is calling me a *bule-mania,* which he started doing after I told him that Selvey did. Actually, I know he is not serious and is just teasing me when he says that. I think he likes to see me angry sometimes, but then he tells me a joke and makes me laugh again and I can't stay angry with him for long.

Now, Ari and I used to see each other all the time when we were growing up but after I graduated university and started work, we didn't see one another every day. He continued studying in medical school and I started working.

Well, back to Charlie. I wrote to him and then I spent ages waiting to see if he would reply. I thought he would reply because he was lonely. I was sorry for him.

In my email to him I wrote that I was happy he had chosen to come and live in my country and I hoped he would enjoy his time here. I told him that Indonesian people are very friendly people and I was sure he would soon have lots of friends. I then added a smiley. Like this: ☺ I don't know why I did that. I hoped he didn't think I am childish. I often use smileys when I write emails to my friends. I think it is a friendly thing to do. What do you think?

I wanted to ask Selvey if she thought it was childish to use smileys but I was worried she would ask me who I wrote to and I didn't want to tell her. Selvey worried too much about me, but I liked her. She was and still is my friend

The day just dragged on and as I was still not very busy I had time to read more on the internet. When I had time like this, I sometimes read stories about my favourite TV shows to find out what would happen in the next episode. I liked to watch programmes from America mostly. I don't really like Indonesian TV or films too much. I think the stories in Indonesian TV shows are all the same. In these shows the women are always crying and the men are always cruel. The men always hit the women and make them fall down and then leave the house quickly. I don't think it is good if the men always hit the women, do you? That doesn't usually happen in real life.

That's why I preferred to watch the TV shows from America. My favourite shows are *Desperate Housewives, Grey's Anatomy, C.S.I, 90210* and *Gossip Girl*. I think these shows are much more realistic, don't you? The men and ladies all seemed to be more independent and cool and that made me think America must be a wonderful place to live in because there everyone seems to be so confident.

I started wondering if Charlie was the same type of guy as the men in these shows. I mean, I knew he was from England and not America, and I knew the men in the shows are only actors and that the stories are made-up and not real and everything, but I just imagined all *bules* must be much the same in real life as they are on TV. I guess I learned the hard way not to judge a book by its cover, though.

Sometimes after work I watched TV with Ari or else went to the cinema with him and we discussed the places in the films and the people. Ari also thinks the films and TV from America are better than the ones from Indonesia but I think he just likes to look at the beautiful *bule* ladies. I sometimes teased him that he should try and find a *bule* girlfriend but then he normally just blushed and said he was not a *bule-mania*. He is a funny boy. I like him and I hope he will have the future he deserves, one day.

I looked up at the clock and saw it was nearly time to go home and until now Charlie hadn't replied my email. I decided to check one more time and then if he still hadn't written to me I would go home and look again the next day.

Wow!!!!!!!!!!! I had a reply from him!!! See, I knew he was a good man! All *bules* are good men! Just like in the movies! Just like Matt Damon and George Clooney and that actor who plays *Maloney* in *Grey's Anatomy* and … ooooh, many others!

Right? Right?

My mind was racing and I was gabbling (internally anyway, in reality I didn't say a word) and a million thoughts and questions were racing through my mind.

What does he say?????? I can't open it, I'm too nervous.

Maybe he wants to meet me and then he will fall in love with me and want to marry me and take me to England and meet his family and we will have many children and they will be semi-*bule* and so cute and everyone will know me as a lucky girl with a great life!

I knew I had to calm down. Ok. Take a deep breath. It's ok.

It's just an email. Just read it and see what he says. Ok. Here we go.

From: Charlie7787@hotmail.com
To: Sarigal80@Yahoo.com
Date: 26 June, 2005

Dear Sari,

Thank you very much for your email. It was a nice surprise to hear from you.

What do you do here, Sari? I work as an English teacher in Slipi. Do you know that place? I should think you do as you said you were born here in Jakarta. ☺

Yes, you are right about Indonesian people being very friendly. Everyone here is always smiling at me and they all want to talk to me. I feel a bit like a film or pop star ☺ but until now I still don't have any close friends.

Well, Sari, I think I should go now because I have to get back to work.

Take care and have a great day.

Charlie

I read his email many times and I was floating. I was so very happy. I thought that was a very nice email and Charlie was a nice man. He was very polite and kind, I thought. I happily read his email many times and it proved what I was thinking: *bule* men were polite and kind and this email was evidence of that. I decided to write to him again later. I would like to be his friend.

He was a nice man, I thought and he even used smileys, the same as me. In fact, he used two smileys. This showed what a friendly man he was. I had to go home, but already I was looking forward to writing to him again.

The very next day I decided to write again to Charlie. I thought about him a lot in the night.

I hoped he was ok the previous night and not too lonely in his house. I hoped he could find some friends here soon. I worried a bit about him.

Ok. This was my email to him.

From: Sarigal80@Yahoo.com
To: Charlie7787@hotmail.com
Date: 27 June, 2005

Dear Charlie,

It is me, Sari. Thanks you very much for your write to me. I am very happy to read your email and you reply to me. Yes, you are right. I do know Slipi because I am live in Jakarta all my life until now☺. My office is in Thamrin. Do you know it? It is not so far from Slipi. I am work for finance company. I like my job but am boring here sometimes.

Wow, you are an English teacher? I hope you are understand my English? ... Maybe you can understand I think.

I hope you will have many friends soon.

Ok, Charlie. I must start my works now. Nice to know you and I hope you have a nice day and write me your news again.

Your (new) friend,
Sari.

I looked at my email for a long time before I sent it. Was it ok? I know my English is not good and, actually, I wanted Selvey to help me but I was still scared to tell her about Charlie. I hoped Charlie didn't think I was a silly girl because I finished my email with 'Your friend, Sari.' Maybe he would be angry because I said I was his friend? I hoped not. I didn't think so. Do you? I just wanted him to know I was happy to be his friend if he did.

Three weeks later my world had turned upside down. There I was, sitting at my desk and feeling angry about it all again and I couldn't think of Charlie as a good man anymore. I think he lied to me and tricked me. I felt sad. I felt like a stupid girl. I was not happy. I was sad.

In the three weeks after I first contacted Charlie, and the almost two weeks since we first met, Charlie made a fool of me. I think he was laughing at me with all his friends and all the other many, many Indonesian girls he knew all along. I am crazy. Ahhhhh ... Charlie! Why?????????

In the beginning everything seemed so nice and Charlie seemed like such a nice man. He replied to all my emails and always showed that he was interested in me and asked me lots of questions and I was always happy when I got to work and checked my email and saw he had written to me.

After a week or so of sending emails almost everyday he gave me his mobile number. Actually, I didn't ask for it; he just put it on the bottom of one of his emails to me. I was confused when I saw it because I didn't know what it meant. I didn't know if it meant he wanted me to call him or if he wanted me to give him my number, or what.

I was not brave to call him. I am a girl. I cannot just call a man I've never met. That is the sign of a bad girl, I think. So, finally I decided I would just give him my number too and then see what happened.

So, that is what I did. I wrote an email to him and finished it with my mobile number at the bottom, just like he did. Then I waited.

The next day he called me! When I heard my phone ringing I looked at the number displayed on it and didn't recognise it but I thought *maybe* it was Charlie. I was so surprised, scared, and happy all at the same time when I answered and it was him.

'Hello, it is me, Sari,' I said.

'Hello Sari. This is Charlie. How are you?' his soft voice said to me.

I was shaking with nerves but I said, 'Oh, hi Charlie. I am good. And you?'

Charlie then spoke to me for a few minutes and I tried very hard to understand everything he said, but it was quite difficult because he spoke quickly and my English was not so good still. After a short while talking together he said he had to go and so we said goodbye.

After we stopped talking, I looked at the phone in my hand for a long time and I felt so excited. I couldn't believe he had called me. I had actually spoken with a *bule* and he was so nice to me! Wow, I felt like I was in heaven. I felt like I was floating.

Then I saw Selvey looking at me.

'*Siapa itu?* Who was that?' She asked me.

I didn't want to tell her, but I was so happy I thought I would burst and so I told her everything. I told her about reading Charlie's post on the forum and the replies he had received to that. I told her about my first email to him and his reply to me, and then the later emails. I even told her about him giving me his number and me giving him mine.

'*Huh. Kamu gadis berani, ya*? You are a brave girl, right?' is all Selvey said to me. She looked very angry and disappointed in me. I don't know why. She made me feel sad right after Charlie made me feel happy.

'*Apa, Mbak?* What, sis?' I said to her. I called her Mbak because this is the polite word to use to a lady who is a little bit older than you are. It means older sister or colleague.

I think she realised I was a bit sad and confused because she was then a bit nicer to me. She smiled and said, '*Tak apa apa, dik* (Nothing, young sis). I know you are not a brave girl, but you are naïve. Just be careful ya?' She said this last bit in English. I don't know why, because she almost never spoke in English to me.

I was still confused a bit but I just smiled and agreed to be careful.

A few minutes later my phone beeped as I got an sms. I looked at it and saw it was from Charlie. My heart leapt again. I was scared again and excited too.

It read, 'Hi sari, thx 4 d cht. hp cn mt sn.Cl' I couldn't understand it. I read it over and over but it made no sense to me. I knew I couldn't ask Selvey because I didn't want her to call me a brave girl again, so I forwarded it to Ari. I explained I had received it from my friend, Charlie, but I didn't understand it.

Ari is a good boy. He is funny, too. At first he just sent me a smiley face in reply, but then a few minutes later he sent me another sms.

'Your friend wrote to you "Thanks for the chat. Hope we can meet soon" … this means little Sari is falling in love????????? See you later, sis.'

I smiled when I read Ari's sms. I am so glad he is my friend. He always cares about me. When I told him about Charlie and the emails he didn't call me a brave girl. He just smiled. He is a good boy. I am proud he is my friend. I said thank you to him and went back to work.

The next day Charlie sent me another sms. He sent it early in the morning and he just asked how I was. I liked it better if he sent sms and didn't call me because I could take my time trying to understand what he said, but in a phone call it is difficult to understand a *bule* speak.

This time it didn't take me so long to understand what it meant and I replied to it quickly. During the day we sent a few more sms's to each other and then he sent one asking to meet me!!! I was very happy but also very worried. I had never spoken face to face with a *bule*. Maybe he would think I was a stupid girl, ugly, uneducated, nothing to talk about, couldn't speak English well. I panicked.

I went to the toilet and took my mobile with me and called Ari.

'Ari, what should I do? He wants to meet me. I am so afraid'

'Ha, sis. You really are funny,' he laughed at me.

'Shut up, Ari. Tell me what to do?

'You want me to shut up *and* tell you what to do?' he was still laughing at me.

'ARIANSA WIBOSO!!!!! I will never talk to you again if you don't help me now,' I shouted.

Then he stopped laughing and he told me to go with my heart. He said I could go and meet Charlie but just to be careful and relax and enjoy myself. I asked him to accompany me but he said that wouldn't be good. He said that Charlie had only invited me to meet him and so if he went too it would look silly. He told me to have a nice time and to let him know what happened later.

He is so good to me. He is my best friend.

So, I went back to my desk and I replied to Charlie. I said, 'k, wld lv 2 mt u. wr + wn?' which meant, 'Ok, I would love to meet you: where and when?'

I was still not sure and I was so scared I nearly changed my mind. After I sent that sms I switched my phone on silent mode and hid it in my desk. I was too afraid to look at it or to hear it beep. I hoped Charlie would reply soon but part of me also hoped he wouldn't reply at all. He seemed so nice and I didn't want to make him disappointed when and if we met.

For the next hour I tried to do my work but my fingers kept going towards my desk drawer. I wanted to check my messages but I couldn't. I wanted to be brave but I wasn't. *Waduh*, I really did feel like the mummy's girl that Selvey sometimes called me.

I knew I couldn't delay forever and so I finally opened my

desk drawer and took out my phone.

I had one message.

I learnt. I learnt that Charlie is not a good boy. Sitting there, the day after our second date, I was sure of it. My mind was racing. I didn't want to see him anymore or be his friend, I mused. I thought he was a playboy who just liked to have fun with girls.

I don't think I am a bad girl or a silly girl, though. I don't think I am a naïve girl or a mummy's girl or a *bule-mania* like Selvey thinks, I think I am just a normal girl who was tricked by a crazy *bule*.

Actually, we have a name for 'crazy westerner' in our language. It is *bule gila*. *Gila* means crazy. Sometimes we join the words and make one new word: *bugil*. I think Charlie is *bugil*.

The next day Charlie sent me many sms and also tried to call me twice. I don't know what he wrote because I deleted all his messages without reading them. I was not angry with him anymore but I was disappointed. I was disappointed that I was wrong about him.

I now knew that Charlie lied to me. He had many friends here. He was not a lonely boy like I thought. He was not a polite boy, either.

The first time we met we just had a coffee in Starbucks in Plaza Indonesia. It was nice and sweet, like we were teenagers. I was very nervous and polite, but so was he. I thought he was so nice then because he didn't want to look directly at me and so I thought he was a shy boy. I remember I called him a 'mysterious boy' because he was so quiet and polite. When I called him that,

I remember, he gave me a funny look. I asked him if I had made a mistake, but he just smiled and said nothing.

I remember he said 'please' and 'thank you' a lot the first time we met and I told him he this was unusual and he didn't have to say words like that all the time, but he said it was natural for him and he even said 'thank you' to the assistant who gave us our coffee. I think it is strange, ya? How can a man be so polite on one side and so impolite and bad on the other?

After our coffee we walked around Plaza Indonesia for a while and he held my hand. It felt very nice and then we watched a film in the cinema. Charlie paid for most things, like the coffee and movie tickets, but I bought us some snacks. Charlie didn't talk very much the first time we met, but he was nice.

After the film I told Charlie I had to go home and so he and I walked to the taxi rank and he wanted to give me some money to pay for the taxi, but I said it was ok and I would pay myself. Charlie smiled and kissed my cheek and said goodbye. Nothing much happened on that first date, but he was nice. Charlie is nice, I thought. I like him. He is a good man.

I was wrong.

After our first date we chatted a bit by sms and also by YM (YM is Yahoo Messenger) but didn't meet again for a few days. When we did meet again we went to the cinema again. Charlie still seemed like a quiet boy, but he looked at me more this time. I could see him looking at me in the cinema even though it was dark. I was a bit surprised, but thought it was ok.

He saw that I had seen him looking at me and then he smiled

and I smiled too. He seemed to move a bit closer to me in the cinema and then he held my hand again.

I felt ok now, still a bit nervous, but ok. Charlie smiled more than before, but didn't say much more. After the film we walked around the mall and had something to eat. Charlie talked to me a bit about his life in England. He said he had one brother and one sister and that they were both married. He said that he didn't think he would ever get married. I was surprised when he said this because in my country everybody gets married.

I asked him why he didn't think he would get married. Do you know what he said? He said he wouldn't get married because he didn't think any girl would ever want him.

Crazy, right?

I told him many girls would want to be married to him and when he asked why, I said it was because he was funny and smart and handsome.

I felt a bit shy after I said that to him, but he seemed to look a bit happier. I think I understand now what he was doing. He was just playing with me.

Ha! I am a stupid naive mummy's girl who needs her bottom smacked, just like Selvey said I do!

I think you can guess what happened next. I am shy. I don't want to tell you, but I want to write down everything that happened and then maybe I won't feel so crazy.

Ha! Crazy, stupid, Indonesian girl!

After I said I thought he was funny, smart, blah blah blah ... he smiled and said nobody had ever said anything like that to him before and that I was a special girl. He said that he felt 'humble'. I didn't know what that word meant and so I asked him to explain it. When he had I think I probably went red again.

After we finished eating, we went to the front of the mall to call a taxi. I thought he would order two taxis, one for him and one for me, but when we got to the taxi rank he asked me if I wanted to come back with him to his apartment.

Well!!! I am not a bad girl! I was scared when he said that and I didn't answer directly. He looked at me and held my hand, but I was scared, scared, scared, you know?

'I don't know,' I said, 'What for?'

He looked down to the floor and I thought then I had hurt him because I suspected him of something. I felt sad. He said,

'Just to watch a DVD or talk, or something. I just don't want to say "goodnight" to you yet, that's all.'

He looked so sad then and I thought I had hurt him. I felt guilty. Isn't that crazy? ME feeling guilty!!! It should be him who felt guilty for what he did to me later!

Anyway, I felt sorry for Charlie and so said I would come with him to his apartment but not for long. He smiled and we got into a taxi.

In the taxi we didn't talk much but Charlie held my hand. I was nervous but I trusted Charlie. Charlie is a good boy, I thought. He won't hurt me or do anything I don't like. He smiled at me again and then I felt relaxed. I was safe, I thought.

Hey, do you know what happened when we got to his apartment building? Well, we went into reception to get in the lift and there was a young man there behind the desk. He smiled at Charlie but he looked at me very badly, I thought. I just scowled at him. I gave him my fierce look. Ari calls it my *galak* look. *Galak* means fierce in my language.

When we got upstairs to his apartment the first thing I did was to take my shoes off. In my country it is always polite to take off your shoes and leave them outside. (Ari says there are some people who go round stealing people's shoes and that's why you sometimes see people going home from the mosque with no shoes on, but I don't think that's true. I think that is one of Ari's jokes.)

Charlie said I didn't have to take off my shoes in his apartment, but I said I didn't feel comfortable wearing shoes in his house. His apartment was very nice and I could see he had a big living room area with a kitchen coming off of it and then he had one bedroom and a bathroom. It was very clean and I was a bit surprised because I didn't think *bules* knew how to clean. I don't know why, but you never see them doing it in the films, do you?

He told me to make myself 'feel at home' and I wasn't really sure what he meant but he was smiling when he said it and so I felt ok. He then went into the bathroom and I could hear him taking a shower. I didn't really know what to do so I decided to just sit on his sofa and wait for him to come back. There were no pictures of Charlie or his family on display anywhere, and I thought that was a bit strange too, because Charlie told me he missed his family a lot

I turned on his TV and had a look through some of his DVDs. He had many films. In Indonesia you can buy very cheap DVD films. They are actually not original films, they are pirate ones. I think we should not really buy pirate films because it's like stealing, isn't it? But ... they are so cheap, you know. They are maybe only Rp 8,000 each while the original film is about twenty times more expensive and even going to the cinema is about four times more expensive than buying a pirate DVD. I usually buy pirate DVDs and I sometimes go to the cinema, but I never buy original DVDs. I am not that crazy.

When Charlie came back I was still sorting through his films. He had changed his clothes and his hair was wet from his shower. I think he had also put some perfume for men on. Actually he smelt quite nice and it was easy to smile at him.

I was sitting on the sofa and he came and sat by my feet on the floor. This felt nice, you know. It felt like he was close to me but not actually in a bad or naughty way. I now felt happy again and so we started chatting once more. We talked about some of the films and which ones we had already seen and which film stars we both liked. It felt nice and ok.

You know, I really don't want to tell you what happened next. I really don't. I know you will think I am a bad girl.

I can't tell you. Sorry, I know I said I would, but I can't. Not everything, anyway. I will just tell you that at the time it felt quite nice but as soon as it was over I felt guilty and sad and like a *pelacur*. This is very bad, because a *pelacur* is a prostitute.

Charlie didn't make me do it, so I can't really blame him completely, can I? He just held my hand and then kissed me. Ahhhhhhhh ... I am *malu*, shy, now. Then we made love.

Oh, my goodness!

Can you believe that?

Charlie and I made love! It's amazing and it's so wrong. We

shouldn't have done that, should we? What do you think of me now? What would Ari think, or Selvey, or my parents or ... or anyone?

After Charlie and I finished, he went to the bathroom again and I just sat on the sofa holding all my clothes to cover my breasts, you know, like they do in the movies. I didn't know what to say or think or do.

Charlie went into his bedroom after he had finished in the bathroom and then I went into wash myself. I got in the shower and I made the water quite hot and I put lots of soap on my body and shampoo on my hair, much more than I normally do. I don't know why I did that.

I just wanted to get dressed quickly and then go home, but when I got out of the shower I had another shock. There was no towel for me to use. Now I was really, really sad. So sad, you know. I was sad because I didn't want to go out of the bathroom with no clothes on because I didn't want Charlie to see my naked body again.

I closed my eyes and prayed for help then, and that is unusual because I never usually pray, and when I was praying there was a little knock on the bathroom door.

'Who is it?' I said, and then nearly cried at the stupidity of my question.

'Who do you think it is?' he said, but not in a cruel way: 'I have a towel here for you.'

He opened the door just a bit and put his hand in with the towel.

'Thanks,' I said, and took it, dried myself and got dressed

very quickly. I came out of the bathroom and I was almost too sad to look at him. I asked him to walk with me and call a taxi to take me home, but he didn't even answer me. He was playing with his phone, maybe sending a text, or something.

I asked him again and this time he looked at me. 'Why don't you stay tonight?' he asked me.

'Oh, my God!!!! What kind of question is that? I am a good girl, I cannot stay!!!' I just started crying and ran from his apartment as quickly as I could.

You know, I thought he would at least follow me or try to make me stop crying, but after I ran out to the elevator I just heard his apartment door close. I was so confused.

I came down in the elevator and into the reception. I saw that nasty boy there again and he gave me another bad look.

I tried to ignore him but then he said, '*Sudah, Mbak?*' which means: 'Already finished, Miss?' This is very rude, because it means he thought I was a prostitute who had just had sex with Charlie for money.

I was so angry now. I stopped walking and looked directly at him.

'*Apa,* what?' I asked him and gave him my *galak* look times one thousand.

He looked a bit less cocky now and said, '*Tidak apa apa, non,* nothing Miss.'

'No,' I said, 'What do you mean already finished? Tell me.'

I was so mad at him, at Charlie, and at myself that I didn't feel shy anymore. He hesitated again, but when I clenched my fist and took one more step towards him he finally answered.

'Nothing, Miss ... Just that Mr errr. Mr ... often has ...'
Now it was his turn to look ashamed or embarrassed.

'Mr often has what, *Mas*?' I asked him, still clenching my fist.

'Erm ... girls come to this room and I thought ...'

What was I hearing? Charlie told me he had no friends and
now this ... *man*, was telling me he had many girls come to his
room, some maybe were even bad girls. I was so shocked. Really,
I was.

'Ah, really? Are you sure? Ha! You thought I was a *pelacur* or
a *gadis nakal*, naughty girl, didn't you?'

'*Maaf, Mbak*, sorry, Miss,' was all he could reply.

I wanted to hit him, I really did, but I just went outside and
called a taxi. I got in it and even though it was already late and
dark I put on my sunglasses so the driver couldn't see my tears.

Charlie had made love to me! Worse than that he had treated
me like a *pelacur* and now I knew he often did that with girls.

I cried all the way home and it wasn't until I got into bed that
I realized that the doorman had referred to the apartment as 'this
room' and not 'his room'.

Fast-forward a couple of weeks and I was back in my office and
starting to put the nightmare behind me. I still felt that Charlie
was not a nice man and I didn't want to see him again or even
talk to him, but I no longer felt as bad anymore. I knew it was
not my fault everything that happened. It was his and I also knew
that one day he would be sorry for how he lived his life now and
he would be the loser.

No. I decided, I won't be sad anymore. I will just learn my

lesson and move on.

For the first time in a while I was feeling really happy again. Selvey was being nicer to me than usual. She had seldom been angry recently and she was laughing a lot. I wondered why? Maybe something good was happening in her life again. I hoped so. She is a nice lady, really.

I didn't tell her (much) about what happened with Charlie *Bugil* – that's what I decided to call him now- except that I wouldn't be seeing him anymore. She just smiled and said 'ok' when I told her that and didn't ask me any questions.

I just didn't want to tell her, or anyone, about what we did. You know, the 'bad' thing, because I thought she might think that was not too good.

I didn't tell Ari much about what happened, either, but I think he guessed. I spoke to him by phone the next morning and I told him I was sad. He asked me if it was because of *bugil* and when I didn't answer he said he guessed that *bugil* had hurt me. He is a good boy. He told me it was ok, and that he was there for me always. He didn't say I was bad or wrong for doing 'that' with *bugil*.

Actually, maybe I should tell you something. A long time ago, when we were in high school, Ari and I made love! We were very young; maybe 17 or 18, and we wanted to know what *it* was like because all our friends were talking about 'it' and so one day when we walking home Ari asked me if I was still a virgin.

I was very shocked and I felt my cheeks burning, but I said

'Ariansa Wiboso! How can you ask me that question! You know I am. Have you ever seen me with a boyfriend?'

He just laughed and said, 'Sorry sis, it's just that everyone in our class is talking about sex and it seems that you and I are the only ones who have not tried it yet.'

I was a bit surprised at first that Ari was telling me this, because his words meant that he was a virgin too, and I knew boys don't like to admit to that.

'Ya,' I said, 'I sometimes wonder what it is like to do "it", but I can't try with someone I don't know well, can you?'

'No, of course not,' he said, but then he looked at me and said: 'but you know me well, don't you?'

'What do you mean?' I knew what he meant, of course, but I just pretended I didn't.

'Well, we know each other and … well, maybe we could find out together?' He was smiling when he said this, but I know Ari. I know when he is serious and when he is joking and at this time he was definitely serious.

'Ok, then,' I said quickly, 'Let's go to my house now and "do it". There's no one there now.'

He was shocked. 'Are you sure? I didn't mean it,' he stuttered.

'Yes, you did,' I said, 'and yes, I am sure. Why not? You think only boys are interested in sex?'

Then I smiled and punched him on the arm and we went to my house and made love.

That's all I'm going to tell you, except to say we never did it again and we never talked about it either. But it was nice and I don't regret it.

After all the nonsense with Charlie, I started writing on my blog again. Do you know what a blog is? I am sure you do. It is kind of a personal website where you can write things or post pictures or do other things. I liked to write about my life and what happened (I didn't write about *everything*, of course. I wouldn't write about *bugil*, for example) and sometimes people read my blog and they posted comments.

I usually wrote in Indonesian and not English, because my English was not so good, and I tried to write most days. I wrote a poem in Indonesian about being happy and never feeling lonely. I don't want to tell you exactly what I wrote because I am a bit shy, but I was very happy when I saw many people (well, seven) had posted comments saying they liked it.

I left messages of thanks for all the people who made comments on their blogs, but there was one person I couldn't reply to like that because when I clicked on their user name 'GarOrl' I just got directed to an email address and not to a blog. That happens sometimes if a user has registered only as a member and hasn't set up a blog.

I wrote an email to this person. I just wrote, 'Dear GarOrl', many thanks for your comment. It is nice to know you. SariGal80' and then I went for lunch.

I had a date that evening to see Ari and his new 'friend'. I say that she is a 'friend' because actually I was thinking she was Ari's new girlfriend, or possible new girlfriend. He is a funny boy. I like him, but he is very shy sometimes. He said he wanted me to meet this girl and see if I thought she was good for him. How would I know if she was good for him? He had to decide for himself, right?

Yes, Ari is a funny boy: a *mysterious* boy.

So, I go to Dunkin' in Citra Raya mall at 7pm as arranged and Ari is already there with his 'friend' when I arrive and when he sees me he stands up and introduces us.

'Sari, this is Wanda, and Wanda, this is Sari,' he says this so formally that I can't help laughing. Wanda laughs too and immediately I think I am going to like her.

'Ari,' she says, still smiling, 'We are not in your father's office now. Just relax, *aja*.'

Ari, the funny boy, just blushes and sits down as Wanda and I go to the counter to order something to eat and drink. She smiles at me and tells me that Ari has told her lots about me and she is really happy to meet me. She says Ari is lucky to have a best friend like me and that she hopes to be my friend too.

She seems so nice to me. You know, most girls would be jealous if their boyfriend, or *maybe*-boyfriend, had a girl for their best friend, but Wanda isn't. As we wait for our coffees she chats about her job as a trainee insurance clerk at an joint venture company in the city and how she met Ari through her friend's sister's friend's brother (or something, I forget exactly) and she touches my arm a lot as she talks, but in a friendly way, and by the time we take our coffees and go back to join *Mr. Funny Mysterious Boy*, it seems we have known each other for years and not just a few minutes.

We sit and chat for a while, us two girls talking much more than Ari, and it all is very nice. We speak in a mixture of English and Indonesian because Wanda says she needs to improve her English for her job.

I tell Wanda about *bugil* and she pats my hand and says that you can never trust a *bule* completely because they are different from Indonesian men. I ask if she has ever had a *bule* boyfriend and she says that she hasn't actually had a *bule* boyfriend, but she has met some through her job.

'You know,' she says, 'Some are handsome and friendly, but they all want just one thing.'

'Ya,' I agree, 'I know what you mean.'

'What one thing is that?' asks Ari, and we both laugh again at the poor innocent boy who just blushes again.

We finish our coffee and decide to go and watch a film in the cinema at the top of the mall, but just as we are arriving at the cinema I suddenly stop dead and I can't breathe. It seems like my heart will jump up into my mouth which is open and closing like I am a crazy woman or a goldfish. I just can't move and it feels like my blood has gone ice cold.

'Hey, what's wrong, sis?' Ari is concerned.

'Yes, whatever is the matter, Sari?' asks Wanda, 'You look like you have seen a *hantu*, ghost.'

'It's him,' I say, pointing at a *bule* walking in front of us.

'Him who? Bugil? Are you sure?' says Wanda, immediately understanding what's happening.

'Yes, yes, of course I'm sure,' I wail. 'That's him! Oh, no. What should I do?'

This time it is Ari who talks, 'Do nothing, sis. We are going to the cinema, remember? Just ignore him.'

Wanda takes my arm and leads us into the cinema and up to the ticket counter. She holds me tightly and when I try to turn round to look if *bugil* is around, she sort of wraps her arm around me and makes it impossible for me to see behind myself properly.

She keeps a tight hold of me as we buy the tickets and then marches me off to the loo, leaving poor old Ari alone in the cinema foyer.

By the time we get into the ladies I have clamed down a bit and am feeling almost ok again. I know that Wanda has helped me and I know now that she is really a very nice girl.

'Wow, thanks Wanda,' I say, 'Sorry about that, but bugil just made me so shocked there.'

Wanda smiles and says '*Tak apa apa*, it's nothing. Come on, let's get out there again or else Ari will think we've fallen in the toilet!' I laugh then and we go back out together, find Ari and head into the cinema.

The film is quite good but I can't help but think of *bugil* during it. I noticed that he was alone when we saw him and I don't know what that means. Does it mean he was on his way to meet someone, had just met someone, or is really as lonely as he says he is? Hmmmmm ... I just don't know.

Anyway, we have a nice evening and then we go home. When we get to the front of the mall Ari and Wanda say they will go home by taxi while I decide to take the bus. As they start to walk away Ari looks back at me and smiles and raises his eyebrows. I know he is asking me what I think of Wanda, so I smile and give him thumbs up, and then he smiles again too.

He is a funny boy.

Finally I get home, tired but happy, although just a *little* bit confused. Ah, bugil, bugil, what are you doing to me? I ask as I drift away.

I woke up early with *bugil* still in my thoughts but I didn't care. I just wanted to have a nice day with no stress. It was Friday so casual day in my office. This meant I didn't have to wear formal clothes and could wear relaxed clothes like a polo shirt or jeans, but not sandals. I was still not allowed to wear sandals on any day of the week.

I chose to wear my denim skirt and blue polo shirt and I got to work early. I should be in my office at 8 am but today I got there at 7.45, and can you guess what? Selvey was already there! I was very surprised to see her so early, and even more surprised when I saw what she was wearing. She was wearing a tight sweater and a short black skirt. It was also very tight. I thought her clothes were very nice, but they were very sexy; you could see the shape of her body very clearly, and you could even see the lines of her bra and panties through her clothes (but just a bit).

I was confused why she wanted to wear clothes like this to the office, but I did think she looked nice. I told her this, and she smiled and thanked me. She also told me she was going to a party in her husband's office later and she wanted to look nice for it. Ah, now I understood, but I still couldn't help looking at her a bit during the morning and I wondered if she knew we could see her underwear.

I started my work and switched on my computer. As usual there was not much for me to do, so I checked my email. There was nothing from *bugil*, but I did have a message from someone called G.Reeve and the title was 'Hi SariGal'. I was a bit confused at first because I didn't think I knew a G.Reeve, but I clicked it open and read.

It read:

Hi SariGal, I just wanted to say I enjoyed reading your poem the other day and to say thanks for your comment to me. How is Jakarta there? I have never been to Jakarta, but I visited Bali for a few weeks some years ago. Since then I've always been interested in Indonesia, and I would like to come back one day. I live here in Orlando, in Canada. Anyway, I hope you have a great day there. Take care. Gary.

I didn't understand at first. Who was this? How did he know my name and where I lived? Why was he writing to me? What 'comment' was he thanking me for? I was confused and so I tied to think hard. Then it slowly came to me. Maybe this was the person who left a message on my blog but didn't have his own blog for me to reply on? Yes, that must have been it. He said that his name was GarOrl. Ah, I deduced, maybe that means Gary from Orlando.

Oh, now I knew. That's nice. I was glad he had written to me again. I hoped he was a nice man, though, not like Charlie. After all, most *bules* are nice, aren't they?

I wrote him an email and I told him I was glad to know him. I wrote a little about myself and what I did here in Jakarta, and I said that I hoped he was well and happy. I also said I was surprised he could understand my poem as I had written it in Indonesian. Then I pressed 'send' and got on with some work.

As the day went on, more things happened. Charlie sent me two texts and called me twice. I didn't know what the texts said or what he wanted to talk about, because I deleted the texts without reading them and didn't answer his calls. Then Ari called me and we talked about last night. He asked me if I was ok after seeing Charlie, and I said it's no problem and I told him about my new friend, Gary. Ari laughed at me.

Huh! The naughty boy!

Then we talked about Wanda and I told him that I thought she was very nice and I liked her. I told him that actually I thought she was too good for him and she should find a better boyfriend. Then he laughed and he said I was the naughty one, not him.

Also, something else happened. Selvey started acting even more strangely. You know, she had been a bit weird for a few days now. She had been very nice to me (I know that makes me sound *jahat*, cruel, but it's true, right?), she had started wearing sexy clothes in the office, and now I could hear her talking a lot on her handphone and in English. Selvey never liked to talk in English usually, but now she was doing it a lot and always laughing when she did so.

Why, ya?

Did she have a *bule* friend, a *bule* boyfriend, even? No, that was impossible, right? She does not like *bules*, and she is married! Hmmmm … I wondered what was up with that lady. It was not my business, though, I decided, and as I didn't want her to be angry with me again, I decided not to ask any questions.

What else? Oh ya, I almost forgot. Gary Reeve from Orlando sent me an email!!!! I was delighted to read it. In the mail he told me a bit about himself and about his life. He lived in Canada where it is very cold and he had his own photography business, he liked travelling and watching sport (he said he used to play ice-hockey but now his 'legs have gone' (I didn't know what that meant) he also said he was 53 years old and had two grown up children. He said he thought my poems on my blog were 'awesome' and he could understand them a little because he had learnt a bit of Indonesian when he had stayed in Bali a few years earlier. He didn't say why he had visited Bali for a few weeks, but he did say he was planning on taking a long journey soon and maybe he would come back again.

I was a bit surprised to know his age and that he had two big children. I don't know why, but I thought he would be young, like me, but it didn't really matter. He also attached a photo of himself and when I opened it I saw quite a handsome man. He was quite small and a little bit chubby but he didn't look too old. Hmmmm … I thought he looked like a professor or a doctor, or something.

'Ok, see you later, honey.'

I stopped thinking about Gary Reeve from Orlando when I heard these words and looked up in surprise. It was Selvey, talking on her phone. I was shocked. Who was she talking to? Who was 'honey'? Would she see him? (It must be 'him' if she said 'honey', right?) I was confused. Surely Selvey knew I was there? She had to know I could hear her.

She finished her call and saw me staring at her. I tried to look away, but she just smiled at me and said nothing.

By now it was nearly time to go home, and so I sent a text to Ari to see what his plans were for the weekend and another email to Gary Reeve from Orlando wishing him a happy weekend and this time I included my photo too. I took one more look at Selvey, in her funny sexy clothes and said 'goodnight' to her and then left. As I did, my phone beeped again with another message from *bugil* / Charlie, which I just deleted without reading.

Two months later and as I sat and looked at my computer all I saw was:

From: Sarigal80@Yahoo.com
To: Charlie7787@hotmail.com
Date: 25 September, 2005

I wanted to write to him one more time and let it all out, but I didn't know where to start. Two months had just rolled by and so much had happened, so now I wanted to get it all down and explain everything. The trouble was, I knew I should just let it go, and so instead of writing anything I just let my mind wander back over everything that had occurred.

Two months in which I became I so sad, happy, disappointed, nervous, worried, excited and afraid all at the same time. Looking back, I don't know how all this could have happened. Let me tell you the position I found myself in and then I will tell you step by step what happened and how I came to be in this way.

Waduh! Am I a silly girl, or naïve, or unlucky or lucky? I don't know, sir, but I do know that both Charlie, *bugil*, and Gary Reeve from Orlando ended up wanting to marry me! Also, Ari told me he would get married too, the silly boy, and Selvey became crazy and made me think she was having an affair!

Oooohhh, my life!

So, how can I tell you what has happened? Well, after what happened with *bugil* in his apartment I didn't want to see him or have any contact with him, but then when I saw him in the cinema that time when I was with Ari and Wanda I felt strange and I couldn't stop thinking about him. He tried to call me a few times and sent me some texts and even some emails, but I didn't reply. I tried very hard to forget him, the silly *bugil*, but I just couldn't.

I started writing to Gary, the guy from Orlando, and then I sort of thought I fell in love with him and he sort of thought he fell in love with me too, and then he asked me to marry him, and then I said yes and I wrote a text to Charlie because I wanted to know how he was and I wanted to tell him my news, but he said he loved me too and that he wanted to marry me also.

That's all.

Wow, I guess I have not really explained things very well, have I? Ok, well now I will tell you step by step.

After Charlie hurt me (I don't want to call him *bugil* anymore, it's not nice) I started writing to Gary. He and I started chatting on YM and I started to get to know him more. He told me that he was 53 years old, but felt much younger (I told him he looked much younger, too) and he said he had been married twice before but he is single now. He said he was only married to his first wife for a short time and it was when they were both young. He said he loved her very much but she died in a plane crash.

He then spoke about his second wife, called Cheryl, whom he married when he was 25. He said they were married for more than 20 years but then they got divorced. I was sad when I heard his stories because it must be very sad indeed if the person you love dies, right? I also think it must be very sad if the person you have been married to for many years suddenly decides not to love you anymore. Gary said that was what happened with his second wife. I felt so sorry for him. It is a sad life, right?

He told me he had two children. They were from his second wife and they were now 25 years old and 23 years old.

Wow, I thought, a kid who is 25! That was my age!

He seemed such a lovely man but so lonely. He told me about the travelling he had done and his journey to Bali a few years ago. He still didn't tell me very much about that trip, and after my experiences with Charlie I did wonder why. I hoped he wasn't being untruthful or holding something back and although I didn't think he was, I decided not to trust him completely at first.

However, I did tell him about my life here. I told him simple things at first about my family and my job and my writing, and he was very interested in what I told him and supported me a lot.

Then I started to tell him about *bugil*, sorry, I mean, about Charlie, and I told him how much he had hurt me and, can you believe it, I even told Gary about making love with Charlie, and I didn't feel shy or guilty. It just felt right to tell him.

Gary was so sweet when I said that to him. He said that he just wanted to hold me and take away my pain and dry my tears. It was such a lovely thing to say and it made me cry a bit. Nobody has ever said such a nice thing to me as that. I felt then that he was the nicest man in the whole world and I told him my feeling. It was strange because I never usually tell anybody directly my feeling like that, but with Gary it all felt so natural and nice.

Then he asked if he could call me and so we spoke by Skype. I felt so relaxed and calm speaking to him, even though it was a bit difficult to really understand everything. We spoke for ages and I felt so close to him. It was a strange feeling but it was a nice one too.

After this first time talking to Gary, I stopped thinking much about Charlie and I looked forward to speaking with Gary every day. Sometimes we would speak on Skype, and sometimes on YM. I loved to talk to him, but I understood more when we were on YM.

One day when we were chatting on YM, I told him that I really really liked him and I looked forward to all our talking every day and he said he did too. Then I said that it was a pity he lived so far away because I would love to meet him, and he said that he would love to come to Jakarta one day, maybe soon, and meet me. I was excited when he said that and I said it would be great and that we could hang out together and I would tell everyone he was my new boyfriend.

Actually, I was just joking when I said that so I was very shocked indeed when he said he would be proud to be my boyfriend. I asked if he was serious and he said he was, and that he did want to be with me.

My heart started beating so fast when he said that. Really, was he serious? I asked him again if he was joking, and again he said he was telling me the truth. I was so happy but also so surprised and a bit scared. I mean, we were so far apart and he was so much older than me, and I had been so badly hurt by Charlie that I just didn't know if I could really trust anyone again so soon.

I didn't answer his YM for a few minutes and then he pinged me. He asked me if I was ok. I told him I was, but I also told him about my confusion and my fears. He said then that 'love is blind' and we could overcome everything.

This made me more worried and scared and happy, because he said 'love' to me. I asked him, 'Do you love me, then?' and he said 'Yes,' and then I said 'I love you too,' and then neither of us said anything for a few minutes.

I felt strange, really weird. I had never been in love before, not really. I mean, I love my family and I love my friends, but I had never really been *in love* with anyone before. It was a really unusual feeling for me when I first felt it and even more when I first said it, but it was nice, too. It sort of made me want to cry, but in a happy way. It made me want to shout loud, but also to be quiet. I wanted to tell everyone and no one at the same time.

I thought I was being a silly girl again, but I wasn't sure. I felt confused. I wanted so much to tell someone, but I didn't know who. Ari was having his own problems (which I promise I will tell you about in a minute or two) and Selvey was also busy (I will tell you about her too soon) and so I had no one to ask or to talk to.

I thought about writing on Jakchat or Expat Forum and asking for people's advice, but I didn't know what to write, and I also didn't feel good about asking strangers to help me. So, do you know what I decided to do finally? I just decided to do nothing at all.

I thought I would just keep my news to myself for now and try to relax and see what happened. I decided I would tell Ari (and Wanda) when I next got a chance, and also I would tell Selvey when I could, but not yet.

Oh my! The next few days were very scary but nice and I felt so happy. I felt really different; like I was floating along and that I was sort of watching the world go by. Nothing I did seemed to be important or have any meaning; whether it was working, eating, sleeping, or anything else: I just thought about Gary.

I knew I was walking around with a big silly smile on my face all day, every day, and I wondered if anyone else noticed. If they did, they didn't say anything about it. I was in a dreamland. Sometimes I told myself that I was being crazy; being in love with a man who was more than twice my age, who was from a different country, who had two grown-up children, and whom I had never even met. It was crazy, I tried to reason with myself, to have these feelings for Gary, but I could never convince myself. I just knew that I loved him and that I was happy.

So, let me tell you quickly about Ari, the silly boy. Remember I told you he would get married too? Well, that silly boy was getting married because he had to. Well, he said he felt he had to, anyway. You see, Ari, the silly boy, made Wanda pregnant!

I don't know how he managed that.

Well … yes, ok, I do know *how* he managed it … I mean, I don't know *why* he let that happen. Everybody now in my country gets sex education lessons in school and so Ari (and Wanda) should know how to take precautions, right? … I mean, I have only ever done *that* twice in all my life and each time I made sure the man was careful (and one of the men was Ari, remember!) so … ah, I don't know.

Ari tried not to show it, but I could see he was a bit excited to get married and become a father, while also being a bit worried too. He was most worried about his many dreams to be a doctor, and I hoped he could still follow his dreams. Ah, the silly boy. I worry about him, but I still love him. He told me his father was so angry when he told him what had happened and his mother just cried. Ari said they soon came round to the idea, though, and even offered to pay for the wedding and to help them rent a house for after they were married.

They will have their wedding soon. It will be funny to see Ari get married, I think, but maybe a bit sad too.

Anyway, back to *my* story!

I got closer to Gary and I told my family about him and our relationship and they were ok about it. Gary called me and asked to speak to my parents. He told them he loved me very much and would always look after me, and I nearly cried again when he said that.

I am not sure how much my mom and dad understood Gary because their English was very limited, even worse than mine, but I helped explain what Gary was saying. My mom was a bit worried at first and told me to be careful, and my dad didn't say much at all. He is a quiet man, really. I know my family love me very much and they just want me to be happy.

It felt so nice and lovely being in love with Gary, those first days and weeks. I felt a peace and a happiness I had never experienced before, but also a desire and a longing too. I thought about him literally every minute I was awake, and I dreamed of him every single night too. Wherever I was and whatever I was doing the picture of Gary's face was in my mind and his love for me was in my heart.

I sometimes wonder now if, whatever happens in the future, I will ever know such feelings again. I hope I will. I wouldn't like to think that the happiest days of my life are already behind me. That would be just too sad to bear, wouldn't it?

So, maybe now you are wondering what went wrong and why I am talking as if my happiness suddenly disappeared again. Well, it's because of Charlie. He disturbed me a bit.

That boy!

It makes me sad now to tell you what happened next, and for ages I really didn't know what would happen or how, or even if, I would ever solve this problem. You see, when I fell in love with Gary I felt that everything would be ok forever and that nothing would ever go wrong again, but after just a few weeks I started to think of Charlie again. I don't really know why, I can't explain it. He just kept coming into my head and I kept remembering the early days in our 'relationship' (if you can call it that) and how I had felt excited and nervous then and had wondered what was going to happen. This remembering the past made me feel a bit unhappy and so I tried to stop thinking about him, but I just felt I had to try and find some way to put the whole experience of knowing him behind me.

I didn't know what to do about my feelings of uneasiness and unhappiness, and so I talked to Selvey about it. I didn't want to, because I thought she would be cruel to me again or laugh at me and call me a mummy's girl but I had no choice. I couldn't speak to Ari because he was too busy and had stress with Wanda and his parents because of his *problem*.

Selvey was actually very kind to me after I had explained my feelings and my problems. She said it was normal to be a bit confused and unhappy about *bugil* (she called him that, not me) because I had liked him before and then he had hurt me. She said I should send Charlie a text or email saying that I hoped he was well and happy and that I had met someone new now and hoped we could be friends soon. I was not sure this was the best thing to do, but Selvey said it would help me to put him out of my mind and then I could concentrate on my new life with Gary.

You know, I was very surprised when she said that. I never thought she would think that Gary and I being together was a good idea because he was a *bule*, he was much older, and etc., etc., lah, but she was so nice to me. She was so kind to me that I could feel my tears coming again and then Selvey hugged me and told me to follow my dreams and my heart. I love her now. Really I do. I will write more about her soon and tell you what happened in her life later.

So, I took her advice and sent Charlie a text. I still have it on my phone. This is what I wrote;

September 26 2005:19.57
Hi Charlie. It is me, Sari. How are you? I am good here and a long time we didn't talk. I hope you are ok. I am happy and I will be married soon (I hope). Take care, Sari.

Charlie didn't reply for maybe one hour and at first I thought maybe he was angry with me, but then he wrote:

September 26 2005: 21.02
Hi Sari. Thanks for your text. I am ok here, I guess. Wow,
you will be married soon? How come? I didn't think you had
a boyfriend. Well, that's great news (but it makes me a bit
sad). I hope you will be very happy, and I will never forget
you. You are special. Sorry for everything if I hurt you. All
my love, Charlie.

You know, I cried a bit when I read that. Why did Charlie
have to be so nice to me now? Why did he have to say so many
nice things now? He said he was sad I was with someone else;
he said he would never forget me, that I was special, that he was
sorry, and that he loved me. Why couldn't he have said all that
before? Why did he treat me so badly? Why did I send him a text
and open all the wounds again?

A million questions in my head.

Then I remembered what Selvey said. She told me to always
be a brave girl and that if I wanted something I should try and
get it. Well, I wanted some answers to my questions and so, after
I had stopped crying, I wrote all those questions (except the
last one, of course) into one text and sent it to Charlie and then
awaited his response.

He sent me a text five minutes later and he said he would
write a real email to me the next day explaining everything and
then after I had read it maybe we could meet and discuss. I said
ok, and then tried to sleep. I dreamt of him and Gary.

The next day I got into my office early and I switched on my computer quickly because I wanted to see if Charlie had sent an email to me yet. I couldn't begin to imagine what he would say to me, I mean, he treated me so badly before so what could he say to me now to make it better?

Nothing, right?

I signed into my yahoo account and there it was; an email from ... from Charlie. It's title was 'I'm sorry!' I felt my tears coming again just looking at that title. I just didn't feel like I could open it and read it. I just can't bear this, I thought, It's too much for me.

I wanted to know what he said but I was scared, so scared. Finally I made myself become angry about being so silly and I made myself imagine Selvey was there and talking to me. Come on, mummy's girl, I told myself, impersonating Selvey. Open it and see what he says! I smiled when I said that to myself because I really think that's what she would have said if she had been there.

I clicked it open and read it slowly.

From: Charlie7787@hotmail.com
To: Sarigal80@Yahoo.com
Date: 27 September, 2005
Dear Sari
Hi, how are you? I guess you are feeling really happy and excited now. It must be a great feeling and you must be really busy making all your plans. When will you be married exactly? I wish you all the luck in the world. I am really happy for you.

Sari, I am so sorry for hurting you before. I really didn't mean to. You are a wonderful lovely girl and so sweet and innocent. You really deserve to be happy and I pray that you will be.

When we were together it just felt so nice and so wonderful. I didn't mean to do anything bad to you that night, I just felt so close to you and so relaxed and happy with you that everything we did seemed so natural. I really and truly had no plan to do anything like that. You must believe that.

I just wanted a lovely evening with you. That's all.

Ah, my Sari. I am really happy for you, truly I am, but I am still sad. After that night with you I tried many times to call you and text you to explain my feelings but I guess you were still hurt and angry and you never replied or answered the phone.

I am so sorry, and I will always regret hurting you, Sari, but worse than that I will always regret losing you. I think we could have had a wonderful life together, but I know I ruined that with my behaviour.

Anyway, take care, my sweet, and be happy. I hope in the future if you ever think of me, the silly bule who came into your life for a few short weeks, you will just smile and think something nice, but I still have slight hopes that you can forgive me and perhaps one day we can be married instead. Am I crazy to hope for this?

All my love, Sari,

Charlie.

(PS: maybe we could meet for coffee and a chat after you have read this?)

I read it and just thought '*hmmmmmm*', nothing more. I mean, what he said is all very nice, right? But it's easy to be nice now when it's too late. It's easy to hurt someone, get what you want, and then just say 'sorry' and expect everything to be fine again.

Now I was starting to feel angry. How could he do like this? I questioned. Better the stupid *bugil* didn't contact me at all again than send me something like this. What did he expect from me now? That I would feel sorry for him, that I would fall for his words and his flattery – in Indonesian language we call this type of talking *basa-basi*, which means 'talking only' – huh!

Yes, I was angry! At first I wanted to ignore him, but then I thought, No, he can't do this to me. I want real answers. So I sent him a text and I just wrote: 'Got your email. Am very angry. Meet me at Starbucks in Semmanggi Mall at 8pm.' Then I switched off my phone because I didn't want to talk to him again until then.

The rest of the day I spent deliberately not thinking about him and being as happy as I could be. I spoke a lot with Selvey, but not about Charlie, and she made me laugh a lot. Perhaps I should tell you now what I thought was happening in her life.

I was beginning to think she was being naughty and having an affair with a *bule*. Really, I know that sounds crazy because she had always said she didn't like them, but for the last two months or so she had been acting very strange. I mean strange in a nice way because she was always smiling and happy those days and always talking in English quietly on her handphone. It was unusual for her to be so nice to people, and also she often came to work wearing sexy clothes and sometimes smelling of perfume.

You know what? A few times she even brought a hold-all to work with her with what I thought was probably a spare set of clothes in. I got to thinking she was sometimes staying overnight with her boyfriend. Maybe my mind was playing tricks on me and I just had negative thinking about her, but I didn't think so. Anyway, if she was being a bit naughty then it was not my business, was it? And anyway I actually was happy for her. Whatever was happening in her life right then was making her happy and a better person, I think. I just hoped nobody got hurt. I knew what that felt like and it sucked.

Anyway, I had a nice day and didn't think about Charlie too much. I thought about Gary a lot, though, and I chatted with him a bit on YM. I didn't tell him about Charlie or that I would meet him because I didn't think it was important, really. I just wanted to talk to Charlie face to face so that we could close the matter and finish things properly. He didn't mean anything to me anymore.

When I got to Starbucks he was already there. I didn't care. Normally I would feel a bit guilty if someone had been waiting for me, even if I was not late, but not today. I didn't want him to buy anything for me so I went directly to the counter and ordered an iced tea while he waited for me.

Good, let him wait, I thought.

Finally I got my drink and went to his table and sat down. He looked up at me and directly tried to hold my hand across the table but I moved it away so he couldn't. I was not going to make this easy for him and fall for his *basa-basi* chitchat again.

He started to talk, to try and explain further the things he wrote in his email and his behaviour with me before, but I was not really listening. All I could hear was *blah, blah, blah* … You know, I felt nothing for him. I knew he was one of the men that Selvey talks about when she describes *bules* as 'players'.

At some point I became aware that he had asked me a question and he seemed to be waiting for my response. 'Sorry, what did you say?' I asked him.

'I asked if it is too late for us; could we try again, please?' he answered.

I looked at him but there was nothing there. No sense, no feeling, no curiosity even. In fact, there was just a gap where there should have been something. I didn't even have to answer. I just looked at him and he knew.

He knew he has blown the best chance he would ever have of being truly happy in his life.

This time it was my turn to reach across the table and take his hand. I gave it a squeeze and I told him to take care, then I got up to leave.

For a second or two I think I saw the beginning of what just might be a tear in his eyes, but even that didn't move me. There had been too many tears already because of *bugil* and so I just left him sitting there.

I started to leave Starbucks and as I was getting to the door two young girls came in. They looked very pretty and one of them smiled as she held the door open for me so I smiled back. As I walked out I heard her friend shout out a greeting to someone;

'Neil,' she shouted. 'How are you?'

I turned and see her go over to Charlie and embrace him.

Neil???????

I was confused and about to go back inside and demand more answers but suddenly I was overcome with a strange calmness and I realised it just didn't matter anymore.

I smiled to myself and started walking back through the mall to where I could get a taxi or bus home. I didn't know what would happen with me and Gary, but I decided I was going to have fun finding out. I didn't know if I really loved him or not but I decided I was not going to be such a naïve mummy's girl again, that's for sure.

I was standing at the bus stop when I suddenly saw Selvey's face looking back at me.

It was on a poster stuck onto the bus stop and I looked closer. It was information about a drama taking place at the National Theatre here in Jakarta and Selvey was acting in it. In fact, she was the star!

Well, I almost peed myself laughing. That was her big secret. That was why she had been so strange recently, speaking a lot in English on the phone. Hahaha ... she had been practicing for her acting!

Oh my goodness!

That's why she had extra clothes in the office and make up and perfume, it was all for her rehearsals!

When I stopped laughing I took my phone out of my bag and I called *Naughty Boy Ari*.

'Ari,' I said, 'You won't believe what I just found out!'

Jack's Story

I am Setiono Jacobsen, but you can call me Jack, and this is my story.

I live in Jakarta, which I am sure you know is the capital city of Indonesia, and I am a poor man but I am on the way up, and it is only a matter of time until I improve myself and my position in life. This is what I tell everybody I meet for the first time, and it is what I say to myself and to my God when I pray.

It is a matter of time. That's all.

I will tell you my story from the beginning up until now and then I am sure you will be able to see why I feel this way and you may even agree with me.

I am twenty-four years old and I am from a small village called Ciang in the centre of Java. Java is the largest island of over one thousand islands in the archipelago of Indonesia. Ciang is about four hundred kilometres from where I live now, which is in the heart of Jakarta.

I was born in a field twenty-four years ago. This was because my mother was a farm worker, and when she was pregnant with me she kept working right up to the day I came into the world. She couldn't afford to take many days off work and so when she went into labour there was no time to get to a hospital or even back to the farmhouse. Everyone she was working with at the time helped with the delivery, and after I was born then my mother and I were carried across the fields to the farmhouse where my mother rested for the remainder of that day and went back to work the next.

I was the sixth child to be born alive and survive in our family (there were two siblings before me who died just after they were born) and another two babies were born to my mom in later years. This meant that our family was of average size for the time and place, and was full of laughter and love, if not money and food.

My parents are good hard-working people and have always looked after their children well and with love, but have never been able to provide as much for us as they would have liked. However, they did insist that all eight of us got at least some education, and both I and my two younger brothers were educated all the way up to junior high school.

My parents are old now and don't work very much. My mother just washes people's clothes or runs errands for them back in Ciang, while my father has a motorcycle and sometimes ferries people around for small sums of money. They live alone now with just a young maid as all us children have left home.

The four boys in our family have all left the village, as have two of my sisters, while the other two girls are still in the village but are long-married with their own families now.

This is a very brief introduction to me and my family, and so now I will give you more details before I get to the main part of my story.

When I was a small boy, I sometimes helped my mother in

the fields or I played with my older brother, Heri, but usually I preferred to be alone. I was known as a 'muser' within my gang of friends and family, as I often gave the appearance of musing, or daydreaming, when I should have been doing something else.

I guess I *was* a bit of a daydreamer in those days, but my musing wasn't aimless or useless even then. I was not idly wasting time, but in reality I was always thinking ahead, planning my strategy, getting my ships lined up, call it what you will. That's me to this day: an organiser and a thinker. That's why I am going to make a success of myself, you see.

As a kid I wanted to learn, to improve, and to get on. I loved reading and writing as a child, and even before I went to school I would look at my older brother and sisters' books and try so hard to work out (or imagine) the meanings of the words in them and copy them over and over again.

In my early pre-school days I was forever plaguing my parents to teach me to read and write properly, and it was not until many years later that I finally realised why they would always smile and encourage me but never actually teach me anything academic. When the penny finally dropped it just increased my love and pride for them. What lovely people they really are.

I was closest to Heri, my older brother, during my childhood. He is two years older than me and he seemed to be everything I wanted to be. He could run faster than any of us other boys in the village, climb trees better, swim further and quicker, had more friends and was the one that the whole gang of us wanted to emulate.

For me he also had one other quality: kindness. He was such a nice guy to be around because he was always kind and friendly to everyone, and I don't just say that because he was my brother. He never picked on anyone for being smaller or weaker or anything, the way that most boys do, and he never excluded anyone from playing with us but instead he made sure that everyone played properly together. He wouldn't tolerate any bullying or being mean, and he wasn't averse to using his fists if he thought that was the best solution.

I guess I regarded him as my hero even then.

I was close to my other two brothers, Yudi and Steffan, but as they were younger than me, I was more interested in being with Heri as much as I could. Steffan and Yudi didn't seem to mind as they were very close to each other, and my four sisters all seemed happy enough to hang out together and not bother us boys too much. Yes, we were a happy enough sort of family but not really much different to most others in our village.

In those days, and perhaps even now to some extent, villagers didn't have much expectation in life. It was just sort of assumed that everyone would have a basic sort of education and then go forth into adulthood in much the same way; males would become farmers or very small business owners within the village, while girls would get married, usually by the age of sixteen at the latest, and perhaps work in the fields or, if the family could afford it, be housewives.

Every year a few of the men, and very occasionally some of the women, would leave the village and go to live in the cities. These would normally be either the few individuals who had a little more ambition for themselves, or those unfortunate few who were forced to leave through circumstance or even scandal.

For example, if someone were found to have committed a crime such as theft or assault then they would normally be 'asked' to leave the village as a punishment. Depending on the severity of their crime, they would then be banished for a certain number of years and not allowed to return within that time frame. This, naturally enough, applied more to the male population than the female one, as more boys than girls tended to commit these crimes.

However, girls could also find themselves under pressure to leave the village in certain circumstances, such as pregnancy outside of wedlock or even, rather unfairly I always thought, in the event of abandonment by their husbands.

A guy may want a girl and so be more than happy to marry her while she was still young and nubile in her mid-teens, but a few years of almost continual pregnancy, childbirth and manual labour soon take their toll, and a village girl in her mid-twenties can often take on the appearance of someone ten or fifteen years older. It is at this point that many men start to look elsewhere. The poor girls involved then usually head off to the cities to seek work, usually as domestic servants.

Growing up in the village I was always happy, but I did wonder just what could be achieved outside its confines. Heri was the same; he was always talking about moving to the city and trying to become rich. He had many dreams and would keep me entertained for hours on end with stories of how he was going to one day move to a big city such as Surabaya or Jakarta and open a motorcycle repair shop. It would, according to him, become the biggest and most famous and popular motorcycle repair shop in the city, and when the time was right he was going to send for me and I would be his partner.

I loved listening to him, and we would stay up all night sometimes going over our plans and hopes. I look back now on those days and sometimes think that they were the happiest, most innocent days of my life, but I also realise that they were much more than that. Those were the days in which my character and personality were, if not formed, then certainly refined and strengthened and my ambitions and goals reinforced. I truly think those all-night chats with my older brother were the making of me.

Anyway, as soon as he was old enough he left for the bright lights of the city and I was heartbroken. I missed him so much and it felt like my life was empty and useless without him by my side. Who was going to take care of me now, to look after me, to organise and arrange our games, to be my hero? I spent much of the next few months not knowing what to do with myself and my only respite was waiting for one of his letters home.

When one arrived, addressed as always to my parents, my mum or dad would always call me and hand over the letter to me. They always asked me to read it out and I was delighted to do so. They would smile as I excitedly told them all Heri's news and they would then tell me they were going to write back to him as soon as possible. However, a day or so later my mum would usually tell me she and my dad were 'far too busy at present' to compose the letter and they wouldn't mind if I wrote to Heri instead. This, of course, was something I loved to do. Again, it was not until years later I realised the significance of this ritual.

My brother seemed to be doing well in his new life in Jakarta. He told us in his letters that he had got a job working in a motorbike repair shop and he was learning about the business and saving as much money as he could in readiness for opening up himself, and in his letters he always had some advice for me, too.

'Work hard at school, bung,' he would say. 'I need you to come here and help me when I set up my business.'

I worked hard. I wanted nothing more than to join him and make him as proud of me as I was of him, but when I was fourteen I had no choice but to leave school. My mum and dad couldn't afford to send me to senior high school and they needed me to go to work and help them to help our family.

I was a bit disappointed to leave school, but I had always known this was going to happen and I considered myself lucky to have had nine years education. People often say your schooldays are the happiest of your life; well, I don't know about that but I know I did enjoy mine. Now, however, I was ready for the next stage in my life.

No matter how much I pleaded with my mum and dad, I couldn't convince them I was old enough or ready enough to be permitted to join Heri in the city, and so I took up as a trainee mechanic in a little shop in the village. I should use inverted commas here while describing my job title, because I received very little in either training or mechanics in general. In reality I was employed as a *pembantu* or 'helper'. It was my job to keep the shop clean, wash the vehicles and generally run errands.

It wasn't the greatest job in the world, but I reasonably enjoyed it. I saw it for what it was; the first step on a very tall ladder. I worked hard again, or as hard as I was able to in such a limited position and environment, and did as well for myself as I could for a couple of years, but then something happened and I ended up leaving the village.

It wasn't my fault and it was most unfair and upsetting at the time, but all has been put right since then and there has been no lasting damage. I can go back to my village now as everybody now knows the truth of what happened but at the time things looked pretty bad for me.

I suppose I should tell you what happened. Well, one day I was working in the garage and the boss, Mr. Simon, decided to go home early. He told me to lock up the garage when I had finished and take the keys home then come in early in the morning so I could open the shop up. I didn't mind this, and so carried on working for a while before tidying everything up and heading off home as instructed.

Well ... the next day when I got to work there was already a large crowd gathered around the place, and as I got closer I could see Mr. Simon. He was very red in the face and was shouting a lot and seemed on the verge of some sort of breakdown. He saw me approaching and flew at me with his fists, screaming, '*Kau babi!* You pig,' over and over. I was amazed and speechless. Why was Mr. Simon, who had always been decent to me, acting like this all of a sudden? What ever had I done wrong?

I tried to fathom out what was going on and why he was so angry, but he was beside himself with rage and I could get no sense from him for what seemed like ages. People were holding him back to stop him attacking me, while others were trying to usher me from the scene. I just couldn't make any sense of it and had no idea of how to deal with the situation.

It was then my father and our village chief appeared and some sort of order started to be restored. Mr. Simon was persuaded by the village chief to calm down and to explain what had happened. He told my father and the chief that his business had been broken into in the night and all the money in the safe had been stolen, along with quite a lot of valuable machine parts and, as I had been given the keys and the responsibility of locking the premises up, I was clearly the culprit.

I was speechless, but luckily my dad wasn't. He is a quiet man and well respected in the village and community and so when he talks people, no matter who they are or what their position or standing is, listen. He quite coolly and calmly told the village chief and Mr. Simon that there was no way I was a thief or in any way responsible for the break-in. He pointed out that if I had been inclined to steal anything I would have had many chances to do on many earlier occasions and as I had been given the keys to lock up there would have been no need for me to come back and break in.

I don't know what was going through my mind at this point, as I seemed to have lost not only the ability to speak but that to think as well. I just stood by mutely as the three of them discussed the matter and tried to reach some sort of consensus. Finally it seemed that Mr. Simon reluctantly accepted what my dad was saying after he had given him and the village chief permission to come and search our house and grounds for any sign of the missing money or equipment.

My dad wrapped his arm around my shoulders and led me back to our house. On the way we didn't exchange a word, and when we arrived home he saw that I was about to speak but he raised his hand to stop me and said, 'I know, son, I know.' He told me he knew I was blameless and that he was proud of me and loved me very much, but that now it was time for me to go and join my brother in the big city. He told me he would find out exactly what happened to Mr. Simon's business and then would get word to me when it was the right time to come back, but that I shouldn't worry about it and he would ensure that there was no stain on my character or lingering suspicion.

I don't think I had ever heard my father speak for so long or so passionately. I looked into this kind, gentle, lovely old man's face and I knew I was blessed to have such a person for a father, and I resolved there and then I was really going to make him proud of me.

The next day I started my three-day journey to Jakarta.

As soon as I arrived in the city, I went and stayed with Heri. He was staying in a small boarding house, or *kost* as we call them, in the middle of the city in a place called Tebet. It was a very small room in a house and there was barely room for one person inside, but he was still delighted to see me and he made it clear he expected me to stay with him.

To be honest, I'd thought he was living in better accommodation than this, and if I had known the conditions of his place I wouldn't have dreamt of imposing on him. However, I didn't know beforehand and besides, I really didn't have any other choice, and so I reluctantly agreed.

I told Heri what had happened to me back on our village and how our father had spoken to me and told me to make something of myself in the city 'the way that brother Heri is already doing'. At this Heri offered a wry grin and muttered something about not knowing if that last part was exactly true.

He did, however, share my frustration and feeling of unfairness at what had transpired, but he told me that for now I just had to put it behind me the best I could and try to get on with things. He said he would help me to find a job and then, when I was ready, a place of my own to stay, and that one day he and I would both return to our village and make sure things got 'straightened out' with Mr. Simon.

I had so many questions I wanted to ask Heri. I wanted to know, for instance, how his plans for owning his motorcycle repair business were progressing, if he was rich yet, when he was coming back to build the big family house in the village he had promised our parents, and about a million other things. Heri merely smiled at my excitement and told me things were proving a bit more difficult to get started than he had anticipated but that he was 'working on it all' and that everything would be fine. He told me he still planned to open a motorcycle business when he had the opportunity, but for now he was working as a labourer. I was a little confused when he said this, because in his letters home he had told the family he was at least working in a motorcycle shop, even if it wasn't his own business. Nevertheless, I decided not to press Heri on the matter, and took myself off for my first night's sleep in Jakarta.

The next day he took me with him to a building site he was currently working on and helped get me a job there. Jakarta is always developing and new buildings are always going up while others are being pulled down. Sometimes a brand new hotel or office building can be constructed in just a matter of weeks, only to be bought and sold and demolished again eighteen months or so later. It really can be perplexing at times, the thinking of people here.

Anyway, as I said, Heri managed to get me employed at this site on a casual daily basis. It was my job to do little more than fetch and carry things for the other workers there, Heri included, and I also got to learn how to do simple things such as chop bricks into the right size and mix cement. It wasn't exactly an intellectual challenge for me, but I enjoyed the work while it lasted. Most of the men there were Heri's age or older but they were very friendly and funny to me.

In the evenings some of them liked to go to the night markets in Godok and pass the time there playing cards or just drinking beer and chatting. I didn't really want to join them in the beginning because I had read lots about the bad influences of gambling and drinking, but then Heri assured me it wasn't like that.

He told me that I wouldn't be expected to drink beer if I didn't want to, many of the guys didn't, and also that they played cards just for something to do, with matchsticks and not money the stakes.

So finally I decided I would come along one evening and when I finally did, it ultimately led to my first real break in the city.

I went with Heri and a few of his friends. There was a man

called Toni, one named Didi, Eko, and an older fellow by the name of Untoro and they all made me welcome enough.

Eko and I were the only ones not drinking and this surprised me a bit because I didn't expect to see Heri drinking, but there he was supping away from a big bottle of Bintang beer he was sharing with the other guys. He saw me looking at him in puzzlement and sort of gave me a sheepish type of grin and a wink that seemed to say, 'I'll tell you about it later.' I remember thinking at the time with fondness and amusement, 'Ah Heri, Heri … what are you doing?'

As we started playing cards, we soon all became engrossed in the game and the intensity in which we all wanted to win was surprisingly high. It was good-natured enough, but everyone wanted to win, there was no doubt about that. As the evening went on, I began to relax more in the company of these guys and to start to feel like a 'real man' for the first time. I mean, here I was living away from home, working, spending my own money in leisure time with people much older than me, and I was feeling a real sense of independence; of having taken the first steps to real adulthood and of having my destiny in my own hands. I conveniently pushed to the back of my mind the minor details of my somewhat cramped living conditions, the dreariness of my employment and the very meagre daily wage that accompanied it, together with the fact that the job, as bad as it was, would probably end soon and then I would be back to square one, and instead just relaxed back in my chair and lost all my matchsticks to my brother and his mates.

Soon even this novelty and feeling of well-being wore off and I began to get just a little bored, so I started taking less interest in the game and more in my surroundings. We were at a small market, which seemed to specialise in selling cheap clothes, perfume and fish! There seemed to be a battle for supremacy going on between the contrasting aromas of inexpensive body spray and various dead sea life, the combination of which was quite an assault on the senses, I can tell you.

I was looking around at the vendors and customers and trying to take it all in, when I became aware of something else going on. All of a sudden, from out of nowhere, there seemed to be an influx of young women milling around. This was somewhat confusing. What were they doing there? They all seemed to be reasonably attractive and quite well-dressed yet they didn't appear to be interested in doing any shopping, and what was more, they were all either in pairs or alone.

I was confused. Confused and naïve as it turned out.

My elder brother saw me gazing around in wonderment, and gave me another one of his knowing grins. 'Hey, *bung*,' he called out to me. 'Do you like what you see?'

'I don't know,' I replied truthfully. 'I don't know what it is I am seeing.'

At this Heri and his friends all laughed, but I got the feeling it was good-naturedly and without malice, as if I had said something amusing and not as if they were mocking me.

Eko took it upon himself to explain the facts to me. 'These girls are the same as you, *bung*. They come here from the villages seeking their fortune but soon find to their cost there is not that big an opportunity for poor illiterate country girls to become captains of industry.'

I was still confused and told Eko this. I asked him what the women were doing now in the market and watched him smirk and shrug his shoulders.

I looked at the other guys and they all had similar expressions and body language and then very slowly the penny began to drop.

'No!' I exclaimed. 'Surely not! Surely these young women are not ...'

'Hush yourself, *bung*,' admonished Heri. 'Don't cause a scene. They will not appreciate the attention and nor will their men. You can be sure of that.'

'What men?' I said my voice quieter now. 'I see no men with them.'

'Oh, they all have men not far away, *bung*, you can be sure of that too. You can't see them but they are here, lurking.'

How fascinating, I thought. Fascinating yet seedy, dirty and sad all at the same time.

I tried to stop looking at them, but it was difficult. It wasn't lust that made me look at these young women; (at least I don't think it was). It was, I don't know, interest more than anything else. They seemed to be at ease with the place and didn't look especially nervous or ashamed or furtive or anything like I would have expected women in such a profession to look, and the men who approached them seemed exactly the same. I saw men walk up to these ladies and talk to them the way I would talk to a street vendor or shop assistant; with no embarrassment or special attitude whatsoever. I found it confusing at first, but then I guess

I got used to it.

I wanted to go and talk to the girls and to find out more about them and their lives but Heri told me that would be an unwise thing to do. He told me that they wouldn't appreciate that because 'time is money' and the guys in the background certainly wouldn't appreciate it either. However, Heri continued, if I was interested in actually going with a girl then that would be a different matter.

I am sure that I blushed when he said that, but something changed right there at that moment. The men, Heri included, didn't laugh at me or josh me any more. They looked at me with neutral yet somehow caring expressions, as if they had decided to stop teasing me and to help me out instead.

I still wasn't really feeling any real sense of lust for these girls, attractive as they were, but I did want to talk to them. I asked Heri what would happen if I went with one of them, where would she take me, how much would it cost, for how long and would I be safe, and he did his best to answer me and put my mind at rest. He said the girl would probably take me to one of the tiny shack-like buildings the far side of the market, that it would cost about Rp 25, 000 for as long as it took, and that I would be perfectly safe because everyone could see I was with him and his friends, and that if I wasn't back safe and sound within a reasonable amount of time, everyone would know they would come looking for me.

I thought about it for a while: where was the harm, I mused. Just go and have a look and a talk, then come back. No harm done, I thought. Then, I thought again. What's the point? Although the situation was interesting to a degree, what would I get out of it other than my curiosity salved and a dent in my wallet? No, I decided, I would just stay where I was and let the evening float by.

So, I watched as they made they way across the market square, half wishing I had the bravery to take Heri up on his offer, and half-grateful I hadn't. There was something captivating about the way all the girls carried themselves; a poise or proud elegance, if you will, that seemed incongruous to say the least considering the circumstances, but it was there nevertheless.

After a few minutes, the procession of nubile young and not-so-young bodies finally left the square and slowly we returned to our card games and drinking. A couple more hours went by and we were beginning to start thinking about calling it a night when my attention was caught by the sound of a commotion coming from the other side of the square.

Where all had been quiet and peaceful enough a minute ago, now a rather large man was cursing loudly and threatening all kinds of retribution on an as yet unseen personage. Although the string of garbled profanities made it difficult to make out exactly what he was complaining about from where we were sitting, the gist of his unhappiness seemed to bear relation to a certain dissatisfaction with a recent business transaction.

'*Pelacur kotor*! *Dia mencuri jam aku*,' is about the politest utterance of his I can relate here. It literally means, 'the dirty prostitute has stolen my watch.' I presumed this meant he had been ripped off by one of the prostitutes we had seen earlier and so I immediately looked to Heri for clarification. Heri confirmed this was most likely the case and we continued to watch the drama unfold.

The man was standing shouting in the square and making

quite a scene, and so I asked Heri why the fellow simply didn't go back to whichever girl had allegedly taken his watch and retrieve it himself.

'No, *dik*,' said Heri. 'He can't do that. If he does, the security guards in the area will set about him, instead. Under no circumstances can the girls be touched or hurt in any way. No, he has to do it this way. He has to make a commotion out here in public and then leave it up to the security to take over.'

We watched as two men emerged from the shadows and gently converged on the guy. Politely but firmly, they took an elbow each and led him to a small food stall opposite us and started the process of trying to calm him down. They spoke quietly to him and listened with what appeared to be sympathy as he, no doubt, outlined his tale of woe. After a few minutes, one of the two men slipped away and headed off in the direction the girls had disappeared a couple of hours earlier, while the other security guy continued nodding and talking to the aggrieved customer.

'Where's he gone, Ri?' I asked Heri.

'To get the girl. The one matey here is accusing of being a thief,' he explained. 'This will be interesting, Jack,' he continued. 'Watch and learn.'

Within five minutes the first security chap was back with a young lady in tow. She looked to be in her late teens or very early twenties, had a small and somewhat skinny body, short black hair and stood, I guess, no more than 150cm. She was, I presumed, the suspected thief.

Upon studying her more closely, I was taken aback by the way she carried herself. I would have expected someone in her position, being practically paraded as a thief in public, to at least look a little apprehensive, if not downright petrified. I remembered my own experience of public humiliation at the hands of Pak Simon when he'd accused me of being a thief back in my village and how utterly numb and incapable of speech I was at the time, but now saw none of the same trepidation present in this particular young lady.

Indeed, she walked towards her accuser with a straight back and her held her head up high, and although I was too far away to make out what was being said, I could see her talking calmly to both the security guards and the guy himself. The guy was still angry and was throwing his arms around as he continued to no doubt cast aspersions on the young lady's character, while she continued to stand her ground.

After a couple of minutes of this stand-off, the girl said something to one of the two security guards. He seemed to do a double-take, then appeared to ask her to repeat whatever it was she'd said. This she did, and then the security guy spoke directly to the punter who initially looked just as shocked as the security guy had a matter of seconds earlier. Nevertheless, the punter put his hand into the back pocket of his trousers and, lo-and-behold, pulled out what was quite clearly an expensive looking watch.

All three men looked dumbfounded. What had just happened? I turned to Heri sitting beside me in the hope that he would be able to shed some light as to what had transpired before our very eyes, but for once even he had no answers for me. We watched as the young lady simply turned away dismissively from all three gentleman and made her way back to from where she had come.

Subsequent to this little unexpected piece of drama, we did indeed call it a night and made our way home. That night, finally alone in the small hubby hole I was sleeping in in Heri's place, I found myself unable to sleep. My mind kept drifting back to what I'd witnessed that evening and especially the altercation involving the working girl.

Who was she, I wondered, where did she come from and how had she ended up in her line of work? Most intriguingly, I wondered how she'd pulled off the trick with the watch. Had she, I mused, somehow performed a conjuring trick to put the watch back into the guy's pocket – you know, a sleight of hand thing- or had she just noticed the dozy chap putting the watch there himself back in the room? It was a right conundrum, I told myself, and make no mistake. Those were my last thoughts as I finally drifted off to sleep.

The next few weeks went by and I started to feel a bit more at home in Jakarta. I started becoming a bit braver and began negotiating the city's public transport systems and learning a bit more about the city and the amazing chorus line of characters it plays host to.

I was starting to learn that it is an unforgiving city in as much as it is survival of the fittest in all walks of life. The city is a contradiction of high-rise apartments, shopping malls and seven-star hotels amongst an array of polluted rivers, crippled and deformed beggars and appalling poverty, and as I took in my new surroundings, I became more aware of why Heri was not as yet living the good life. Notwithstanding this, still I didn't feel despondent regarding my own chances of making a go of things. On the contrary, whereas I could see the challenges ahead, I could also see the opportunities too.

I carried on working with Heri and his friends at the building site, and although I was grateful for the work, it wasn't long before I started getting itchy feet and started wanting to see what other alternatives were out there. We would work until just before 6pm, or *magrib* evening prayers, each day before usually heading out for a walk or just hanging around the settlement, known locally as a *kampong*, where we lived.

We would sometimes head back to Godok and the site of the adventures of my first night in Jakarta, but such trips were rather rare as most of us were keen to save what money we could and on the rare occasion when we did venture there, I found to my mild disappointment there was neither a repeat of prior histrionics nor any sign of the girl responsible for them.

I actually spent rather a disproportionate amount of time thinking about that particular young lady for some reason. I guess I was slightly in awe of the way she had held herself together and conducted herself that night, and couldn't help but continue to compare it with the way I'd practically hidden behind my father when I'd been in the same situation back home. This girl was a bit of an enigma to me, and I decided that if I ever got the chance I would like to talk to her – just to try and get a bit of a handle on her and see what made her tick.

As it happened, I didn't have long to have to wait. A couple of nights later and the usual suspects had decided on spending the evening in Godok. As usual, I was invited along and as I agreed,

I started developing a plan of action. I would, I decided, try and get to meet her, and if all went well, I would attempt to put my curiosity to rest. The only problem was I didn't know how to approach her except by way of presenting myself as a willing consumer of her goods for sale, if you get my drift. I remembered Heri's initial warning to me that these young ladies were not tourist attractions to be gawped at or to have their time wasted by the likes of me asking inane questions, so I knew I would have to pretend to be interested in her services.

I decided if I saw her walking across the square tonight I would simply go through with a charade of pretending to be interested in her in the normal consumer manner and see what happened.

This meant, though, the embarrassment of having to broach the subject with Heri. I decided to keep things brief and not tell Heri of my plans in advance, rather I would bring the subject up only if I saw the young lady and then I would try and let Heri know I wished to take him up on the kind offer he and his friends had previously extended.

The evening panned out exactly the same as previous ones spent in Godok. We found a spot and some of the guys ordered beers while Eko and I just sipped iced tea and water, and we played our games of matchstick-cards while chatting amiably and watching the world go by. At about 10pm the usual procession of girls started as the young ladies made their way round the enclosure of small eateries, or warungs, and that's when I saw her and made eye contact. She smiled at me and my heart started to beat just a little faster. It was now or never.

'Ri,' I nudged my elder sibling.

'Hmm?' he was preoccupied talking to his friend, Untoro, and paid me little heed.

'Heri,' I persisted. 'Ri.'

'What is it?' he muttered, now annoyed that I was disturbing his flow.

'That.' I said, nodding over in the direction of the nameless lady who continued to give me the slightest hint of what could be construed as 'the eye'.

Now Heri caught on.

'Ahhhhhh, I see,' he sort of smirked. 'Leave it with me.'

Heri had a quick word with his friends who all grinned at me, and each contributed Rp 4,000 leaving me to pay the remainder.

So, this was it. I took a deep breath I got up out of my chair and went over to her.

She smiled at me and we started chatting in what we call *basa-basi*, or small talk. I was once more aware of the fact that I shouldn't take up too much of her time lest she think I was just playing with her. Heri had warned me once again to get right to the point as quickly as possible, and so after a couple of minutes I did.

'Would you like to spend some time with me, Non?' I asked.

'Sure, *sayang*. You know time is money, eh?' she replied, still smiling.

'I do, Non,' said I, the smooth operator that I am, and we left together for the row of shacks just visible the other side of the market.

As we walked together I felt self-conscious and shy. I was sure that everyone in the market would be looking at us and knowing who we were and where we were going, but I needn't have worried because a quick glance around assured me that no-one was paying us the slightest bit of attention. People were just getting on with shopping, selling, talking to their friends or whatever it is they were doing. I was heartened by this and began to relax a bit more. I did wonder, however, just what the hell I thought I was doing and why. I was telling myself I was just curious and I just wanted to know more about her, about things and about life in general. I was arguing with myself that my curiosity was natural and harmless, but it was an argument I was in severe danger of losing.

We reached the row of tin shacks and the girl, Devi was her name, produced a key and opened one and led me inside. It was tiny, probably smaller even than Heri's room in his *kost*, and all it contained was a mattress on the floor, a chair piled up with clothes, a fold away table also piled with clothes, some cutlery and crockery, and in the far corner, a tap and a bucket – presumably for washing clothes, cutlery, crockery and bodies.

Devi was nice to me. She could see I was nervous so she did her best to put me at ease. She smiled easily and chatted pleasantly as if we were old friends as she moved around the tiny place. She told me she was going to take a wash first and suggested I had one too.

She was nice. I was relaxing and felt ok.

However, I had a problem. I didn't want to make love with her; I only wanted to talk to her. This had seemed like a good idea before but now my natural shyness was taking over and I was trying not to panic. I just wanted to get out of the situation without annoying her or losing face too much.

How was I going to manage that?

It wasn't that I didn't find her attractive, or that I was saving myself, or I was some sort of puritan. It was just that I didn't want to. I was just interested in the whole scene and I wanted to learn more, or that's what I was telling myself, anyway.

I watched her take her skirt and blouse off and squat down in the corner with the tap. There was barely a trickle from it but she used it to wash some of the sweat and grime off her legs and stomach before signalling for me to do the same and going over to the bed.

I had a sudden idea. I would feign impotency.

Good idea? Not quite.

'What's wrong, sayang?' she said when she saw me reluctant to get undressed.

I stammered something about not being up to the job and changing my mind but still, of course, paying her, but she wasn't having any of that.

'Come on, Sayang. I will assist you,' she said, helpfully.

I wasn't banking on this, but she came to me and wrapped her arm around my shoulder and breathed warm scented air into my ear. I had no chance. Nature took its course as I involuntarily appeared on the parade ground, in a manner of speaking.

'Seems alright to me,' she giggled as she wriggled out of her underwear.

It *was* nice. There is no getting away from that, I enjoyed it and although I felt a certain guilt, I didn't feel particularly dirty as I thought I might, even though this had not been my intention at the start of the evening. Devi was kind to me and helped me through with my somewhat clumsy and inexperienced fumbling without complaint, unlike the other couple of girls I had been with back in my village, and all in all I would say it was worth every rupiah.

I still wanted to talk to her, though, and to find out more about her and how and why she was doing this job, and in particular what had happened with her customer on the night I first saw her. My gentle probing in this direction wasn't very fruitful initially, but as we lay there post-coital, she began to open up a bit. She told me she came from a village similar to mine and initially she had worked as a maid to a Chinese-Indonesian family in one of the nicer areas of the city, in a place called Pondok Indah, but she had had to work so hard for so little money that she after a few months she had left and started working in a bar in a position one of the local motorcycle taxi drivers, *tukang ojek*, had helped her get.

From there she had ended up working here in the market. I asked her why she had left the bar but she just shook her head indicating she wasn't going to tell me and I didn't push it.

I told her what I was doing at present and that while that was fine for now I would want to move onto something a bit better in time. Devi listened to me with what appeared to be genuine interest and I found myself definitely taking a bit of a shine to her. Not in a romantic way, you understand, but she did seem to be a genuinely pleasant and nice person who was easy to listen to. I told her I was sure I could be a success in my life if I just got the chance but I was finding it a bit difficult to make the breakthrough.

Devi was quiet for a while but then started to speak,

'Well, I think someone like you should be able to make a go of things here.'

I was confused: 'Someone like me?'

She grinned. A cute smile. 'Yes, a smart nice lad. You could go far. I could, I suppose, help you.'

It was then that she made a suggestion that helped to turn things around for me.

'Why don't you come and work for Pak Neil?' she asked. 'He is always looking for smart young men.'

'Who is he?' I asked.

'He is this *bule* guy who has a many bars and apartments around the Kedoya area, where I used to work, and he employs chaps such as you to help out.'

'Doing what?' I was intrigued now.

'Doing whatever is needed,' she replied, just a little tersely. 'I can make a call if you like, let people know a bit about you and see if we can fix you up.'

I agreed, and she sat on the bed and made a called on her mobile. She turned away from me so I couldn't hear too well what she was saying but finally she turned back to me and said that it was all fixed – Pak Neil would see me tonight at the Club Mexicanas in Kedoya.

I was still somewhat concerned about what sort of job I was looking at but nevertheless I could see that this maybe held half a promise for the future. I thanked Devi profusely and gathered up my clothes and got ready to leave. As I was about ready to go she walked with me to the door and put her arms around me.

'*Hati-hati*, be careful, Jack. This is my mobile number so please let me know where you are and what happens, ya,' she said.

I kissed her nose and thanked her again. I made a promise then that whatever else happened in my life I would never forget Devi and the kindness she had shown to me. It was only as I made my way back to Heri that I remembered I hadn't even asked her about her experience with the john and his watch.

My erstwhile brother and his friends were still drinking and playing cards and barely looked up as I sat down at the table, but finally Heri ventured,

'So, how was it?'

I told him what had happened and about the introduction Devi had made for me with Pak Neil. I asked him if he knew of this guy and what I should do.

Heri seemed to hesitate a bit before answering, but when he did he told me that Pak Neil was a rich expatriate (*bule*) well known in the city for running clubs and karaoke bars. Eko joined in and told me that if I could get a job working with him it would be a step up, the salary would be higher than at present and I would get a good 'street rep'. People would respect me if they knew I was working for him.

I decided that I would go and meet Pak Neil and see what the deal was, but I was still a bit apprehensive. I didn't want to get mixed up in anything illegal or immoral. I know that sounds slightly hypocritical seeing that I had just spent time with a lady of the night, but sleeping with such a girl and getting involved in, say, procuring them was totally different.

Anyway, I decided that there was no point in worrying too much about anything until I knew more information. With that in mind I bade farewell to my brother and his mates and headed off to Club Mexicanas by *ojek*.

Kedoya is in the south of the city, and is a fairly run down yet not desperately poor area. There is a strip of what might reasonably be called low-grade shopping malls and pubs or clubs. There are also a few karaoke places and one or two slightly dodgy-looking massage parlours. However, it doesn't really have a reputation for being a den of vice, just for being a bit seedy.

Upon arriving at Club Mexicanas, I was made to wait in the lobby for as few minutes and I took the time to take in my surroundings. The first thing that struck me was that place was very dark even in the reception, so much so that I could hardly make out the features of people walking in front of me.

Music was pumping out from the main part of the club, which was through a thick set of double doors from where I was sitting and even where I was there was an over riding smell of cheap beer and perfume.

I was quite nervous at the prospect of meeting Pak Neil and this wasn't helped by the fact that I was left waiting for almost half an hour before this really massive guy came through the double doors, introduced himself as Yusuf and told me to follow him.

We went back through the double doors into the club proper and into almost pitch-blackness. I was petrified I would lose Yusuf in the darkness and Heri and my parents would never see me again, but somehow we made it over to the other side of the club with me more or less keeping up with him and we entered a small corridor. Here at least the lighting was almost normal and I was able to see again.

Yusuf stopped outside a door on the left, knocked once and was called in. I was left waiting in the corridor for another couple of minutes and then the door opened and I was beckoned inside.

Yusuf stepped out and I was left facing Pak Neil. He was not anything like I had expected. I had anticipated coming face to face with a much bigger man (I don't know why I thought that, except maybe because successful *bule* businessmen often *are* big and fat) and I thought he would be perhaps in his fifties or sixties.

Instead I found myself in front of a small, frail-looking guy in his early to mid-thirties. He was red-eyed, as if he'd been up all night, or had been crying, and the first thing that struck me was how vulnerable he looked. He didn't look like anything I imagined a 'big boss' would look like, but if I had suspected any weakness about him I was soon to be put right on that score.

He looked up at me with if not exactly kindness in his eyes, then at least amiability. He sort of grinned at me and motioned for me to sit down in the rickety chair opposite him.

That was another slightly confusing thing about him: his office. It was rather small, was sparsely furnished with an old practical-looking desk, a threadbare sofa, and a couple of what appeared to be prints of paintings lifted from a cheap motel room.

For all that, I immediately felt calm and relaxed in this old man's presence.

'Jack,' he said. 'What can I do for you and, more importantly, what can you do for me?' He spoke to me in passably good

Indonesian with just a hint of an accent and only slight grammatical errors.

'I dunno, sir,' I stammered. 'I have just recently arrived in the city and I am looking for work. I am a hard worker, smart and am ready to learn.'

'Hmmmm ... you are smart?' he mused. 'Not too smart, I hope. I don't trust smart people too much; they are almost as dangerous as stupid people.' This was said with a twinkle in the eye and another slightly mischievous grin.

'Let me tell you what we do in these here parts and then you can decide if you want to work with us,' he started. 'We are here basically to give people what they want and to make a good profit at the same time. Many people want to relax, have some fun and forget about their troubles. You know, Jack, Jakarta is hard. Life is hard. We must be hard too, but we must always remember that we will finally answer to a higher power. Do you believe that, Jack?'

I nodded, but to tell the truth this old coot was losing me. I didn't know what he was on about, but he continued nevertheless.

'Jack, I need people I can depend on; people who will help me to help others. I have many pies in which I have fingers and despite what I said a few minutes ago, I need smart young men,' here he paused, 'such as yourself to help keep my finger on the pulse of it all.'

He continued, 'Now, listen Jack, Devi is a nice girl. One of the best I have met and one of the best I know. She has recommended you to me. I don't know how you know her or how well, and I don't want to know, but her word is good enough for me and if you are up for it then you can start here tomorrow night.'

I didn't know what to say or think, but I knew I was right about Devi, she was a lovely girl.

'What would be my responsibilities?' I asked.

'Yusuf will fill you in tomorrow night. I will pay you two million rupiah a month to start with and we'll see how you get on,' he told me.

My mind was spinning. Two million? That was crazy and far, far more than I could have ever hoped for. I merely nodded my agreement and shook his outstretched hand.

'Good. That's settled then,' he said and led me back out to the corridor. Once there, Yusuf took charge and led me back to the reception area.

With a gruff, 'See you tomorrow,' I found myself back on the pavement outside.

I was in a bit of a state of shock as I took another ojek back to Heri's boarding house but I knew this was a golden opportunity that I couldn't afford to pass up. I was under no illusions that Pak Neil was going to want a return on his monthly investment and that I would be expected to perform and to perform well, but I had no worries on that score. In all modesty, I knew that I was reasonably intelligent and definitely hard working.

I was aware that perhaps not all aspects of that esteemed gentleman's business interests would be completely legitimate, but I felt sure I could keep an eye out for trouble and be ready to adapt to any situation if needs be.

I told Heri about what had happened and he reinforced my thinking. He said that it was a good chance for me to start making something for myself, but that I should also be careful as there was bound to be some dodgy aspects to my new-found employment.

It was agreed that I would continue staying with him until I received my first month's salary and then I could look for somewhere on my own to stay which would afford me a bit of independence. Heri also said I should go to work with him once more just to show my gratitude to his boss for giving me the opportunity in the first place and, of course, so I could say goodbye to the guys who had been so welcoming and friendly during my brief employment there.

As on my first night in Jakarta, I once again had trouble drifting off to sleep. This time, though, there was a multitude of questions and emotions swimming through my head. I was happy, excited, nervous, worried and a little confused all at the same time, and not for the first or the last time during my life in Jakarta the face of Devi was last thing to bother my consciousness before I finally found sleep.

The next evening I set off to the Club Mexicanas and the next instalment in my life: one which I hoped would lead to the fulfilment of my hopes for a better future.

I arrived early, around five pm, and the place was not surprisingly empty. The only people around were some of the staff getting things ready for opening time, which I learnt was at seven although not much in the form of customers was really expected until at least ten.

I introduced myself to a few of the workers and wandered around aimlessly for a bit while sort of half-heartedly looking for

Yusuf. I didn't quite have the confidence to go into the back of the club into the corridor I had been the previous night, and I just hoped he would come and find me. After a few minutes this was indeed what happened.

He came out of the back corridor, saw me and then beckoned me to follow him. Without speaking he led me down into what was obviously the cellar and with the minimum of words introduced me to a guy named Endy. With that he left.

Yusuf was not, I gathered, a great conversationalist. Endy, however, turned out to be the exact opposite. He was a youngish man, perhaps in his mid-thirties, and was skinny to the point of emaciation. He was already losing his hair and had a couple of missing teeth, but despite this rather gawky looking appearance he had the most engaging smile and, as I was soon to discover, personality.

He explained the way things worked in this particular area of the club; that he was the purchasing manager and that his responsibilities included making sure the club was fully stocked and loaded and that, most importantly, the beer never ran out. He said Yusuf had told him to expect me and that I would be working with him for a week or so then I would be handed over to another area of the club's business.

It all seemed relatively straightforward to me and I didn't envisage that there would be any problems in picking up the job and what to do. Endy showed me how to get the barrels in place and ready for the 'lads' to install. That's what he called them -'lads'. He explained that the club hired some young chaps on a freelance basis to do all the manual work and 'other bits and bobs', while the permanent staff, which included us, mainly supervised them and told them what to do. He told me that the job was a pretty decent one and as long as one kept his nose clean and didn't try anything stupid, like ripping Pak Neil off or upsetting Yusuf, then one could be set up in a very nice number indeed.

I did wonder briefly at this point exactly what he meant by the 'lads' doing 'other bits and bobs' and also just how exactly I was going to actually earn the rather large salary I was on, but I figured it wouldn't be prudent to ask too many questions at that point, and anyway, things would probably become clearer over time.

Endy showed me a few other things that first evening, such as how to make out orders and to check invoices before they were sent to the accounting and finance department, how to ensure there was enough stock for any one particular night, and what factors to take into consideration when planning ahead. For example, early weekdays such as Mondays and Tuesdays would obviously usually be quieter than days later in the week, especially Fridays and Saturdays, while the club hardly had any customers at all on Sundays yet still opened for business. I wondered aloud why Pak Neil bothered to open on Sundays as Endy told me he probably made a loss on that day of the week, but Endy just smiled again and shrugged, so I left it.

For most of the rest of the evening, Endy and I just chatted amiably in the cellar area but a couple of times we went for a walk around the club to see what was going on. It was just as dark as I remembered from the night before but slowly my eyes got used to the darkness and I was able to see a little bit more of what the club was like and what was going on.

The club was made up of two bars on different floors and a set of karaoke rooms off to the left of the bar on the lower floor. The upper room bar ran along the full length of the room and this area had a number of sofas and tables where patrons could sit and order food. While not exactly the height of luxury, this bar had a certain refinement to it and it seemed to be the place where genuine couples, rather than those who had just met, could come and talk and enjoy an evening out.

The downstairs bar was a little different. Both the entire room and the bar itself were a lot smaller than those upstairs, presumably because the upstairs bar also overhung the reception / entrance area, and it just seemed a little seedier all round. There were almost no chairs and certainly no sofas, and so the clientele had to stand. It seemed more like a pub than a club to me, not that I had had much experience of either at that point.

When Endy and I first walked around the club it was around ten-thirty and the place was still no more than about one third full, but when we had a second stroll around about an hour and a half later things were much different.

By then the club had filled up, especially on the lower level which was now really rather crowded. Music was blazing out again and it was hard to talk so Endy just led me around and pointed out a few things to me. First he pointed at a couple in the corner; a rather large gentleman, perhaps in his early fifties, was pawing at rather an attractive young girl who was trying to escape his clutches and who didn't look that unlike my friend

Devi (although it definitely wasn't her). Endy just grinned and started counting on his fingers – ONE, TWO, THREE … before he got to FOUR the largest man, certainly the largest Indonesian man, I have ever seen had flown across the room and picked Mr-Gropey-Sweaty-Pants up by his collar and was ushering him out of the club.

Next Endy nodded in the direction of another couple. This time it was two men trying to talk over the noise of the club with little success and then suddenly one of them made a jerking movement with his head indicating that the other should follow him out to the gents' toilet. I looked questionably at Endy who once again grinned, and then pinched his right thumb and index finger together and then put them up to his nose as if he was sniffing them. It took me a moment or two to work out exactly what he was saying, but then the penny dropped; the two men were off to the lavatory to take or sell drugs.

Then Endy took me through to have a look at the karaoke rooms leading off the lower barroom area. There was another small corridor to go, not unlike the one the other side of reception in which Pak Neil and Yusuf's offices were located, but this corridor had about eight small rooms adjoining it, four on each side.

I looked in the first of these rooms and I was astonished. It was full with the most beautiful girls I think I have ever seen and they were all sitting on or around one single sofa watching television. There must have been around fifteen or twenty of these stunning looking girls and at first I couldn't understand what they were all doing. Were they all customers, perhaps girls from a factory or shop or something all here for a night out? In that case why were they all here watching TV and not in the bar enjoying themselves?

Endy looked at me and gave me one of what I now realised was his trademark grins and then, once again, the old penny slowly began to drop.

Endy explained that these girls were not prostitutes as such; rather they were 'companions' for any man (or the occasional woman) who wanted some company while they sang in the karaoke rooms. What would happen, Endy explained, was a man (or a woman) would ask for a girl to accompany them while they sang and they would pay the club RP 65,000 an hour for the privilege, of which the girl would get RP 25,000. The customer would then invariably buy the girl some drinks and probably food too, and if both parties agreed, then they might hook up for more intimate relations later. If this happened, Endy explained, then the customer would pay the bar another RP 65,000 to take the girl away and once again she would get RP 25,000 and would be free to negotiate any 'extra' from the customer which she would keep.

I must have looked a bit shocked because Endy then explained a bit further that all the girls were well looked after and that none of them were ever forced or pressurised to go with any of the customers, or even to stay in the room for more than the initial hour. He told me that no physical contact at all was allowed in the rooms and that 'the lads' came to check discreetly through the outer windows every few minutes just to make sure nothing untoward was happening.

After one hour's karaoke the girl had to make an excuse to leave the room and report back to the waiting room. Here she would give a quick report on what the customer was like, whether he was drunk, mistreating her or generally being obnoxious and if she was happy to continue for a second hour with him. If she didn't want to, for whatever reason, then she would be replaced in the room by another girl and that particular customer would not be permitted to take any girl home that night nor welcomed back into the club for a while. 'The lads' would politely point out the error of his ways at the end of the evening as they called him a cab or saw him to his car.

Endy also said no girl would have to ever go home with a customer if she didn't want to. He said that a customer who wanted to take a girl home would be expected to ask her himself and then respect her decision, and he even told me that once or twice a girl had supposedly 'agreed' to go home with someone but had looked very unhappy or distraught about the idea and so the club had not permitted it.

I found Endy to be a wealth of information in those early days, and I would often pick his brains about the workings of the club and how to get on and make sure I progressed up the ladder as quickly and effectively as possible. Endy was always ready with a snippet of advice or information and we got along famously. I asked him what he knew about Pak Neil and how come a *bule*, a white foreigner, had ended up owning the bar. Here, though, Endy was a little less forthcoming and a bit more guarded.

'I don't really know that much about him, to tell you the truth,' Endy explained one day when I asked him again. 'All I can say is one day we all came to work a year or so ago and everything had changed.'

'How do you mean?' I asked him.

He thought for a moment before replying. 'Well, the club used to be run by an Indonesian guy when I started working here two years ago, and it was a bit of a state, to be honest. It was a rough club, there was always trouble with gangs and fighting, and police raids were not uncommon. I stuck it out because I needed a job, but it was clear that the club was failing and it was only a matter of time before it closed down.'

'So, what happened?' I pushed a bit more.

'Well, like I say, one day we got to work and saw there had been changes,' Endy explained. 'The old owner was nowhere to be seen, and in his place was Pak Neil. He told us that he was running things now and that there were more changes on the way. Then, true to his word, things did change. The club went slightly more upmarket, the trouble stopped, the police stopped visiting so much, and normal regular punters came back in droves.'

I decided to give one last push: 'But Pak Neil? Where did he suddenly come from?'

Endy just looked at me. 'Nobody is quite sure, and nobody is really brave enough to ask too many questions.'

I wasn't sure if this was meant as a warning to me to desist, but before I could say anything Endy continued anyway.

'It is rumoured that he lives outside the city somewhere and that he has been here in Indonesia for a long time. Some say he has even married a local woman and has a kid or two, but nobody has seen them and he has never spoken to anyone about that side of his life at all. All I know for sure is he's often gone for long periods of time and he's a pretty nice guy. Nothing more I can say than that, really.'

I knew that was all I was going to get out of Endy and so I decided to drop the subject altogether and get back to work. I would, I decided, not ask any more questions or try and dig into Pak Neil's story or background. After all, I reasoned, what was it to me? All I knew was I had a good job and I was being well paid to do something I reasonably enjoyed, and I wasn't doing anything illegal or potentially shameful to my family. That was what was important.

I did see Pak Neil around once or twice, however, and one time I even ended up being given a lift home by him. It was late in what had been a run-of-the-mill kind of evening when Pak Neil showed up at the club with two other people in tow. I had never seen these two other guys before – both Indonesian – but the three of them disappeared into Pak's office and I thought nothing more of it. After a few minutes, Pak Neil emerged and walked his guests through the club and back to the entrance. As far as I could see, they didn't stop to talk to anyone on the way and nothing was out of the ordinary, or so it seemed.

Pak Neil, upon coming back into the club after seeing his guests off, appeared slightly out of sorts, however. Instead of either going to his office or taking a walk around the club as he usually did when he made an appearance, he now made straight for the bar where I was on duty. I had never seen him take a drink before, but now he ordered a large whisky and he even appeared to be trembling slightly.

'Are you OK, Pak?' I ventured as respectfully as I could.

'Umm?' was all I got in reply. I decided it wasn't worth

pushing it and so I carried on cleaning up. After Pak Neil had finished his drink he seemed to regain a bit of colour in his cheeks and a bit of a spring in his step once again, as it were.

'Jack. Get your coat. I'll give you a lift home.' This was somewhat unexpected as Pak Neil had never been known to give anyone a lift before.

'I haven't finished here yet,' I said, aware of how weak it sounded even as the words left my mouth.

'Ah, leave it. Endy will close up here. Won't you, Endy?' This last utterance was accompanied by a raised eyebrow aimed in my colleague's direction.

Endy looked less than enthusiastic about the prospect, but nodded his acquiesce anyway, and I went and got my stuff ready to meet Pak Neil out the front.

Pak Neil brought his car round, and I was a bit taken aback. I don't know what kind of car I was expecting Pak to own, but this wasn't it. He was driving a Kijang hatchback, which is a kind of jeep-type vehicle with five doors, and it is a perfectly respectable kind of car but not one you would expect a captain of industry to be seen in, let alone driving. I was also surprised to see Pak Neil driving himself, as I had assumed he would have a driver. I thought it best, however, to keep my thoughts to myself at this point and just climbed in.

We drove in silence for a while with Pak Neil concentrating on manoeuvring the car out of the small car park and onto the main road. Other than checking my address, our silence continued for the next few minutes before Pak Neil finally spoke.

'Jack. Sorry for being a bit, ah, unbecoming before.'

'That's OK, sir.' I managed in reply.

Pak looked sideways at me as he drove. 'Please, call me Neil, and anyway, as I said, sorry about that. I'm just a bit tired and nervous, maybe.'

This was a surprising admission to say the least. 'Nervous Pak? How come?'

Pak Neil didn't immediately answer. 'Umm?' he finally offered.

'You said you are a bit nervous. About what?' I asked.

'Did I? Ah, sorry Jack. I'm not with it properly tonight. Just ignore me.' This was said in a somewhat resigned tone of voice if anything, and did nothing to allay my suspicions that something was not quite right with Pak tonight.

'OK.'

At that response from me, at least, Pak Neil gave a little grin and we carried on in silence once more. He dropped me at the top of my road, and other than a cheery, 'See you, buddy.' Not another word was exchanged between us.

After this strange little encounter with Pak Neil, I carried on working and within a very short time working with Endy, I started to find my feet and then I moved around the club spending a little time in each of the areas as directed by Yusuf.

During that time, I worked behind the bar, in the reception, as one of 'the lads' (although thankfully for only a couple of days) in the kitchen, and in the offices as 'management'.

I found all aspects interesting, and in the main most of the employees were very friendly and helpful. I guess I found 'the lads' work the most interesting and varied but the least suitable for me. What they had to do, basically, was the security work and the running around that fell into no-one else's direct remit.

They would have to watch out for unruly customers both inside the club and out, help with the manual work such as fixing the barrels onto the bar and carrying out small repairs around the place, look after the girls in the karaoke lounges, and then generally be at the beck and call of all the other departments.

The management area of the club was also interesting. It involved making sure the security laws and regulations with respect to things such as overcrowding, fire escapes, kitchen and bathroom cleanliness, etc., were being complied with, as well as controlling employee matters such as complaints from and about them, absenteeism, tardiness and general staff well-being and unhappiness.

After about six weeks, Yusuf called me into his office and I had the longest conversation with him yet: it lasted 15 seconds.

'You have done ok. We are keeping you. You will work in management. Your salary is now three million a month. See you tomorrow.'

Not much I could say to that, except, 'See you tomorrow.'

During this time, I was still seeing a lot of Heri whenever I could although I had moved into my own room at a slightly more upmarket boarding house a mile or two closer to the club. He seemed to be pleased for me and kept imploring me to make sure I continued to work hard and keep 'my nose clean'.

'You can do it, bro. Make us all proud of you,' he would say.

That was all I ever wanted to do: to make him and my parents and other siblings proud of me. I was determined to do so one day and repay their faith in me.

Time went by as 'management' and I grew into the job. There weren't really that many problems on a day-to-day basis and I found the work interesting and varied rather than truly challenging.

I got to know all the club employees naturally, and most of the regular customers too. They were, in the main, gentlemen who worked in the business and industry sectors in downtown Jakarta. They were not a young crowd and tended to edge towards early middle age in years rather than anything else. This meant that there was rarely ever any trouble in the club, because the clientele came looking to relax and unwind at the end of a days' work rather than in search of a punch-up.

I also got to know the girls in the karaoke sector fairly well and began to understand them better. They told me similar stories to the one Devi had told me; namely that they were poor girls from the villages who came to the city looking for work and for one reason or another ended up working here. Some of them were quite open in admitting they slept with the customers if they liked them and if they felt there was a good chance of getting a decent pay-off from them, while others adamantly refused to ever go with a man no matter how much money he had or offered them.

They were almost all without exception nice girls, though, and I came to like them all and feel rather protective of them.

As my first year at the club came to an end, I found myself in the position of having saved enough money to put a deposit down on a small house in a kampong, or inner-city village / compound, on the edge of Depok, a place to the south of the city. This was the first real sign that I was becoming established and it was a proud day for me when I signed the lease.

I asked Heri, by now finally working as a mechanic for a Toyota workshop and doing quite well himself, if he wanted to come and move in with me, but he just smiled and said he would prefer to stay in the middle of the city near his job and his friends. He did tell me, however, over and over again how proud he was of me.

During this time I managed to go home to our village just one time. That was at Idul Fitri, the culmination of the Muslim fasting month of Ramadan when everybody who can is expected to travel to their place of origin or home town or village. I was able to go home for quite a lengthy three weeks because the club was closed for the entire Ramadan month.

It was another awful multi-hour journey by bus and public transport to get home, and when I arrived I was hot, sweaty, and exhausted. Not really the best frame of mind to meet my family after almost a year away, but that all changed when I saw my parents and the rest of my family.

They were as delighted to see me as I was them, and we spent the next few days catching up with each others' news and gossip and having a great time. I told them all about my new house and how well I was doing in my job, although I didn't tell them I was working in a nightclub. Instead I just told them I was working for a rich businessman. I felt a bit guilty not being totally honest with them, but I didn't think they would really understand or approve if I told them everything and anyway, I didn't actually tell any lies.

My father told me the problem with Mr. Simon had long been sorted out and he, Mr. Simon, now knew that I wasn't the culprit responsible for breaking into his shop. My father told me it had been discovered that the true villain was none other than Mr. Simon's nephew who had gotten drunk with a few of his friends and then broken into his uncle's shop.

My dad told me that Mr. Simon had been so heartbroken when he discovered what had really happened that he promptly closed his shop down and left the village. I felt sorry for him to a degree, but I remembered how I had felt a year or so earlier when I had been almost forced to leave the village in shame, and to tell you the truth, now had difficulty in feeling too much pity for Mr. Simon. What goes around comes around.

After too short a time, I had to head back to the city and resume my duties. On the bus on the way back to the city I reflected on the changes in my life and in those of some of the people around me. My parents, of course, were still just the same as they had ever been, as were the majority of my siblings and their families, but without doubt I had changed and so had Heri.

He had not wanted to return to the village this year, stating that he was too busy in his job and also that he wanted me to go on my own. At first I wondered why this was, but then I realised it was because he wanted me to have the opportunity to bask in a little bit of glory upon my return home without running the risk, however slight, of him overshadowing me. What a nice guy he is.

I did, of course, tell our parents how well he was doing and how happy he seemed in his life and watching my parents beam at this news made me feel almost as happy as I did when they told me they were proud of my achievements. What a lovely family I have.

Accompanying me on the bus back to the city were a number of people from my village. Some of them I knew and some of them I didn't, but what they all had in common was that they were on their way to try and seek a better life for themselves. I couldn't help wondering what was going to happen to them all over the next year. Some would make it big, no doubt, and some would be abject failures, while the majority would probably lie somewhere in between, but all had their dreams.

When I got back to the city, I found that Yusuf had left a message for me to call in at the club as soon as possible, even though it wasn't due to open for a couple more days. This was not that unusual, although I did wonder why he hadn't tried to call me or leave a message on my mobile.

Anyway, I turned up at the club later that afternoon and my meeting with Yusuf was characteristically short. He told me in as few words as possible that Pak Neil wanted me to branch out more now and to see more of his businesses. I asked him what exactly that would entail, but he just said that I would soon find out and it would be good experience for me. He also told me that from now onwards my monthly salary would be five million rupiah.

Pak Neil had a lot of businesses all over Jakarta and not just strictly in the entertainment industry; he also was involved with lots of shops and properties and had many other investments. However, he was usually conspicuous by his absence and we really didn't see very much of him at all. I remember thinking that for someone who was still relatively young, Pak Neil had done well for himself but I couldn't really see how, as he hardly ever seemed to be around in those days.

Anyway, the first place I was detailed to work in was one of his apartment buildings in Slipi. I had to work there purely as a liaison clerk to start with and my task was to just to make sure the tenants were relatively happy.

I had to act as a sort of go-between for them and the various departments of the building management. For example, the building had a security system and employed an outside firm on a contract basis. It was my responsibility to make sure the security firm were happy with the precautions and systems in place (fire alarms, id checks, emergency escapes, sprinkler systems, etc.) while not intruding on tenants' privacy. I had to also liaise with the tenants' organisation which was supposed to meet monthly and would air complaints or feedback on a manner of things ranging from rent payments to parking spaces to noise complaints. I also dealt with the rents collection agency to ensure that tenants were paying up on time, and then there was the repairs maintenance department to handle, the shop tenants who took up space in the basement of the building, the small restaurant that provided limited room service and a thousand other jobs and responsibilities that lay outside the direct remit of any of these departments.

I found the work to be a lot more demanding, and to be truthful, a lot more satisfying than working in the club. I had so much more to do and I found myself exhausted at the end of each day, but I also had much more of a sense of achievement because I felt that I was actually earning the exorbitant amount I was being paid in contrast to feeling a bit of a fraud when I worked in the club.

I didn't really have an office that I worked out of – instead I was stationed mainly on the front desk of the lobby. This enabled me to act as a kind of receptionist as well as my other jobs. This suited me fine because I was able to get to know most of the residents this way.

There was quite a wide mix of people who were staying in the five-story, sixty-apartment building, with some being local middle aged families, some young single people, some old and retired couples, and even some expatriates, or *bules* as we call them.

I hadn't really met that many *bules* when I had been working in the club, except for Pak Neil, of course. Endy had told me that they sometimes came in but usually preferred the clubs in the Blok M area of the city or the restaurants and bars in Kemang. Both of these areas were just a little more upmarket than we were and perhaps that's why they preferred them.

I got to know a few of them in the apartment, though, and found them to be reasonably friendly. Some were a little quiet and didn't stop for a chat too often, but some others were very talkative and liked to spend time talking with me. This was great for me because it gave me the chance to practice my English which I hadn't really used that much since leaving school.

These *bules* were in Jakarta for a short time only, usually a year or two years, and so were keen on having a good time. They almost always were single people or else friends sharing, and they often had parties or brought back girls to their apartments. This was no problem as long as they didn't stay too long or cause any trouble. It did lead to one or two awkward situations, though.

I remember Pak Neil used to call round sometimes and this was the first time that I really got to speak to him on a regular basis. He would sometimes turn up late at night, either alone or with a young lady in tow, a 'naughty girl', usually, and then disappear upstairs to 'his' apartment.

On the nights that Neil came round on his own, he and I would sometimes get the chance to 'shoot the breeze', as he put it. He would just accompany me in the reception area of the apartment and he seemed content to put his feet up and get away from the stress of running his businesses. He told me these nights gave him the opportunity to 'escape from it for a while' and although I wasn't really sure as to what he was alluding, I was happy to hang out with him and chat away. Most of these chats we had were really rather inconsequential and consisted of not much more than passing the time together. I was mindful of what Endy had implied about asking too many questions, and also of Heri's warnings to 'be careful', so I took steps to ensure our conversations didn't stray into dangerous waters.

Over time, though, I told Pak Neil more about my background and family, and also about my reasons for coming to Jakarta along with my hopes and aspirations, and Pak seemed to listen attentively. He would rarely interrupt but would prefer to let me talk and he'd interject only when he wanted to clarify something or help me out with my still-poor English. He seemed genuinely interested in me and my life and whatever pearls of wisdom I was trying to impart, but one thing about him that never changed was the fact he was always very guarded and hardly ever spoke about his own private life.

What little information he did let slip was just fairly routine stuff. He told me, for example, that he had been born and raised in the UK and had come to Indonesia for the first time about fifteen years earlier. He said he enjoyed living here 'to an extent' and when I asked what he meant by that, he just replied that here life was fairly good for those willing to work hard. I remember saying I thought life in the west must be easier than in Asia because his country was rich while mine was poor. Neil just smiled at this and replied that I shouldn't believe everything I saw on TV or read in the papers.

The only time we did have one conversation in which he opened up a bit to me, however, came a little later and in hindsight considering what was to end up happening to me, I wished I had paid more attention to his words them.

One night we were sitting together in the reception area of the apartment building just filling in time and trying to stay awake when Pak Neil suddenly said, apropos of nothing:

'You a dreamer, Jack?'

I was a bit confused by the suddenness if not the meaning of the question and so didn't answer immediately. Pak Neil for his part just looked at me sideways and then closed his eyes.

'Ah sorry, Jack. None of my business. Ignore me. I'm just in a funny mood today.' It was true that he looked different than normal; more ill at ease or uncomfortable, if you like. Less self-assured, possibly.

'Why, Pak? Anything the matter?' I tried to help.

Pak Neil kept his eyes closed. 'No, not really. It's just that …

… Well, sometimes, life doesn't go the way you think it will, does it? Then you end up over compensating for disappointments.'

Well, I found myself struggling to keep up, but I felt he wasn't really looking for much of an input from me anyway.

'Has something happened, Pak?' I timidly ventured.

A sigh: 'No, that's the trouble. Nothing's happened. A whole lot of nothingness and emptiness.'

I chanced a glance at Pak at this point and to my eyes I have to say he seemed far away; distant even. For the first time in the period I'd known him, Pak Neil looked less than in control. If it didn't sound so silly I'd even say he looked down beaten, as if life in general rather than anyone thing was getting him down.

Again I tried: 'Really, is there anything the matter? Anything I can do for you, Pak?

'No, Jack. Just promise me a few things, will you?'

'Sure. Anything.'

'Just don't hope for too much in this world, mate. Don't put all your eggs in one basket, and never, ever depend on anyone else for your happiness. I did that and now look at me.'

I found this last statement particularly confusing. I mean, it looked to me that Pak Neil had everything a man could want. He was rich, important, good-looking, owned many properties and businesses, and seemed to me to be living the ideal life. I risked a little and told him this.

'Ah, Jack,' he reasoned for the second time in a matter of minutes, 'appearances can be deceptive, you know. But, at the end of the day, that's what it's all about, isn't it?'

'What?'

'Appearances, young Jack, appearances. I appear to have it all but, in reality, well … let's just leave it at that, shall we?' This last utterance was accompanied by a finality that indicated I had no say in the matter and so no response was required or forthcoming.

Over the next few weeks, Pak Neil started coming round a bit more often and he seemed to step up his liaisons with young ladies. At one point he had a steady stream of late-night companions who would be on his arm as they arrived and then accompany him upstairs to his apartment.

This wasn't really his own apartment, as such, as he never stayed there alone but it was the one he used when he was, ahem, entertaining. These girls would invariably leave the next morning or later the same night. This was quite a regular occurrence for him and I didn't really think that much of it one way or another, after all, who was I to be moralistic about making love with a 'naughty girl' for money?

Anyway, one night he brought another girl home with him and as they went to the lift together I happened to look at her and she caught my eye. Instead of giving me a grin as most of the working girls did in that situation, she sort of scowled at me. I didn't think much of it at the time and when the same girl arrived back in the reception area an hour or two later I made the mistake of saying, '*Sudah, Mbak*?'

This I shouldn't have said because it means 'Already finished, Miss?' and in the wrong circumstances it can be very rude.

It turned out that this was the wrong circumstance.

The girl was very angry now and stopped walking to look directly at me.

'*Apa*, what?' she asked me.

I was really embarrassed and said, '*Tidak apa apa, non*, nothing Miss.'

'No,' she said. 'What do you mean 'already finished'? Tell me.'

I hesitated again, but when she clenched my fist and took one more step towards me I finally answered.

'Nothing, Miss ... Just that Mr. often has ...'

'Mr. often has what, Mas?' She asked me, still clenching her fist.

'Erm ... girls come to his room and I thought ...'

'Ah, really? Are you sure? Ha! You thought I was a *pelacur* or a *gadis nakal*, naughty girl, didn't you?' she screamed at me.

'*Maaf, Mbak*, sorry, Miss' was all I could reply.

It was not my finest hour, and I felt guilty and ashamed for a while and I also worried for a long time that she would make a complaint about me, but in the end she didn't. I did learn from that experience, however, not to judge people or to be quick to rush to form opinions of them.

During this period still I made sure that I kept in close contact with Heri as much as I could, because above everything else I still valued his words of wisdom. Although I knew he was proud of the progress I was making, he would still insist on exhorting me to 'be careful'.

At first I thought it was just *basa-basi*, or empty words, that he was spouting, but as time went on and still he persisted with his warnings, I began to wonder if there wasn't more to it than met the eye, and if Heri wasn't in fact referring to something in particular that I should be wary of.

Anyway, after around another six months I was once again moved on, this time to work in one of Pak Neil's hotels. I was officially without title in the time I worked at the Rose Garden Hotel, but my brief was pretty much the same as in my previous positions; namely to learn as much as I could and also, although this was unsaid, to try and show leadership or management qualities.

I have to say I didn't really enjoy the position in the hotel that much. I am not sure why; maybe it's because I ended up getting arrested!

Like my problems before with Mr. Simon, it wasn't my fault, not really. I think the only thing I could be blamed for really was my naivety. It all started when I was working as a Floor Manager at the RGH.

You see, what I had to do was be in charge of one floor of the hotel and to make sure everything was going ok. Like in the apartment, I was the liaison between the various departments, but I had the brief that the guests were the most important. If they had any problems or complaints then I was the one who had to sort them out.

One day I was making my rounds, just walking around and making sure that security was ok, housekeeping was doing its job, and any guests around were happy and had no problems, when I came across a room with its door open. This wasn't unusual because many guests leave their doors slightly ajar, for any number of reasons, such as they are waiting for someone to come back, are expecting a visitor or room service, are in a big group which has taken many rooms and so now they are leaving them open to allow for easy access or many more reasons. So, I wasn't unduly worried or surprised to see the door of room 624 slightly open.

I did what is protocol in those situations and just knocked gently on the door.

'Come in,' said a female voice in English. I did so. In later days I wished I hadn't, but by then it was too late.

I was greeted by a western lady wearing just a short nightdress, a baby-doll, we call it here – and a smile.

I was embarrassed.

'So sorry, ma'am. I saw your door was open and so I was just checking that everything is ok,' I said in my far from perfect English, but I think she understood me.

'No problem, dear,' she smiled. 'It's good to know there's someone who still cares about other people.'

'Erm, I was just doing my job,' I stammered. 'I will be on my way, then,' I added, nodding at the door but unable to take my eyes of this very attractive lady's legs.

She saw me looking at her and gave another grin as I no doubt blushed deep red. 'Are you sure you wouldn't like to stay for a cup of tea or coffee?' she asked, while giving me what even I in my limited experience of such matters knew to be a look of amusement and fake innocence.

'Erm … I'd better be getting back to work,' said I, Mr. Smoothy.

'Nonsense,' she insisted. 'I'll fix you a coffee. Wait there.'

I did.

She went over to the mini bar and I have to admit I enjoyed

watching her walk. She was, I guess, in her mid-thirties, was around 150 centimetres, perhaps 50 or so kilos and was very, very attractive. She had short brown hair cut in a sort of bob style and a nice suntan. Her white baby-doll dress was short, to just above her knees and, as it was a little tight fitting, it showed the curves of her rather attractive body nicely.

I tried to keep my eyes off her but it wasn't easy. To make matters worse I think she was fully aware of the effect she was having on me.

She walked over to the mini-bar and turned away from me, glancing ever-so-sweetly at me over her shoulder. She then made what appeared to be a great show of bending forward to look for the coffee while keeping the palms of her hand on her thighs. She knew what she was doing; she was teasing me. She knew that by adopting this pose her baby-doll would draw that bit tighter around her and show off her assets even more.

I wasn't going to look; I wasn't! I was going to be strong on keep my eyes and mind elsewhere. I could do it, I knew I could.

I couldn't.

'See anything good here, darling?' she teased.

Hmmmmm … it was wrong. I shouldn't have done it and I know I have only myself to blame, but it's natural, isn't it? It was her fault for teasing me and for driving me to it.

So, here I am now; on trial for rape.

I didn't rape her. I have never raped anyone. She wanted to make love with me; she was just as willing as I was.

I have a lawyer. His name is Mr. Bambang Yohannes. He is

good and he believes in my innocence, I think.

We are in court now and he is asking me questions about what happened that day. He is gentle with me and I answer him the best I can. I tell him what happened with the open door, the invitation to have a drink, the lady in little more than her underwear. I tell him how she teased me and let me know, or at least think, that she wanted to make love with me. I then tell him what happened after she asked me if I saw anything I liked. I forget to tell him, however, that she called me 'darling'.

He seems happy enough with my answers and thanks me before sitting down.

That wasn't so bad, I tell myself. I look around the courtroom and I see people I know. I see Heri, who has come here with some of the old gang from the building site. I am happy to see them. Mr. Yusuf is also here. He does not look happy. He is only here because he has been sent by Pak Neil. Pak Neil is not here himself but I know he is responsible for paying my lawyer. I am very grateful to Pak Neil because without his help I would never be able to afford a lawyer and I would surely go to prison for a long time.

Mr. Joko Hardono, the prosecuting lawyer / attorney / barrister / whoever, stands up and approaches me. I had forgotten about him. He is not so nice to me. He doesn't ask nice easy questions like Mr. Bambang did. He doesn't seem to think I am innocent.

No, in fact, he is not a very nice man at all.

'Why did you kiss her? Did she ask you to kiss her? Did she tell you to stop kissing her? Why didn't you stop when she asked you? Why didn't you think she was serious when she said to stop kissing her? Why did you put your arms around her? Did she ask you to? Did she tell you to let her go? Why didn't you let her go when she asked you to? Why didn't you think she was serious when she said to stop holding her?'

So many questions, so fast. I try to answer but can't. Confused. Want to cry. Help. Make him stop. It's not fair. It wasn't like that.

He continues.

'Why did you throw her on the bed? Did she ask you to do that? Did she tell you to let her get up? Why didn't you let her get up when she asked you? Why didn't you think she was serious when she said to let her get up? Why did you take off her dress? Did she ask you to? Did she tell you to stop? Why didn't you stop when she asked you to? Why didn't you think she was serious when she said to stop doing what you were doing.'

Help! It's not fair. No! It didn't happen like this.

Nobody helps me. Nobody makes Mr. Joko stop, until, finally, he does.

I am exhausted and dizzy. I don't know where I am or what's going on. I am aware of being led away and a few minutes later I arrive in a small room where I am left to sit on my own for a few minutes. I put my head on the table and it feels so cool.

What is happening? What is going to happen next?

The door opens and in walks Yusuf. Not happy to see him, and he is not happy to see me. He slaps me hard around the face twice and swears at me.

'You fool,' he hisses. 'You told us you are innocent. That's why Pak Neil agreed to help you.'

'I am innocent,' I insist.

'No,' says Yusuf: 'You are not innocent. You know that and so do we.'

I am stunned. What to do now? Is Pak Neil going to stop helping me? Without his help I am surely going to hell, or at least prison.

'You fool,' Yusuf repeats. He adds nothing else for what seems an eternity; he just stares at me.

Finally he shakes his head and swears again.

'It is going to cost Pak Neil so much more to get you out of this. If it were up to me he we would leave you to do the forty-year sentence the judge is surely going to hand down. However,' he adds, giving me the slightest glimmer of hope, 'Pak Neil thinks it will look bad for him and his businesses if any of his employees are sent to jail, especially for rape. So, against my judgement, I must confess, Pak is going to get you out of this.'

I don't know what to say, and as it happens I don't get the chance anyway as Mr. Yusuf clearly decides he's had enough of my company and leaves the room without another word.

Afterwards I am taken back to Pak Neil's office to see him. This is not a meeting I am looking forward to, but I have another surprise waiting for me when I get there.

I am ushered into his office and the first words he says to me are, 'Get married.'

'I'm sorry?' I stammer.

'Get married,' he repeats. 'Find a girl, maybe Devi, she is a nice girl, and get married.'

'I don't …' I start, but he holds up his hand to cut me off.

'Enough,' he says. 'I can't have you making mistakes like this because your dick is ruling your head. Marry Devi. I will help pay for the wedding and to start you off somewhere.'

I realise that this is not a suggestion and it is not negotiable, so I just nod and try to stammer a thanks, but again Pak Neil cuts me off.

'Don't thank me, Jack,' he says, 'because you are going to pay me back out of your future wages. Just as you are going to pay back to me every last rupiah I had to pay to get the charges dismissed. Understand?'

'Yes.' I am shocked. That is why I was able to walk out of court a free man. Pak Neil paid for the right people to be bribed. Oh, my goodness!

'One last thing, Jack,' he looks at me.

'Yes?' I reply.

'You will never be so stupid again. Will you?' Just for a flash, the avuncular uncle act he likes to play disappears and I see ice in his eyes: the ice that has led him to the top of his world and mine.

'No. I won't. I promise,' I say and I mean it.

So, that is me, Jack, and that is my story so far.

I am on my way now, I really am.

Tess's Story

Hello everyone. My name is Tessinda Alya Avery and I am ten years old. People normally call me Tess or Tessy, but my daddy calls me many different names. These include: penguin, pixie, bebek (which means duck in Indonesian language), tesscot, tinkle, tixy, trouble, tussy, tusscy and Tesco's. My daddy never calls me by my real name unless he is angry with me, and that is not often. My daddy loves me very much.

Anyway, I want to tell you the story of my life until now and so here goes. I will write down everything that I can remember about all the things that have happened in the ten and a half years that I have been alive and I hope you won't get too bored reading my tale. After I have done that, I will tell you more about my life now, and then I will tell you what I hope will happen in my life when I am older and grown-up even.

I was born in a place called Sidoarjo in the country of Indonesia in November 1997, and although I don't remember being born, of course, I stayed in hospital for just a few days before my mummy and daddy took me home with them. I was born in the middle of the night, and my mummy had to have a special operation to cut me out of her tummy because I was too big to come out the normal way. This operation hurt my mummy for a long time afterwards and she couldn't walk properly for many weeks afterwards. I know this is true because my mummy has told me many times.

Usually she tells me this story whenever she thinks I am being naughty.

I am a girl from two countries because my parents come from two different countries. My mummy is from here, Indonesia, and her name is Yossy, and my daddy is from England, and his name is Neil. They tell me I am lucky to have two different countries and I think they are right, but sometimes it feels a bit strange, too. I am the only kid in my class at school who has two countries and I am the only kid who looks like I do but I am not the only kid in my class who can speak two languages, though.

When I was very little, my mummy and daddy and me lived in a house near the hospital I was born in. I don't really remember that much about there, but I do remember some things. I have lots of photographs from that time because my parents liked to take pictures of me when I was small, and they are all in albums now. My mummy and daddy used to tell me lots of stories about that time, and also before then when they first met and got married, but they don't do that anymore. I think that is a pity because I used to like listening to their stories.

If I look at the pictures now I can sometimes just about remember things, or at least I think I remember them. It could be that I don't really remember them and my mind is confusing me, or I am just remembering the things my mummy and daddy told me about the events in the pictures.

I think I remember my first birthday party, though. I know I have many pictures of that day and I know I was wearing a white fairy princess dress. My house was very busy with lots of people coming to visit and play with me. My house was sort of a school as well as it had a classroom built into the garage and my mummy (and my daddy sometimes) used to give English lessons in there. On the day of my birthday, we had my party in there and we had a clown come and do some tricks, and then we ate some cake, and then everyone gave me lots of presents. This is my first real memory, I think. I remember we had lots to eat and my daddy was not happy about the food for some reason. I'm not sure why. My daddy often is not happy about food here in Indonesia and he often says that people ask for too much and then don't eat it all. Maybe that's what Daddy was unhappy about on that day. Who knows?

When I was very little, we moved house. We didn't move very far away, just around the corner, and I still went back to see my old house all the time. This is because all of my old house became the school for my mummy and daddy and not just the garage. They had lots of students wanting to join the school and so finally they turned all the rooms in the house into classrooms and we had to find somewhere else to live.

My mummy usually was the teacher in the school at that time while my daddy got in his car and went to Surabaya every day. Surabaya is the name of the big city near where we lived in Sidoarjo. Now, my daddy was also a teacher but he didn't teach kids much then. He told me he taught grown-ups in their offices and also big girls in an academy. At that time I was a bit confused about why grown-ups or big girls would want to study English, but Daddy explained that sometimes people didn't get the chance to study much when they were little like me and so when they got bigger they would study again. I guess it kind of made sense, but I didn't really think about it that much for very long, anyway.

Sometimes, but not often, Daddy used to take me to Surabaya with him when he went to teach the grown-ups. One day we went very early in the car to an office in Surabaya where Daddy had a lesson. This was fun for me because I didn't usually get time to see Daddy that much during the week and so I was very happy. Our driver took us in the car and Daddy sat in the back with me and kept making me laugh. He kept playing silly songs on the car cassette machine and then singing along but making up silly words to the songs. Finally I had to tell Daddy to stop being silly because he was making my tummy hurt through laughing too much.

When we got to the office where Daddy was teaching there were some people already there. I remember the people there were very nice to me and gave me some orange juice and some drawing paper, but there was one man who was a bit annoying. I realise now that he was just teasing me, but at the time I was only a little girl and so when he kept telling me that my daddy was not a teacher and was really a *'tukang becak'* (which means becak driver), I became very angry with him and said, *'Ngak, kamu nakal'* – which means 'No, you are naughty.' When I remember that time now I smile to myself.

When I got a bit bigger, I started nursery school in Surabaya and Daddy and me used to go in the car together most mornings.

As I said before, we had a driver because Daddy said he didn't like driving in Indonesia. When I asked him why not, he just told me it was difficult for him because driving in Indonesia was different to driving in England. In Indonesia, he said, all the drivers were 'bebek gila' or 'crazy ducks'. I laughed again when Daddy said this. Daddy always made me laugh a lot when I was a little girl, and he still does now.

In my nursery school I made many friends and I always had lots of fun. I have some pictures of my third birthday party at school, and I really can remember this one. The same as with my first birthday party, there was a clown and we played games and ate ice-cream and lots of other food. My mummy and daddy are both in these pictures. We are all smiling and looking very happy.

Because Mummy and Daddy were both very busy when I was little, I sometimes spent a lot of time being looked after by other people. For example, we had a maid or nanny who lived with us and she would help me to get ready for school and to have my meals. Her name was Sri, but we called her Mbak Sri or just Mbak. Mbak means Miss, and it is a polite way to talk to an older lady when you are a kid, or a younger lady when you are a grown-up. Mbak Sri always played with me everyday when Mummy and Daddy were busy, but she could only speak Indonesian and not English. This meant that when I was small I grew up speaking Indonesian better than I spoke English. Mummy used to talk to me mostly in Indonesian and Daddy used English. If I didn't understand Daddy when he spoke English, he sometimes tried to use Indonesian but his Indonesian wasn't very good and Mummy and me sometimes used to laugh at him and then he would pretend to be angry and tickle us both!

On Saturdays, my daddy was usually still working so even though I was not in school then, I didn't see him very much. On Sundays Daddy played football very early in the morning near where we used to live and sometimes I watched him play with his friends. All his football friends were Indonesian but I think Daddy was the best player even though he never scored a goal and he fell over a lot. After he finished football, Daddy always went to lie down in his bedroom for a long time because he said he was very tired.

Mummy didn't watch Daddy play football very often. She said that football was silly and was just a lot of old men running about getting hot and angry for no reason. I thought Mummy was wrong, though, and now I am (nearly) a big girl, I play football in my school for my school team. Mummy didn't really like many sports when I was little, but she did sometimes join in the neighbourhood fitness club. This was a club that had aerobics in the road and any of the neighbours in our complex who wanted to, could come and join in. It was usually just the ladies in the complex who joined, but sometimes some men did, too. I joined sometimes if I didn't go to watch Daddy play football, but I didn't really like it that much.

Daddy told me when he was little he was a good runner too, and he used to run in races back in England. One time he showed me a picture of him running in a race in England. He looked very different in the picture he showed me, because he had long curly hair and he looked very skinny. When I was a little girl, Daddy never had long hair, and now he has almost no hair at all!

Mummy told me once she used to do karate before she met Daddy and one time she showed me some pictures of her, too. She also looked very different because in the pictures she had long black hair and also was very skinny. I asked her why she was not skinny anymore and she told me it was because I had been in her tummy and made her fat and she had stayed like that forever. When she said that, I saw Daddy smiling but later when I asked him why he wouldn't tell me.

Mummy and Daddy say that I was a smart little girl and that I always liked books and watching TV when I was a little kid. I don't really remember that too much, but I do remember always being around the school that Mummy and Daddy used to have. Like I said, it was in our old house at first and then Mummy and Daddy opened another one or two schools (I forget which) also in Sidoarjo, and so everyday after I finished in my nursery school, Mummy's driver picked me up and took me to whichever school Mummy was in and I would stay there the rest of the day. If Daddy was not too busy in Surabaya, he used to come to the school later. I decided at that time that I wanted to become a teacher too when I was grown up. I watched the way Mummy was very friendly when she was teaching and I decided that I would also be a friendly teacher. She was always laughing with the students and playing games with them, but Daddy was a bit different. When I saw Daddy teaching his lessons he always seemed to be more serious and his lessons were always quieter. I don't think the kids enjoyed Daddy's classes as much because they always seemed to have to do lots of writing. This actually was a bit strange for me, because I didn't understand why Daddy was always so serious in teaching, but so funny with me at home. At home he was always laughing and telling silly stories and singing silly songs, but at school he never smiled very much. I wondered why that was.

There were lots of other teachers at the schools Mummy and Daddy owned, of course, but Daddy was the only teacher from a different country. All the other teachers were from Indonesia and some were women and others were men. I liked them all because they were all nice to me and all of them played with me if Mummy and Daddy were teaching or busy. Because we knew them well and they were close to us, I called them all either *'um'* which means uncle, or *'tanta'* which means 'auntie' together with their first names. For example there was: Um Didik, Um Kasi, Um Yanto and Um Arin and Tanta Ida, Tanta Della, Tanta Tine, and Tanta Nurul.

Mummy was very good in training the other teachers to be good teachers and she helped them with lots of things. They didn't just teach English language, like Daddy did, but also physical activities for the little kids. It was like a kind of nursery or playschool as well as a language school and I sometimes joined the classes too, but not often.

When I was maybe three or four years old, my mummy and daddy and me went on a long plane journey to England. I remember we stayed with my Nana for one or two weeks and we did lots of exciting things there. We went to London (I think) and we went to many famous places there – but I forget the names of these places now. I will ask Mummy if we have some photos somewhere and then I will describe them more later. Also, I know we went to the beach even though it was quite cold and I rode on a donkey for the first time. Daddy said he used to ride on a donkey sometimes when he was a little boy living in England with Nana, too. I wonder what Daddy looked like when he was a little boy? I have never seen a picture of him when he was little. I wonder why.

England was nice, I think, but it was very cold. I think we went there in winter maybe. I met my English cousins and played with them, but I think they didn't understand me much because I couldn't really speak English very well then.

When we came back from England, Mummy opened a new school and was very busy getting everything ready for that. There were many things to buy and she had to go to many places so she wasn't at home or in the schools much when I got home every day from my nursery school. Luckily though, she had Um Arin to help her. He used to go with her in the car everyday and they would drive around for ages buying things for the new school while the other uncles and aunts did the teaching in the old schools.

I liked Um Arin especially, as he was always nice to me and Mummy. He had funny curly hair and I always teased him and called him 'Um Cribo'. Cribo is the Indonesian word for 'curly' you see, so I was really calling him 'Uncle Curly'. Funny, right?

Um Cribo and Mummy and me went one time to a place called Malang. This is a town which is near where we lived in Sidoarjo but it is a bit cooler because it is in the mountains. When we were there, Mummy and Um Cribo met some people and talked about something connected with Mummy's job, and then we spent the rest of the day playing and walking around. It was a lovely day and we played in the park and ate ice-creams together and Mummy and me laughed a lot at Um Cribo's jokes. It was nice because Mummy was so happy then. Sometimes Mummy was not happy in Sidoarjo, I know, and so it was a good day for us all there. The only pity about that day was that Daddy wasn't there because he was busy working again. I told Mummy that I missed Daddy, and she just said that he could come with us next time.

Soon after that day we did go to Malang again and this time Daddy did come too. In fact almost all the teachers from the schools came and we all stayed in Malang one night. That was a good day too.

I told you that sometimes Mummy was not happy in Sidoarjo, right? That used to make me sad too if Mummy was unhappy. Sometimes she cried and other times she just looked sad or angry, but I never really knew why. If she was sad then I always wanted to cuddle her and make her happy again and I used to say to her, 'Don't cry Mummy. We love you,' and then she would cuddle me and say she loved me too. I am sad now if I remember those times.

My daddy was usually happy with me, though. I always saw him smiling and laughing when he came home or when he woke up in the morning. Mummy and me slept in the same bedroom and Daddy slept alone because he didn't want to be disturbed, but when he woke up he always chased me around the house and tried to tickle me or sing a song into my ears and give me goose bumps. If we were awake at the same time in the morning, then Daddy and me always had breakfast together. Mummy didn't sit with us for breakfast because she used to eat chicken and rice while we always ate cereals. Daddy and I ate Cornflakes or Rice Krispies usually.

Daddy still played football sometimes and I still watched him play in his games. One day he played a game in Surabaya and he took me with him. It was just me and him that went to this game and we had a good day with lunch and games in the mall before going to the football field. I was still a little girl then, so when Daddy was playing football he asked one of his friends to look after me on the side of the field. His friend was a very nice lady called Tanta Jolie. She was very pretty and not so old like Mummy. She told me she was Daddy's friend and that I was very lucky having a daddy from England because when I grew up I would be able to speak English very well. I said, yes, but by the time I could speak English my daddy would already be *very* old. Tanta Jolie just laughed and gave me a cuddle.

When I was about five, or nearly five, Daddy and Mummy were not happy together anymore and that made me sad. They sometimes were angry and had arguments, and sometimes they were both quiet and didn't talk to each other for a long time. I don't know what the problem was or why they didn't like each other anymore, but I knew they still liked me, because they told me that many, many times.

One day, Mummy and Daddy went into Daddy's bedroom for a very long time and they talked and talked. I remember that while they were talking in there I had time to watch three whole Disney films on VCD. That shows they must have been talking together for hours and hours. When they came out of the room they said they wanted to talk to me.

I was sad and I started crying because I knew what they were going to say: they were going to tell me that they didn't want to be married anymore. I just cuddled my daddy very, very tightly and told him I didn't want him to go. I told him I loved him and I wanted him to stay. I didn't want him to go.

My daddy cuddled me tight and told me he loved me too.

Then he told me that he was going to go to England for some time and that Mummy and me would stay in Indonesia for a while. He said he was going to try and save lots and lots of money there, and then when he had, Mummy and me would come and stay with him. He told me again that he loved me very much and then I asked him if he still loved Mummy. He cuddled me more, and he told me that of course he still loved Mummy. He said that he would always love me and Mummy forever and ever, lots and lots and lots.

When he said that, I felt a bit happier but I cried even more. I know that's strange, isn't it? Then my daddy cried too, and so did my mummy. Then we all cuddled each other and then we all stopped crying and then we all had our tea.

So, Daddy went to England and me and Mummy stayed in Indonesia. I remember the day Daddy left very well because he nearly missed his plane. There was a football match on TV and Daddy wanted to see the end of it before he went to the airport. I think England were playing in the World Cup but they lost to Brazil, so Daddy was not happy and we had to drive to the airport very fast or he would have missed his flight.

I was sad that Daddy left, but at least I knew we would be

together soon and Daddy said he would call me often from Nana's house. We kissed goodbye at the airport and this time nobody was crying and when me and Mummy went home in the car with our driver she cuddled me all the way home and told me funny stories like she used to when I was very little.

I missed Daddy a lot, of course, but I thought about him every day and I tried to be a very good girl so he would let me and Mummy come over to England quickly like he said. He called us every week and I always looked forward to his calls. I was now in the second year of kindergarten school and I told Daddy about my new friends and teachers, and all about my new games and toys and all the things I was doing. Daddy told me he was working very hard, but this I already knew because my daddy always works very hard. I think he gets too tired sometimes from all his work. I asked him if he still played football but he said he was either too tired or too busy to play football anymore.

Mummy talked to Daddy on the phone as well, of course, but she didn't talk to him for as long as I did each time. Mummy said that was because it was very expensive for Daddy to phone from England, and so she let me speak for longer than her. Daddy asked me how Mummy was and I always told him not to worry because Um Cribo (Um Arin) was often with her and he made her smile. Daddy said that was good.

It was true that Mummy did seem happy again now. Everyday she smiled a lot more and she hardly ever had any headaches anymore. She was still very busy and every day had to go to lots of meetings or else teach in the different schools, and I didn't see her too much during the day, but I saw her almost every night now. I didn't really understand why she had so many meetings except it was something to do with the schools. I think she wanted to make or open more schools in different places, and many people wanted to help her by giving her or lending her money, or something like that anyway. I was still a little kid, really, and so all of that kind of stuff was boring and confusing for me.

I do remember there was one thing that did make Mummy a bit sad at this time, though, and that was when Um Cribo decided to stop working with Mummy. I remember Mummy was very, very sad and cried a lot. This made me sad too, but I didn't cry. I remembered Daddy told me I had to be a brave girl without him and if I was brave and good, then he would be able to be happy and work even harder so Mummy and me could come to England quicker. So, I didn't cry when Um Cribo left even though Mummy did, but I did cuddle her and try to make her happy again.

Mummy wasn't sad for long as she still had many things to do and she had lots of other friends. We sometimes went to see her mummy, my grandma, and I called her Oma. Oma is the Indonesian word for grandma or nana, I guess. My Oma looks like Mummy because both of their faces are round. I asked her why once and she said she has a round face because she likes to smile a lot. I thought that was a good answer. I don't have a grandpa because he died before I was born and not long after Mummy and Daddy were married, but I have seen pictures of him. He looks like he was a nice man and my daddy said if grandpa knew me he would play with me lots. Daddy said he was very close with grandpa and they spent lots of time together when Daddy first came to Indonesia. Actually, now I think of it, Daddy always looks very sad when he talks about grandpa.

When Daddy was in England we had Ramadan and then Idul Fitri. This was the first year for me to really join in and do everything properly. Ramadan is the Muslim fasting month when all Muslims are not allowed to eat or drink anything from very early in the morning until the evening. I was still little, of course, but I did fasting until lunchtime while Mummy and her friends did it all day. At the end of the fasting, at around 6pm, everyone ate lots of food and almost every day Mummy got a tummy ache in the evening.

I spoke to Daddy on the phone and asked him if he was doing fasting in England, and he said he was. He said it was easier in England because it was winter there. I asked him why that made it easier to do fasting, and he explained that people only did fasting during daylight hours – the time when it is light- and in England in winter it is only light for a few hours each day. Daddy said if it was summer time then it would be very difficult to do fasting in England because in the summer it can be light for fifteen or sixteen hours every day.

Mummy continued with her work in the schools and continued with her meetings and travelling to Malang and other places, and lots of people always came to our house, and lots of times the telephone was ringing all through the day and into the night. It was a very busy time and so Mummy decided to disconnect the phone and not to answer the door to people so much. Sometimes Mummy even used to hide in the bedroom and tell mbak to tell people knocking on the door that she was not at home. I asked Mummy why she did that, and she told me she was just too tired to talk to all the people who wanted to talk to her. I asked her how Daddy could call us if the phone was not connected, but she told me it was OK and she would call Daddy if there were any problems.

At about the same time as Idul Fitri that year, I met Um Ritchie for the first time. He was to become a very important man in my life, and in the life of my mummy and my daddy, but at that time he was just a new worker in Mummy's school. He was about the same age as Um Cribo, I guess, but he was taller and skinnier. He was a quiet man when I first knew him and Mummy always seemed to boss him around and he just agreed, but he was always friendly to me. Soon he seemed to take Um Cribo's place and become Mummy's assistant in the school and they did lots of planning and talking together. I sometimes joined them when they went for lunch together but they always wanted to talk about work things and so it was quite boring for me.

They didn't often talk about Daddy, though, and I hoped this didn't mean Mummy was forgetting about him and that we were still going to live in England soon. I missed Daddy a lot and I missed especially his cuddles and funny stories. I told Mummy this and then she cuddled me and told me that Daddy missed me too and was always thinking about me. I asked Mummy if she missed Daddy and she said she did.

Then Mummy had a good idea. She said we would get some proper photographs done in a studio and send them to Daddy so that he would look at them and be happy. I was very happy about this idea, and so I spent absolutely ages choosing which clothes to wear so that Daddy would see how pretty I was and how grown-up I was becoming.

We got ready and Mummy and I got in the car with our driver, and then Um Ritchie also got in the car. I was surprised because he also looked very smart in his best clothes. I asked him if he was going to have his photo taken too, and he said he was. Anyway, we went to the studio and a nice man took lots of pictures of us all. He took pictures of Mummy and me together, me by myself, Mummy by herself, Mummy and Um Ritchie together, and Mummy and me and Um Ritchie together. We had a nice time and I was sure Daddy would be happy when he saw all the pictures of us.

I wrote Daddy a nice letter with mbak's help and I put it in the envelope that Mummy put the pictures in. Mummy sent the pictures of me, of her, and of me and her together, but she didn't send any pictures with Um Ritchie in.

Soon after this, I had something very exciting happen to me. I went on an aeroplane for the first time! It was so exciting! Um Ritchie and Mummy and me all went to Singapore first and then we went to Bali. After that, we came back to Surabaya. It really was the most fun thing ever and I was even allowed into the place where the man flies the plane (the cockpit, Um Ritchie says) and I showed the man a picture I had drawn of the plane and he said it was very good.

We went to Singapore not for a holiday, Mummy said, but to get a special letter that would allow me to live in Indonesia longer.

I didn't understand really, but Mummy said it was something to do with me having an English daddy and so I had to get permission to stay in the country. It still didn't make sense to me, but I didn't complain.

After that we went on another plane and we flew to a place called Bali. Mummy told me that Bali was not a different country like Indonesia, but another island. Bali was very nice and very hot. We stayed at a nice hotel and every day we played on the beach and ate really yummy food. I remember that one day we went to a park with lots of slides and swimming pools and Um Ritchie and I had lots of fun sliding and splashing in the pools. Mummy didn't go on any of the slides, and instead sat in the shade.

A few days after we got home from our holiday, I had some more very good news. Daddy was coming home! I was so happy when Mummy told me this but I was surprised. I thought that Daddy was going to stay in England and Mummy and I were going to there later when he had enough money, but Mummy explained that Daddy was just coming back to Indonesia for a visit and then would go back to England again. I was a bit sad when Mummy told me this, but at least Daddy was coming and I would be able to play with him again.

I was very excited and I remember I kept counting the sleeps I had left until Daddy arrived. I wondered if he still looked the same. I wondered if he would bring me any presents or sweets from England. I also wondered if he and Mummy would be happy or if they would start arguing again, but that idea made me sad so I didn't think about it too much.

On the day Daddy arrived, we went to the airport to pick

him up and I was so happy, excited and nervous at the same time. I wanted to go to the airport early to make sure we didn't miss Daddy, but Um Ritchie explained that wasn't necessary and he told me to be patient. I did try, but it was so difficult. Mummy warned me that Daddy would be so tired when he arrived and so probably wouldn't be able to play with me straight away for one or two days, but I didn't care. I just wanted to see him.

Finally we got to the airport and there were many people there. It was very hot and we had to wait behind a barrier but Um Ritchie lifted me onto it and I sat there waiting for Daddy. Finally I saw him and I jumped down off the barrier. Mummy and Um Ritchie tried to stop me, but I started running to my daddy and I called his name many, many times. Daddy saw me and he ran to me too. He picked me up and swung me round and round and I held him very tightly. I was so happy.

I told Daddy I missed him and I kissed him many many times, and he kissed me and told me he missed me very much too. It was the happiest moment of my life up until then.

Daddy stayed with us for a week and we had lots of good times together. We played in the park near our house early in the morning and again in the evening almost every day, and Daddy also took me to school and met my new friends and teachers and me and Daddy talked a lot and I told him all my news. I told him all about my school and my friends, and all about the schools Mummy was opening and the journeys we had been on to many places like Malang and Bali and Singapore, and Daddy listened to all my stories and was very interested.

We had lots of McDonald's to eat, which was good because Mummy normally didn't let me eat that food, and Daddy gave me some toys that he had brought with him from England. It was such a happy week.

On one day Daddy went somewhere by plane (to a big city called Jakarta, I think), but he came back in the evening and played with me before I went to bed. I was worried that he and Mummy would argue again, but actually they didn't. They did talk to each other quite a lot, but they always talked quietly and seriously without any shouting, and I was pleased about that. Um Ritchie wasn't there very much for that week.

Quickly it was Daddy's last day in Indonesia and I became sad again. I tried not to cry because I remembered that Daddy said I had to be a brave girl and then I could come to England soon, but it was very, very difficult. I think it was difficult for Daddy too, because he cuddled me and he cried a bit. This made me cry a bit, too.

Then Daddy spoke to Mummy.

He told her he had made a decision and he was going to come back to live in Indonesia. Mummy looked a bit surprised and asked Daddy why. Daddy just said it was too hard to leave us again and he didn't want us to live apart anymore. Mummy didn't really say anything very much then, but I was so delighted. I asked if this meant that Daddy was not going to go back to England today, but Daddy said he still he had to go but he would be back very soon. When I asked him how soon, he said it would be just one month. Well, that still sounded like a long time to me, but Daddy explained it wasn't really and it would soon go quickly.

Daddy said he wasn't sure if we would live in Surabaya or in Jakarta but he would know soon and then tell us. Again, Mummy didn't say much.

So, we all went back to the airport. Again. And we all said goodbye. Again. And we were all sad. Again.

Soon, though, things got better. I knew my daddy was coming back to live with us in a short while even if I didn't know where exactly. Mummy was still a bit quiet for a few days after Daddy left and she seemed to talk often with Um Ritchie about grown-up things during this time. They both looked a bit sad and not really excited like I was about Daddy coming back to live with us and I didn't know why, but after a week or two they seemed to be happier and they told me they were looking forward to living with Daddy and me in Jakarta.

I didn't really know much about Jakarta except that it was another city in Indonesia and that it was quite a long way from Sidoarjo and Surabaya. Mummy told me that Daddy had decided to take a new job there and so we would all move together and we would all be happy together again. This was all I ever wanted to hear, and I started looking forward to it right away, but Mummy told me I had to finish my kindergarten in Surabaya and then we would move to Jakarta in time for me to start primary school. In the meantime, she explained, Daddy would go to Jakarta and start his new job. Well, I told Mummy that all of this just sounded the same as before, Daddy still wouldn't be living with us. I told Mummy I was not happy at all about this idea but she explained that it was different because now at least Daddy was in the same country and we could see each other more often. Mummy said we could go to Jakarta and see Daddy and also that Daddy would come to see us in Sidoarjo.

Well, this made me feel a bit better, and a short while later we got on another plane and went to see Daddy. This time it was only Mummy and me that went on the plane and Um Ritchie didn't come with us. I think I was more excited when we got on this plane, because I knew that not only was the journey going to be fun, but at the end of it my daddy would be waiting for me. When we landed I was right. There was my dad! It was his turn to wait outside in the hot weather but he told me he didn't mind and now we were going to have lots of fun again.

Daddy was staying in his own house and it was a bit bigger than our house in Sidoarjo. When I came inside it, the first thing I saw was the pictures Mummy and me had sent to him when he was in England. Daddy had put them up on display in his living room. He had also made a bedroom ready for me, and I spent some time putting my toys inside it and arranging them all while he and Mummy spoke outside on the sofa. I don't know what they spoke about, but when I came back out of my new bedroom they stopped talking and just smiled at me. Daddy asked me if I liked our new house, and I said of course I did and I was so happy we were all going to be living together again and I was sure I had the best mummy and daddy in the whole wide world. They both smiled when I said that.

My time in Jakarta didn't last long that first time, just a couple of days, and then Mummy and me had to go back to Surabaya and Sidoarjo again. I wasn't too sad this time, though, because I knew there wasn't much longer to go until we all lived in the same house forever again.

We went back home and Mummy carried on working with the schools, while Daddy kept his promise to come and visit us in Sidoarjo a couple of times over the next month or two. Um Ritchie and Mummy were still busy, though, and I didn't see them very often. I was usually at home alone after I got from school and I spent more time with Mbak. I drew many pictures of our new house in Jakarta and I also drew some pictures of what I thought Daddy looked like in his new office.

One day, Mummy told me she was going to sell all the schools. This was so we could all start our new life together in Jakarta with Daddy, she said, and also because she was too tired. I asked her why she was too tired always and then she told me it was because I was going to have a little baby brother. I was confused again. How come?

Mummy told me there was a baby growing inside her tummy and the doctor had told her it was going to be a boy.

Wow! I was going to get a new house, a new school, a new bedroom and now a new brother as well. What a lucky girl I was.

The big day finally arrived and we flew to Jakarta to be with Daddy. Some things were exactly the same as before: I drew a nice picture and the nice lady on the plane who looked after the passengers gave it to the man who flew the plane who then invited me into the cockpit to have a look and to talk to him. Some things were different, though. For example, we flew in the evening so it was dark when we arrived, and also my daddy didn't pick us up at the airport. I asked Mummy why not, and she said she wanted to surprise him by just coming to his house. Mummy said Daddy didn't even know we were coming and so it would be fun to see his face when we arrived. I giggled then, and said that sounded like a good idea.

Our taxi drove through the dark streets until we arrived at the complex where Daddy lived. Mummy told the taxi driver which house was Daddy's and we stopped outside. I think Daddy was inside watching TV or something, because he didn't come out while Mummy paid the driver and he helped us with all our bags.

I asked Mummy if I could be the one to knock on the door and she said I could. So, I gave three knocks and then waited. I could hear the TV inside (I was right, he was watching it) and then I heard the locks being turned and ... Daddy opened the door!

Wow! He was so shocked!

He looked really amazed to see us and for a few seconds he didn't say anything at all, but then he picked me up and threw me up in the air like he always used to do, and then we came inside.

Once he had helped to take all our bags inside the house, I ran to my new bedroom and started playing and jumping on the bed while Daddy said to Mummy again how surprised he was to see us all. I heard Daddy ask Mummy why she hadn't let him know earlier, but I didn't hear Mummy's reply.

Now, I have just remembered something. Sorry, I forgot to tell you guys that it was not just Mummy and me who came to live with Daddy. Um Ritchie also came to live with us too.

Well, that first night I was quite tired so I didn't play for too long and I went to sleep not long after I went to my bedroom. When I woke up, I was a bit surprised that Mummy and Um Ritchie were also asleep in my room. Mummy was sleeping on the same bed as me while Um was sleeping on a mattress on the floor. I got up and went outside into the living room, and Daddy was already there watching TV and talking on his phone. Actually, he didn't look very happy when I first saw him, but after he saw me he smiled and looked a bit happier.

I came to sit with him on the sofa and he talked about our new life here in Jakarta. He told me he had found a nice school for me near our home and he also told me that I could join lessons in the English school he taught at. I asked him if Mummy was going to come to his school and be the boss there too, but Daddy just smiled and said no. He then asked me a few questions. He asked me if I knew Mummy was going to have a baby and I said I did. He asked me if Um Ritchie often slept in our house in Sidoarjo and when I said he did sometimes, Daddy then asked which room Um usually slept in, and I told him that sometimes he slept in the living room but usually he shared a room with Mummy. Daddy didn't ask any more questions after that.

So, the next few months were like that. Daddy took me to school most days early in the mornings and then he went to his job. He worked in an English language school which was in the mall and he was the boss or the director, or something. I came there to study two times a week in the afternoons and I liked it because I made more friends and I met more people from different countries.

Most of the teachers there were like me and Daddy – they were *bules*. *Bule* is the name Indonesians give to people who have white skins and there were not many people like that in Sidoarjo, or even Surabaya.

We lived in a nice place called Cikarang. This is kind of a small village or town outside the main part of Jakarta. Although it is hot, of course, it is not so busy or noisy as Jakarta or Surabaya. It is a bit like Sidoarjo, I suppose. I mean, we could ride our bikes in the morning or evening if we wanted to, and Daddy could go running, too. There were lots of big roads with lots of trees on them and so we didn't get too hot.

In Cikarang there was a big mall with lots of shops and a cinema and a big playground too. Daddy and me, and sometimes Mummy, went there a lot when we first arrived there. There was also a bus service that took us from our house to the mall. This was good because Daddy's new school where he worked was actually inside the mall.

Daddy had lots more friends now. His friends were the other teachers and they came from many other countries like America, Canada and Australia. They were all very nice to my daddy and also to me, and my daddy started smiling a lot more and I think he was really happy. I told him this and he agreed, and said that he was happy because he had a good job, more friends and most importantly, he had me to play with every day. I cuddled him when he said that.

Most nights Daddy came home after I was already asleep because he had to work until late in his new job. I felt sorry for Daddy because he always worked hard, but he said it was ok as he didn't start work in the morning until later than before, and also he said he only had to work in one place, while when we lived in Sidoarjo he had to work in many different places.

Mummy didn't seem quite so happy, though. She didn't have so much work to do now because she didn't have a job and I think she was a bit bored. Um Ritchie was looking for a job, Mummy told me, and so Mummy and he sometimes went into the centre of Jakarta together, but mostly she stayed home. She told me that she didn't have much money now because she had no job so if I wanted any toys or sweets I should ask Daddy and not her. Also, Mummy's tummy got bigger as my baby brother continued to grow inside her.

Then, one day, just about when I was six, Mummy had to go to the hospital to have my baby brother. I was a bit excited because I thought it would be cute to have someone little to play with and so I helped Mummy to walk to the car. Daddy and Um also came to the hospital, of course.

We got to the hospital and Mummy got ready in the bed. She smiled at me, and then Daddy spoke very quietly to her in her ear and I don't know what he said, but I could see Mummy nodding her head and then she held Daddy's hand and he kissed her head. I saw and heard Daddy tell Mummy he loved her very much and she said the same to him and they both had tears in their eyes. Then the bed was rolled out the room and my little brother was born.

My little brother's name is William Akbar Avery. He was very funny when he was born: very small and wrinkly but very cute. I was happy when he was born, but he didn't do anything! He just lay in his cot and went to sleep all the time. I thought I was going to have someone to play with, but that didn't happen straight away, and it was quite boring having a little brother that did nothing but sleep and cry.

Daddy was a good daddy to William and used to play with him and cuddle him and give his milk, but Daddy never changed William's nappy. I asked him why not and he just smiled and said because William was too stinky. Daddy said he never changed my nappy when I was small either because I was too stinky also. Mummy usually changed William's nappy or else Um Ritchie or Mbak did. Um Ritchie still didn't have a job, so he stayed with us for longer and he spent some time looking after William while Daddy was at work and Mummy was getting better after her operation to have William taken out of her tummy.

When she was strong again, Mummy started working once more and Um Ritchie helped her with that. In the beginning, Mummy had a little business buying and selling clothes, and then a bit later she started teaching English again. She was teaching English to people in their houses and sometimes in our house, but she wasn't as busy as before.

After a few months, Um finally got a job and moved out of our house. I think he got a job as an engineer or something, and he moved very far away. I am not sure exactly where he went but I think he still phoned and texted Mummy sometimes. Daddy didn't say anything when Um left, and Mummy didn't seem very sad, either. It was not like when Um Cribo left and Mummy was very sad for a long time.

The next two years or so were kind of uneventful, I guess. I moved through Primary 1 and Primary 2 in my school; William got bigger and started walking and talking and being someone for me to play with; Daddy still worked in the mall school and I still studied there twice a week; Mummy did more teaching and had more new friends with the neighbours; Um Ritchie visited sometimes but not often; but other things were totally different from before. For example, there were no arguments or shouting between Mummy and Daddy; nobody calling our house late at night; nobody coming in their cars and parking outside all night, and nobody was unhappy anymore.

I learnt more in my school and I became smarter. I learnt about the world and about different places and things started to get less confusing for me. I was always confused why I was different from the other girls in my class, but now I began to understand why I didn't look the same as them. Sometimes when I was little, I would be walking in the mall with my daddy and people I didn't even know, strangers, would pinch my cheeks as they walked by and call me *lucu* – cute. That used to really annoy me (and my daddy, too) but I learnt that they did it because I looked different. Actually many people here think *bule* kids are very beautiful. Well, maybe, but they still shouldn't pinch my cheeks, right?

My daddy gave me lots of advice about being a little white kid in Indonesia. He said people would always look at me because I was different, and although most people would be kind, some would maybe say cruel things or do things that annoyed me (like pinch my cheeks, for example!) and that if they did, then I had to ignore them. Daddy said everywhere he went people always looked at him because he was white and almost every day people called out to him if he was walking or out running.

He said it was very annoying wherever he went to hear people shouting, 'Hey misterrrrrrr, misterrrrrr ... misterrrrrrr bean, misterrrrr bean, *bule* ... *bule* bean ...' and so on, but he just didn't listen and if someone shouted at him or called him 'mister' 'bean' or '*bule*', he just totally ignored them. He said to not even turn my head or look at them when they did this, don't raise your eyebrows or shrug or look away, just don't do anything at all and show absolutely no reaction whatsoever, and then the person or people would feel stupid and stop. After all, he said, would I keep shouting at someone in the street if they weren't paying me any attention at all?

I tried to do as my daddy said and it worked. Now I don't care about them anymore.

When I was nine, I moved school again. This was a new school nearer the centre of Jakarta, and Mummy and Daddy said it would be better for me. I didn't mind, actually, because although I liked my current school, it wasn't very big and it didn't have a sports field or swimming pool like my new one did. The only problem was it was quite a long way from our house and so Daddy couldn't take me to school in the mornings anymore.

Not long after this, Mummy and Daddy bought a new house and Mummy opened a new school teaching English there. It was the same as our old house and school in Sidoarjo, but this time it was a bit different because we didn't live there. It was a very long way from our house, even further than my new school, and it took almost two hours to drive there every day. After I finished my school, our driver sometimes took me to Mummy's school where I did my homework, and sometimes took me straight home.

Now that I was bigger, I had lots of new hobbies and games. I liked to play football in my school and with Daddy outside our home, and I liked to play with William and help him to dress and feed himself, but I was not a little kid anymore. I was still very close with Daddy, of course, but now I spent more time with Mummy or at home with William. Daddy was busy and got home late still, and often had to work on Saturdays or travel to different places so we didn't have so much time together. That made me sad a bit, but as I said, I was not a kid anymore and so I didn't get sad so much anymore.

As Mummy's school got bigger and more students, the lessons finished later and later every day, and sometimes Mummy was too tired to come home to Cikarang, and so she would sleep in the school. At first this was only once or twice a week, but soon it became almost every day. Mummy said it was better for me to also sleep in the school and we would make one of the rooms there into a bedroom and so I could go to my school and back directly from there each day. I asked Mummy if Daddy would move there too, but Mummy said that would not be a good idea because Daddy still had to go to his work in the mall in Cikarang each day.

I agreed with Mummy that was the best idea because I saw how tired Mummy was if she did too much travelling every day. I was worried about Daddy, though, because who would look after him and clean his clothes or cook his food if Mummy and me and mbak weren't there? Mummy said Daddy could cook for himself and we would still see Daddy at the weekends and mbak could clean his clothes then.

When we told Daddy our plan he was OK. I thought he might have been a bit upset or angry, but he agreed it was a good idea and he said it wouldn't be much of a change from the way things were, because we didn't all see each other very much now anyway. He said he would miss us all, and I had to make sure I looked after William especially.

Well, that was about one and a half years ago.

Now things are different again.

Mummy and Daddy are not married to each other anymore and sometimes I feel a bit sad about that. I am not sure when and why exactly they decided to not be married anymore, but I think really that is probably the reason Mummy and William and me moved to stay in Mummy's school.

To start with, we used to see Daddy every weekend, but after a few months it was only 'most' weekends and we stayed more often in Jakarta centre and did not come back to Cikarang. I never forgot about Daddy and I always spoke to him on the phone and we had lots of fun when we met, but I think I knew after a while that Daddy and Mummy wouldn't be married anymore even before they told me.

When they did tell me, I was upset but not surprised. They said they were both tired and getting old and wanted to be happy in their lives, and although they loved and liked each other, it wasn't enough for them to be happy anymore. I just listened. I think they expected me to cry and beg them to stay married, but I didn't. I just kind of agreed with them. I think it is important to be happy, right?

Now, my daddy has just got married again. I didn't go to his wedding to his new wife, but I have met her a few times and she seems OK, I guess. She is nice to me and William, and Mummy also says she is a nice lady who makes Daddy happy so we should try and like her too.

My mummy will also get married again next month. She will marry Um Richie who now has a very good job and has bought us a very big house to live in. Mummy says I cannot call him *Um* anymore, though, and now I have to start calling him *Bapak*. Bapak kind of means 'father' but not exactly. I think I have to call him this because he will be kind of my dad but not exactly. William will also call him Bapak.

So, that is the story of my life until now. I have had a happy life, mostly, but maybe a little bit of an unusual life too. I am still young and I want to do lots of things when I grow up, but for now I will be a good student, a good daughter and a good sister.

Thank you for reading my story.

The General's Story

Neil has been, shall we say, known to me, or on my radar at least, for many a year now, and the balance of our friendship, relationship, cooperation – call it what you will – has shifted considerably more than once over that time, but, basically, and he might not agree here, he has mainly been beholden to me during the vast majority of our years together.

Yes, our conjoined tale makes for interesting reading, but before I really get into that I guess it is prudent for me to start at the beginning and fill you in with at least some perfunctory details regarding me and my background.

I was born in Surabaya, the capital of the province of East Java, in 1959, and lived there as well as other places until 1996 when I finally moved lock, stock and barrel to Jakarta, where I have remained ever since. In between, I spent some considerable time moving around (for reasons that may or may not become clearer later) but always returned to my base in Surabaya.

I am of mixed heritage – Chinese Indonesian and indigenous Indonesian – and, as will also perhaps become clearer over the pages that follow, this has proved to be both a blessing and a drawback. My father was indigenous and my mother of Chinese descent

Some elaboration regarding citizenship and heritage matters in Indonesia is perhaps called for before we progress much further. As the results of a 'mixed' marriage my parents both suffered to a degree through the 'years of living dangerously' in the mid-sixties, when there was a reported coup attempt by the Indonesian Communist Party, who allegedly attempted to seize control of the government in 1965. Their attempt failed and the communists were promptly outlawed and anything remotely 'red' looking either banned or persecuted. This included people of Chinese origin.

There followed a period of murder and mayhem in Indonesia whereby anybody suspected of having communist tendencies or sympathies had very real reason to fear for their lives. Both my parents had family members who simply disappeared during this time never to be seen again. It was by all accounts the most horrible of times.

One of the by-products of this so-called coup attempt was that people of Chinese origin were deprived the same rights as indigenous Indonesians. This meant they found it very difficult, if not impossible, at one stage to secure employment or education for their children. They weren't allowed to own property or to even have 'Chinese-sounding' names and this led to my mother being re-christened Elizabeth Mary Chantmo, and my own name being changed from Xien Chan to a more acceptable Henry Chantmo. This was as, my father told me, many Chinese people based in Surabaya chose deliberately 'English' sounding names for themselves and their offspring in an attempt to crook a nose at the authorities.

Other by-products of this discrimination included mixed-religion marriages being forbidden, the state of Israel as well as the religion of Judaism no longer being officially recognized, and atheism and agnosticism also no longer being official options for citizens.

It was further announced that with immediate affect, all adults would need to register for an identity card and on which they would need to state which of the five approved religions they followed. These were: Islam, Protestantism, Catholicism, Hinduism and Buddhism. Confucianism was outlawed due to its perceived popularity in communist China. Finally, Chinese language schools and courses were banned and Chinese writing symbols forbidden. Some of these rules remained in force for over fifty years.

In 1967 the government went so far as to set up a committee to discuss the Chinese Problem or *Masalah Cina* as it was known in Indonesian. Possible solutions debated included the forced repatriation to China of all people of Chinese descent, and when this was declared 'impractical' other solutions were sought instead. It was decreed that Indonesia would attempt to find ways to take advantage of the economic and business skills of the Chinese-Indonesians whilst ensuring they were no longer in a position to uphold economic dominance.

As years were put between the so-called coup and the present, discrimination against ethnic Chinese continued on one hand, whilst perceived economic inequality existed on the other. A system of belief bordering on myth sprang up that 'the Chinese' were all rich and were squirrelling away the wealth of the country whilst employing indigenous Indonesians in less than salubrious working conditions. As time progressed, an uneasy kind of truce existed, but with racial undertones that would one day again bubble over and cause internal mayhem.

Anyway, this was all still to come as I continued my education and became a young man.

My early education was uneventful and reasonably happy until the time of the aforementioned aborted coup and the 'years of living dangerously' epoch that followed. My father worked as a civil servant in the land transmigration department and by all accounts was well liked and respected by his colleagues and business associates. This meant when the racial instability of that time transposed into something far more dangerous and sinister, he was in a position to be able to call in favours and thus protect his family.

His wife, my mother, would have been at serious risk of the mobs due to her ancestry had she not had my father and his connections to protect her, and, by extension, me. As it was, we were moved from the small private dwelling we rented into the relative safety of an army compound, and it was here that I proceeded to continue my studies until graduation from senior high school in 1977. By this time my father had carved out a second career for himself whilst laying down the foundations for my own.

Dad was still working for the government but in more clandestine areas of expertise. He was not permitted to talk too much about things, of course, but many years later I learnt that a by-product of the horrors of 1965-67 was the setting up of a government agency with connections to the intelligence services. The intelligence services in those days went by the acronym of BIN – which stood for Baden Intellijen Negara (State Intelligence Agency) – and dad worked for an offshoot of this organization. As the male indigenous partner in a mixed marriage, who just happened to already be working for the government, my father was deemed to have the special insight and skills required to be able to understand the sociological conflicts, concerns and underlying problems facing society under the rule of President Pak Soeharto's New Order government.

My father was often away from home and his journeying included several trips overseas. As far as I am aware now, he was responsible for learning and then training recruits in the arts of subterfuge. It was also his remit to oversee the setting up of very small, localized agencies that would be run on the ground in a literally street-by-street or *kampung* basis. Simply put, each area or municipality was instructed to appoint a local head or chief. This head would be responsible for the registering and observance of citizens within a collection of maybe two to three streets. All these citizens would report to the local chief their personal details that included obvious information such as name, age, and address, but would also include details relating to ethnicity, religion, political leanings, property holdings and even bank account details.

The neighbourhood chiefs would be charged with keeping an eye on those citizens within their locality and then reporting upwards to the village or kampung chief, who would in turn report upwards to the local municipality chief, and so on and so forth. It sounds complicated, but it was basically the establishment of a 'spies charter' and it remains in place today.

The whole system was very much self-financing, with citizens paying 'administration fees' to register with the chiefs who likewise paid upwards. My father was, by all accounts, near the top of this particular food chain and so did reasonably well financially, and this in turn led to us living in relative comfort.

In 1977 it was time for me to consider my future. In reality, though, there was not much considering done by anyone as it was decreed that I would take up a post at Yogyakarta Military Academy to undertake Officer Training while ostensibly studying for a degree in political history.

Fast-forward almost twenty years and Neil and I first entered each other's orbits. At the time, I was moving towards the end of my spell in the military and was beginning to branch out and look for investment and opportunities within the private sector, and Neil himself was, I suppose, trying something similar in as much as he was teaching English and trying to make a living and even a business from doing so. Although he says he can't remember our first meeting now, it is still clear in my mind. He was doing some freelance work for a language school in Surabaya called (I think English Education Classes – EEC) and as a 'native speaker' he was sent out wherever he was needed to teach. Now, my dear old mum, who would have been in her early sixties at the time, decided she wanted to brush up on her English and take some private lessons. She got in touch with EEC who duly sent Neil round to mum's house twice a week for a couple of hours or so, and we briefly met one evening when I popped in for a visit while he was giving a lesson.

As I recall, we exchanged pleasantries and, using my years of training and through force of habit, I garnered a little information about him, his background and personality and promptly salted them away for future reference. As I say, Neil insists he can't remember this meeting and therein, I think, highlights one of the many but subtle differences between the pair of us: while I generally speaking don't miss a trick, Neil can sometimes be said to be not entirely on-the-ball, and this is why he is prone to the odd slip or sometimes displays an inability to make the most of a given opportunity.

About eight or nine months after this introduction, I did indeed find myself on the brink of my first truly solo business venture. I decided to invest in buying a franchise in the well-known English Plus Language Corporation. This is a corporation that is involved in the foreign language sector, and includes (amongst other things) a chain of language schools across the world. Each branch is in itself a franchise and 'owners' are beholden to the corporation as an entity, and I invested in one of the first ones opening in Jakarta, Indonesia.

As it ultimately turned out, this didn't turn out to be a fantastically lucrative first dip of the toe into the private sector, and although the schools still operate today and I haven't actually ended up losing money, nor have I exactly made a mint out of it.

More of that to come later, but at this point I was more interested in ensuring I had a good team of teachers for our opening. Being a bit of a greenhorn when it came to the education business, I initially tried to recruit by word of mouth and this is when I remembered Neil and so approached him in order to see if he would be interested in coming on board.

It wasn't difficult to dig up his personal details, and so one day my wife and I made an appointment to go up and see Neil together with his wife, Yossy, at their house in Sidoarjo.

I guess Neil must have been about 27 or so at the time and Yossy a couple of years younger. As we settled down to chat in his living room, I took the opportunity to take in my surroundings. His home, although not exactly salubrious, was certainly respectable in size and décor, and he seemed to be doing reasonably well for himself. His house was a single-story dwelling but had three bedrooms, a large living room, and, no doubt, a kitchen and bathroom in the back. He and Yossy had tastefully furnished the house with a nice line in contemporary furniture and had adorned the walls with what appeared to be a couple of original pieces of artwork. They looked to me to be a young couple with a plan and a future ahead of them.

I outlined my plans regarding EPLC and he seemed interested although non-committal. I said I saw him coming on board and working with me for a few years and then being in a position to either branch out on his own, or else move up through the Indonesian education system and get into the really lucrative teaching world of bona-fide International Schools. I said that in time I would assist him to gain the additional educational qualifications which he would ultimately require should he have serious designs on staying in the teaching industry, and in turn he could assist me in providing some knowhow and experience in what was sure to be a trying time as I attempted to get the business off the ground. I advised him that as much as he might enjoy doing what he was currently doing; namely, lots of teaching in various locations all over the city, he wouldn't be a young man with lots of energy forever and what I was offering him was a chance to build a career.

Although he was friendly enough and seemed to be listening to me, I got the impression I wasn't really getting through to Neil. I felt he was perhaps reluctant to move to Jakarta at that point in his life, or maybe he felt he could do better financially working on his own than the package I was offering him, and thus the vibes I was getting from him didn't look promising. I noticed that every time I asked him a question or made a general statement about something, his attention would momentarily flick across to his wife, Yossy, before offering up any sort of response. He also spoke very carefully and in measured tones as if he was weighing up how much information to impart, which I found slightly unusual in someone still relatively young.

Ultimately, I decided to take the bull by the horns, so as to speak.

'Yossy, may I speak to you outside a moment?' I ventured.

They both looked surprised, but finally Yossy answered. 'Me?'

'Yes, if you don't mind.'

She didn't look it, but she replied, 'Sure.'

We spoke briefly and quietly in Indonesian outside on the small patio there while my wife and Neil stayed inside.

'I can see you are the 'boss' in this marriage. The decision maker,' I started.

She tried to protest. A token protest, I thought. 'I don't think so.'

'Oh, you are. I can see that. Look, Neil has potential,' I pushed on. 'I like him. But he needs a bit more drive: a bit of a push. Try and persuade him this could be a good move for him. For both of you.'

I saw her hesitation and so decided to try a different tack.

'I have wide contacts in Jakarta and I can soon get you a position in an airline there, if that's what you personally are concerned about.'

Still Yossy seemed unconvinced: 'It's not that. It's just that I think Neil enjoys more or less working for himself.'

'Well, I can understand that,' I countered, 'but I think flying all over Surabaya chasing the bucks will soon get old. Look, I tell you what. I'll leave it with you guys for now and get out of your hair. If you feel this is something you'd like to look into, then you've got my number, but if you both feel the time's not right at the moment, well, that's fine too.'

Yossy smiled and said she would work on Neil and see what she could do, but she didn't hold out much hope, and nor did I to be honest.

I was proved right to be pessimistic and it would be another seven years or so before Neil finally did come to work for me.

My business, as I've said, turned out to be a lot of hard work for not an awful lot of gain, at least in the beginning. The first thing to deal with was the fact that the franchise purchase fees were rather exorbitant at $50,000 and then 10% of gross income, which proved not far short of crippling once start up and running costs were factored in. It took an inordinate amount of time and effort to recoup just the initial investment, but after three or four years we were finally showing a slight working profit and turnover was increasing.

The mistake I made back in the beginning was trying to do everything by the book and above board. By this I mean I felt all eyes would be on me as a former TNI operative, and so I would have to be squeaky clean – I should have known better, really, but I learnt! I learnt the various little scams and tricks involved in staying ahead of the game. For example, the most obvious scam was to not declare the correct number of students to Head Office and so pay less commission. This wasn't hard to do, but it was a little risky because if a franchise didn't show sufficient profit it could, technically, find its licence being revoked. There was also the risk of spot checks and audits from HO, but these were rare and far from stringent. Other little tricks included obtaining contracts to teach in businesses at lucrative rates and not declaring them at all to HO. Again, a risk was involved, but generally speaking it was minimal and as long as HO got a reasonable lump sum quarterly they were quite happy.

What was expensive, though, was the employment of teachers. The unique selling point of the business was it employed 'native speaker' teachers instead of 'local' teachers. This meant that the majority of teachers were from countries where English is the first language – the UK, the USA, Australia, Canada, New Zealand, etc. – and this meant, theoretically at least, a higher quality of teaching. Of course, the reality was nothing of the sort. The vast majority of teachers we employed may have been natives, but they were certainly no better than the Indonesian teachers. In fact, in many cases they were severely lacking in even rudimentary knowledge of the grammar and structure of their own language. They were, as I say, purely USPs for the business. They did, however, cost a lot to employ as one had to fork out for their work permits and visas, pay the government tax on their employment, and then lay out a disproportionate amount on their salaries – on average they earned (and I use that word loosely) four times that of a (better qualified) local teacher.

I discovered there were ways of reducing costs here too, though – again with an element of risk involved- and so improved my margins slightly. The way to get round these costs was to employ the foreigners on business visas rather than working ones. This was much cheaper as they didn't then require work permits and no tax needed to be paid. There was a risk of raids from immigration or other such authorities, but even then a word in the right ear – if you get my drift – would ensure advance notice of such raids and thus ample time to take such cautionary measures as to simply tell the *bules* to stay home that day. The greater risk was actually to the teachers themselves, as the business visas were only good for a maximum of three months before they had to be renewed or extended. Too many trips out of the country could lead to suspicions being raised at the airports and so it was all a bit cat-and-mouse.

A few years after the inception of the company, racial undertones in the country once more came to the fore and the country again erupted. The Asian economic crises of the late nineties had a terrible effect on Indonesia, and once again ethnic Chinese were blamed in some quarters. Riots, demonstrations and racially motivated attacks took place throughout Indonesia, and within Jakarta particularly. Although the number of fatalities was much fewer than of those thirty-three years earlier, the consequences were just as far reaching. The incumbent President Soeharto was forced to step down after more than three decades of iron-fist rule and the value of the Indonesian rupiah collapsed by 85%. It was a time of worry and concern and for a while it looked as if Indonesia was on the brink of total anarchy and disintegration. However, things calmed down and the first totally free and independent elections were held and the country stabilized once more.

A few more years passed and finally the business started to pay better dividends. It was the start of the internet boom and people were becoming more aware of the necessities and advantages involved in learning English and so were keen to take courses and enrol with us. We began to get bigger and we took out two further franchises at more favourable rates and started to push the business forwards a bit.

This was, if I remember correctly, the dawn of the new millennium. I was by now employing Indonesian Business Managers to look after the mechanics of running the schools and expatriate Directors of Studies to run the academic side of things, while I took a step back and looked for more lucrative and less stressful ways of making a living.

I realized I needed to broaden both my horizons and my education if I was really to succeed in the private sector, and so I set about learning about the world of finance. I called on my old contacts and started networking, picking the brains of former colleagues, associates and friends of friends, while also taking courses in banking and investment. I learnt how to trade in futures and options, how to spot-trade without too much risk, and how to take advantage of the currency markets. This took time, about two to three years to really get on top of, but I could see this was where the future was at.

The best decision I made at this time, however, was to learn how to leverage low risk loans at favourable interest rates. Done correctly, an individual or company is given the means to obtain loans and advancements of cash that enable he or it to purchase companies and businesses without providing any upfront capital of their own. Basically put, the company they are purchasing is then saddled with the debts incurred from the takeover and not the individual or company making the purchase. This is perfectly legal but is subject to adherence to a host of rules and regulations. Again, these can be bypassed or at least relaxed through simply knowing the right people.

Back to Neil. In early 2003 we needed more teachers for our schools and so our BMs made the decision to advertise for some on the internet. This was usually a successful method of recruitment but things could still sometimes go wrong. As almost all of the candidates we received applications from in this manner were based in their home countries, we would have to invariably conduct interviews over the phone rather than face-to-face and occasionally we would end up getting things wrong.

Sometimes a candidate would be accepted and then would turn up in Jakarta as agreed but then, for one reason or another, turn out to be totally unsuited to life in Asia. The reasons for this were varied but usually contained some element or trace of immaturity. The teachers we employed were usually first-time teachers in their twenties or early thirties who fancied a year abroad and for whom the idea of living and working overseas for a while represented a challenge or an experience rather than a career choice. This could lead to problems such as them arriving and instantly becoming homesick, or failing to adapt to Indonesian culture and the people. The most common problem though, came from the young men we employed who got carried away with the pleasures Indonesia has to offer. I lost count of the number of guys who had their heads turned by the attention their white skin and 'westernness' provoked and then ended up getting into trouble with local girls or their families, or, more seriously, the local police and other authorities due to drunken mishaps.

It was for this reason that we preferred to recruit teachers we felt would be here for the long haul and ones who had at least an inkling of the country, its mores, and what was expected of them. Admittedly, though, it was hard to attract such candidates because they would be a little older and so probably more experienced and qualified and thus less likely to accept the salaries we were offering, which although good by Indonesian standards were a long way behind those advertised in international schools and the like.

Well, to cut a long story short, we received an application from Neil who, as far as I knew, was still living in Surabaya at the time. Although I didn't usually get directly involved in the recruitment process, in his application letter addressed to our BM he had written that he and I knew each other, and so the BM handed over his application to me. Thinking Neil was in Surabaya, I invited him over to Jakarta for a chat, and it was then he informed me he was actually in England at the moment but he could come over and meet me the following week.

So, a few days later and Neil and I sat opposite each other after a gap of seven years or so. He hadn't really changed much in the interceding years: he still had that slightly awkward air about him – a kind of sense that he could hold his own in any situation or conversation, but would rather be left alone if it was all the same, thanks very much.

We chatted amiably enough and I asked him why he was currently in England and what his future plans were. I was interested to know why he wanted to come and work for me now having been so keen to work for himself the past seven years. He was a bit evasive at first but then lightened up.

'Well,' he started, 'I just think it's time for me to settle down and start to build a career.'

'Why now?' I questioned. ' I mean, I don't want to say 'I told you so' but 'build a career' are the exact words I said to you back in Sidoarjo all those years ago.'

He was quiet for a minute then continued: 'Well, I think

Yossy and I have done well enough in our ventures, but it's hard. It's hard having to deal with immigration for visas every year and having to chase around looking for work all the time. I need something more permanent and stable now I'm no longer young.'

This last utterance was said with the finality of someone much more advanced in years and took me aback slightly.

'How old are you, by the way?' I asked.

'I'm 34 now.'

'Well', I countered, 'that's hardly old, is it?'

'No,' he said, 'but it's time to really get cracking and start providing for the future.'

'Hmmm,' I said. 'So, anyway, why are you living in England at the moment, and without Yossy?'

He then explained his reasoning behind his going to England and although I still got the feeling there was something, or some things, he was holding back, I think we both knew I was going to offer him the job and he was going to accept.

Actually, I needed a new Director of Studies for a new school opening as well as teachers for all the schools, but although I mentioned this to Neil we didn't really discuss the prospect of him becoming the DoS at that time. Again, I got the impression that he was a little bit backwards in coming forwards and I wanted to see if he would push himself for the position, but he didn't.

Anyway, we ended our meeting cordially enough and he then headed off to the airport to catch a plane back to Surabaya where he was spending a few days with his family before heading back to England.

I mulled the situation over in the next week or so and an idea began to form in my mind.

My other investments were beginning to pay small dividends and I was now ready to move things to the next level. Amongst my new business partners I had often heard it said that investment in property was a sure thing in terms of long-term growth. They argued that in contrast with even the safest of financial money market trading, the value of bricks and mortar structures hardly ever depreciated and in fact almost always rose. It therefore stood to reason that if I were able to leverage enough capital to get started, then property management and development would be the next logical step.

A word here regarding my 'new business partners': these were in fact a conglomerate of people I had known from my days in the military together with some friends of theirs. These were an amalgamation of people from various walks of life and a mix of cultural, ethnic and religious backgrounds. The Group, as they were loosely known as, was a highly motivated and financially astute collection of individuals who had interests, financial and otherwise, in any number of business markets and ventures across the archipelago. Gaining access to and acceptance by The Group was not an easy thing to achieve, and one had to have both financial clout and impeccable contacts in order to gain entry to their inner circle. Thanks to my security services background, I had the contacts, and now with the help of my loan systems, I was able to contribute financially too.

Neil came to Jakarta a month or so later and started work in the new EPLC school in Cikarang Mall. I pulled a bit of a fast one on him on his first day by welcoming him to the branch and then showing him directly to his office.

His face was a picture of bafflement. 'What's this?' He said. 'Why am I getting an office? I'm just a teacher, right?'

I just grinned.

'Nope. You're the new Director of Studies. Congratulations. Evie here is the Business Manager. She'll fill you in on the details. Good luck.'

And with that, I left them to it.

While Neil got on with the intricacies of being a DoS, I continued to build up my portfolio. Together with a kind of sub-committee consisting of some of The Group members, I started investing in property and getting involved in leveraged buyouts of existing businesses. Starting small, we took over a couple of restaurants in the Depok area of Jakarta and bought up empty lots of land in the Serpong principality. This land buying was with the long-term future in mind, because we knew this area would be developed intensely over the next decade or so and as a result we wanted to get in on the ground floor, so as to speak.

Business-wise I was learning. I was learning not just how and what to invest in, and how to find a bargain or a good deal, but also how to deal with people in the private sector. My years in my first career had taught me about discipline and how to follow it as well as instil it in others, as well as the value of having subordinates and outsiders alike if not exactly fear you, then at least wary of you and the power you yield. In business, I realized, while there were certain parallels, there were also some major differences too. For example, people in the private sector were greedier and more self-absorbed and less likely to do something they didn't want to do just because the boss was telling them to. Job fluidity in Indonesia is particularly commonplace with nobody tending to stay in any job very long. It is not uncommon for a well-educated professional to have three or four jobs within a five-year span, and this fluidity of movement is much greater amongst the semi and unskilled workforce. This meant a different approach to man-management from the one I had been used to was called for. No longer could I expect people to turn up to meetings on time, for example, or for something to be done just because I was requesting it. No, I had to find other ways to handle people and instil loyalty.

As I said, people are basically greedy and have loyalty only to themselves and, possibly, to their families, so I learnt that the way to get people onside was through their wallets. I resolved to pay good wages with decent perks to get the people I wanted in place in the first instance, and then lay down the law in order to keep them in line the best I could. I found that a stern face devoid of smiles or laughter was pretty much all I needed to display in the majority of cases, and this in fact led to me building up an aura of being a bit frightening and thus kept most people in line.

Some things, however, remained the same as in my previous world. My skills included being able to read people and being able to sniff out any weaknesses or deficits in character as well as strengths and plus points. This meant that, by and large, I recruited well and so was able to let my managers and their staff get on with the day-to-day running of the various businesses while I took a bit of a back seat and looked to increase the financial backing and security of my portfolio.

Working together with The Group wasn't ideal, and I would have much preferred to have been in a position back then to have gone alone, but it wasn't financially possible at the time, and anyway, I knew that the contacts and security The Group offered were an insurance for the future.

Meanwhile, Neil was settling into his role as the Director of Studies at EPLC in Cikarang and, I have to say, making a decent fist of things. That said, though, it would be hard not to being doing relatively well in what was basically a captive market. We had done our due diligence with regards to market research and marketing, and had secured a prime location and then set about on a top-notch advertising campaign. The students were rolling in and all it needed was someone to keep a lid on the quality of academic teaching, which Neil was doing a good job of, to be fair, and in no time at all the school was showing a working profit. This was despite the rather high rental and employment costs involved.

I didn't see that much of Neil in this time as he worked closely with Evie, the BM, who reported directly to me, but I would pop in from time to time to see how he was doing and just to keep him and everyone else on their toes a bit. Neil was, as ever, pleasant enough and hard working without ever really giving the impression of being awe-inspiring. He was what I used to describe as 'clever but not too clever' or perhaps even a bit of a 'mysterious boy'.

Evie, the Business Manager I had deigned to work with Neil, was in fact a distant relative of my wife's, and it was her remit to maintain student numbers, organize marketing and promotions, and deal with the financial side of matters with a number of staff working directly under her. I also requested her to keep a close eye on Neil and report back to me anything noteworthy at all. When she pressed me on what I would consider 'noteworthy', I explained that I was looking for information regarding not just his performance in the job but how he dealt with people, his communication skills, the friends and relationships he appeared to have or be forming, as well as other more off-beat aspects of his character and actions such as where he went for lunch, who he called on the phone during working hours, his internet browser history and how others viewed him. Evie agreed to do so without ever questioning me why I wanted such information. This was just as well, because by now a new plan was beginning to form in my mind.

I needed a face: someone I could put in overall charge of my fledging empire, as it were, and let get on with it, but it had to be the right person. It couldn't just be anyone I knew or even trusted. Whoever it was had to be exactly the right fit and tick all the boxes without exception. This person, whoever he or she were, would need to be approachable, industrious, well respected, diligent and, above all, smart but not too smart. In a word: Neil.

Now, why him you may wonder. Well, I had seen enough of

him at relatively close quarters to know that he was ambitious without being cut-throat, and intelligent without being a genius. I knew I could trust him because he was one of the good guys; he was honest and sensitive to others, and he could adapt to situations. I knew that after living in Indonesia as an expat for as long as he had, he had to have a certain determination about him and the potential to be of use and benefit to me.

In fact, the one consideration I did have to ponder was the very fact that he was not Indonesian. This could be both an advantage and a drawback. The positives of employing an expat in such a position included: he would bring a fresh perspective to the business; he would garner respect by virtue of being a 'westerner; he would act as an attraction in certain quarters and aspects of the business; and he would add a certain mystique to our businesses, too. Against all this I had to weigh up some drawbacks too. For a start, a *bule* could sometimes be taken advantage of due to naivety or be seen as an easy mark to tap up for money or a sob story. I didn't have many worries regarding Neil, though. I trusted him well enough, and according to Evie, he was doing just fine with man-management of staff and dealing with customers at EPLC.

No, the only real concerns I had regarding Neil related to his personal life.

I wasn't totally aware of what was going on between he and his wife, Yossy, but I felt something was up. He had informed me that Yossy was pregnant with their second child but according to my rudimentary grasp of mathematics, the months didn't add up and I didn't see how she could have conceived his child in the time span being talked about. That in itself was none of my business, but I had to be sure that he wouldn't let this interfere with the business. Of a slightly more pressing concern was the reports I was getting back from Evie that Neil could be a little bit of a flirt and perhaps a bit of a budding ladies man. According to my erstwhile Business Manager, Neil enjoyed a good chat with some of the female staff and the older female students. For example, we had a few Housewife Conversation Classes in the mornings and Neil taught these personally, and from the reports I was hearing Neil employed a 'cheeky chappie' persona in these lessons. Nothing necessarily wrong with that of course, and there were even possibilities to turn that into an advantage, but again, precautions and care would need to be taken.

The other consideration to bear in mind, of course, would be the immigration status and work permit situation. As EPLC was sponsoring him, he should not by rights work elsewhere, but as long as we did a bit of tap dancing and I called in a few favours, that too should be no problem.

I called on him bright and early one morning and directly I cut to the chase. 'Neil. How would you like to make some real money?'

'Doing what?'

'Working for me.'

Neil looked confused: 'I am working for you.'

He had me there. I grinned: 'I mean, really working for me. For real money.'

He looked interested so I outlined what I had in mind for him. When I had finished he looked at me some more.

'How about EPLC? Would I still work here, too?'

'Yes, at least in the beginning. It would be good for appearances if you were here in the school at least some of the time, but we both know that this place practically runs itself now you and Evie have got it up and going.'

We chatted a bit more and discussed how things would work and also his personal terms. I offered him a three-fold increase on what he was currently earning as well as a profit-sharing scheme that had the potential to make him rather a wealthy man in a few years if he worked hard and kept his nose clean.

'Keep my nose clean?' he played innocent. 'What do you mean?'

'Nothing, Neil. Not at the moment, anyway.'

I didn't say anything more; I didn't have to. He knew, and he knew I knew that he knew.

So, I started Neil of as General Manager of a small and rather dingy bar our consortium had bought in Kedoya in the south of Jakarta called Club Mexicanas. I told him that he would be working with my associate Yusuf who would be his right-hand man. Yusuf was an extremely large gentleman with a propensity for mindless violence if pushed too far, and extreme amiability if not. He would get on perfect with Neil, I surmised. I told Neil that as he was now technically a partner in the business it would be perfectly acceptable, indeed preferable perhaps, if he were to let on to others that he was indeed the full owner of the place. Neil looked a little confused at this point, but didn't question matters.

Neil worked closely with Yusuf, even though the big man was a chap of few words, and soon showed an aptitude for running the bar. It was a bit dark and gloomy there when we bought it and certainly not the sort of place I would frequent – either as a patron or even as an owner if I could help it – and so I was very happy to take a back seat and move onto frying bigger fish. I let Neil and Yusuf have their head there and make the changes they wanted to within reason, and by all accounts they did a good job in making the place a bit more presentable and appealing to a slightly higher class of customer.

The reports I was getting back on Neil from people at both EPLC and Club Mexicanas was that he was a considerate boss who was learning to be a bit stricter and a little less naïve. He was able to show a bit more steel over this time than he had before and this included moving people out in the two businesses if they were not performing up to scratch. I had worried a bit that he was too nice and that he wanted to be liked rather than respected, but over this period of a couple of years or so, he was happily proving me wrong.

The school was doing well, the club was doing well, I was doing well, The Group was doing well, and Neil was doing well. We were all doing well.

This period saw more investments undertaken and more loans procured and facilitated. We diversified into leasing and freeholds on apartment buildings, hotels, boutiques and further restaurants and clubs, and in doing so undertook more debts – on paper at least. It would have been easy and indeed a cliché to have Neil be responsible for signing the paperwork on such deals and therefore becoming responsible for loans and debts incurred, and indeed the thought did occur to me, but I resisted the temptation to do that. I didn't exactly need Neil as such, as I could have got any number of people in to carry out the role he was doing, but I had known him for some time now and I did feel a degree of affection for him, I guess. I knew that he was struggling with his home life, and I knew he was devoted to his little daughter, Tess, and so I chose to help him as long as he was capable of helping me. Besides, I reasoned, there was no shortage of other people I could put up as fall guys if all the business deals did indeed go south.

After a period of consolidation, I did very occasionally drop in at the club as I wanted to see the changes to the place and also see how Neil was doing. He seemed a little heavier in build when I clapped eyes on him for what must have been the first time in perhaps six months, but he also seemed a little bit more confident and relaxed. He was able to hold a conversation a bit better now, whereas previously, and notwithstanding his liking of the ladies, he had sometimes given me the impression he'd rather be stuck in a good book and not speak to anyone unless he totally had to. He showed me around the club and pointed out the bars and the karaoke parlours. He explained how they worked, that originally Yusuf had been the one to come up with the idea and that they were serious money-spinners. I was a little concerned when I saw these, to tell the truth, and took the time to take Yusuf aside and grill him a little.

Yusuf explained security was tight around the club and the girls were all well looked after and under no pressure to do anything they didn't want to do. I said that was all well and good, but I was more worried about Neil. I knew of his reputation for enjoying flirting with girls and told Yusuf I couldn't be having that kind of carry on in the club. He assured me that Neil was pretty clean in that area, and he never dabbled with the staff or any customers in that way and the only liaisons he did enjoy were very discreet and never interfered with business at all. Back to the karaoke parlours, and Yusuf explained that Neil never really went near them but they were successful in as much as they were places where businessmen could bring their clients for a piece of almost innocent fun with no risks. I just nodded.

As our/my portfolio grew, I gave Neil more to do and so he was even busier. He was now charged with looking after apartment rentals and leasing in various areas throughout the city as well as looking for other opportunities. He provisionally proposed getting involved in export of textiles but I felt that almost all export deals involve too much unpredictability and so opportunity for things to go wrong. I preferred to deal more within Indonesia as I am a creature of habit and I know Indonesians. I know the fears, interests, needs, desires and foibles, of us Indos, whether indigenous or otherwise, and so I decided to stick with what I knew and soldier on accordingly.

Taking a stake in the palm oil business was another possibility put to me by Neil, and again while I was impressed with his proposal and the way he was thinking outside of the box, I turned this down too, Now, why did I, by now a hard-nosed businessman, reject what could have been a rather lucrative deal? Well, as daft as it sounds, I did so on moral grounds. The palm oil business is responsible for the destruction of rainforests in both Indonesia and Malaysia at alarming rates and, while I am certainly no dyed-in-the-wool environmentalist, I do believe we should take a degree of care of the world around us, and certainly not look to profit from its destruction. I know that such a view is far from universal in these days of get-rich-quick, and may even be seen as slightly hypocritical coming from me bearing in mind some of the strokes I've pulled in my time, but there you go.

No, Neil was doing fine and I was quite happy with him until one unfortunate incident after he'd been in charge of the club for some time, and not totally unsurprisingly it had its origins in the karaoke parlours. Neil and Yusuf had explained to me that the girls there were little more than part of the scenery and were definitely not for sale. There were safeguards in place, supposedly, to ensure both their safety and that of customers, as well as the name and reputation of the club itself. On this particular night, however, these best-laid-plans all somehow went astray, and we were left with a potentially disastrous scenario.

It seems it all started when a group of perhaps four of five guys turned up at the club a little worse for wear and demanded entry. Now, ordinarily anyone in an inebriated state would be refused entrance and turned away, but on the night in question the door was being manned by a couple of newer doormen, and they were perhaps a little intimidated by the government civil service uniforms these guys were wearing, and so let them in when more experienced staff would have been braver and known better.

The gentlemen ordered drinks and then moved into the karaoke area of the club where they were confronted by Neil. According to Neil, he was perfectly polite and respectful in explaining that the rules of the club did not permit intoxicated customers onto the premises, and so he would have to insist the gentlemen undertook certain guarantees that they would act in an appropriate manner if they wished to stay. The civil servants evidently took Neil's words in good humour and assured him they would behave accordingly.

All went well for an hour or two, with the men ordering some food and drinks and enjoying the fairly innocuous company of the hostesses, when it seems things started to go wrong. One of the hostesses, a girl named Devi, left the room and complained to Neil that she was feeling uncomfortable in the presence of the men in the karaoke room. They were, she said, beginning to act offensively to her and the other girls by making lewd comments and suggestions as well as taking liberties in the form of groping and stroking them. Neil sent Yusuf and another guy, Endy, to talk to the men and to issue a final warning. Neil also told Devi that he would change her and any of the other girls in the room who didn't feel comfortable remaining there, but by all accounts Devi simply thanked Neil and decided to return to the karaoke room.

Well, what Neil should have done, of course, was to call time on this motley little crew and bounce them out of the club there and then, and his failure to do so led to matters escalating out of control.

Yusuf later filled me in on the details: Devi returned to room and the girls and the men enjoyed a few more drinks. About thirty minutes later a scream and a lot of shouting was heard coming from the room; Yusuf and two other security 'lads' rushed in the room to be greeted by the sight of Devi straddling the prostate overweight figure of one of the government workers and screaming like a banshee as she scratched his face and neck with her two-inch finger nails; the rest of the room was also in uproar as the guy's friends attempted to assist him while the other girls jumped on their backs and did everything they could in order to prevent them from doing so. It was a right mess.

Yusuf and his men were able to break up the fighting quickly enough, but ironing out the repercussions took a lot longer. I was forced to make one of my irregular appearances, and considering the hour it is fair to say I was not best pleased. After a lot of negotiating and arguing, we came to an arrangement that the gentlemen would not be presented with a bill for the evening's entertainment but nor would any of them be welcome in the club again for an extensive period of time. In addition, I ordered Yusuf to be more diligent in training and supervising his doormen and I informed Neil that Devi would have to go. Neil tried to defend her, but I made it clear that I held the two of them equally responsible for the night's events and either Devi could go on her own, or Neil could join her. Either way, Devi had to go.

I know Neil felt sorry for Devi, and I have the feeling that he personally made arrangements to help her out somehow, but I was not privy to the details and I didn't push for them.

By now we were well into 2007 and life was busy, eventful and, in the main, fun. I was still embroiled in negotiations with The Group, but I was becoming less dependent on them for backing my deals and ventures. I continued to learn, to study, to consider and to educate myself regarding matters financial and business and I continued to reap the benefits. On a personal level my own family was growing up, and although I had no intention of stepping back from work altogether, I did wonder if it was time to scale things down a little in terms of my personal involvement and so have the opportunity to enjoy more quality time with them.

Around the fall of that year, I undertook a longish sabbatical to Europe with my wife and our three sons, and took the opportunity to really have a look at some of the places I had promised myself I would one day return to. While the trip was not exactly a trip down memory lane, this time around I was at least able to see the different sides of places such as Paris, London, Berlin and even Moscow. We saw and visited places on the tourist trails and although I could sometimes feel and sense the ghosts of the past lurking in the shadows, all-in-all the trip was a cleansing and cathartic exercise, and I came back feeling revitalised, rejuvenated and ready to go again.

I did indeed take a slightly more relaxed outlook on life and on business in general following our sabbatical, and certainly started to get a little more enjoyment and sense of tranquillity from life than before. The investments and portfolios I was now entrusting other people to develop and nurture continued to pay dividends and I was able to devote more time to my family and leisure pursuits. Now, as I approached my late forties I found for the first time in life I was actually finding some kind of balance and fulfilment.

Neil moved around within The Group and broadened his horizons, too. He was still nominally in charge of the schools and he had to spend a certain number of hours in each of the three premises we had in Jakarta, but he'd come on a long way in a short time. The problem with Devi was never repeated and Neil was normally able to deal with situations and occurrences as they arose without usually having to involve me or call on the backing of The Group.

The one exception to this involved a rather naïve and gullible worker at the Mexicanas called Jack who let himself be taken advantage of by a woman who was old enough to know better. Neil did was what necessary to clear up the matter, however, and it all blew over in a matter of weeks thanks to contacts and backhanders in the appropriate places.

Neil himself was going through changes in his life at this time. He'd been struggling for some time at home, I knew, and although he'd tried to keep a lid on things in the main, it was obvious he was having difficulties. By this time I'd long given up asking him anything about Yossy, and I would keep any and all enquiries regarding his family perfunctory in the extreme and limited to Tess and the boy, William. I knew the two children were the glue that kept Neil going at times, and as much as I felt for him, there was nothing I could, or was prepared to, do.

Since getting back in touch with Neil and inviting him into EPLC, my contact with Yossy had been somewhat limited, and I had no real idea of how she was or what she was up to these days. All those years ago back in Sidoarjo I had earmarked her as the dominant force in their marriage, and although I sensed a change in their dynamics had since taken place, I wasn't aware of to exactly what extent. I did get the feeling, however, that things were going to come to a head sooner rather than later.

This inkling was to prove well founded in early 2008 when Neil came to me and announced he was getting married again!

Well, although I had been expecting something – some kind of announcement or life-shifting change – this was a bit beyond my expectations, to say the least. I mean, as far as I knew he was still living with Yossy and the kids.

We sat down and had a chat:

Well, this is a surprise', I started: 'When did all this happen?'

Neil explained he had met the young lady he intended marrying on a chat site, and seeing my raised eyebrows, he grinned slightly sheepishly before continuing: 'Yes, I know. But she was different, Pak' – All these years we had known each other and he still he insisted on dressing me as 'Pak' and not by my name.

'Different how?'

'I don't know. She just seems to "get" me. I know it sounds a bit waffly, but she just makes me feel safe.'

I just nodded: 'How about Yossy? I didn't even know you'd split up.'

He looked sad momentarily and then went on: 'Well, actually, she left about eighteen months ago, but funnily enough we get on better now than we have done for many years. I think she will probably get married again soon, too.'

Again I nodded. 'You mean to the boy's fath … ?' I stopped myself just in time and now it was Neil's turn to simply nod.

I told him again I was pleased for him, and when I met the young lady for the first time a week or two before the big day, I was taken aback by her presence and charisma. She seemed totally different to how I remembered Yossy as being – a total contrast in terms of character and personality. While Yossy was, I recalled, a bit of a livewire and a chatterbox and seemingly fully driven, Neil's bride-to-be was altogether more relaxed, naturally friendly and innately confident, and I could see the calming influence already at work on Neil.

Later, looking at the two of them together on their wedding day, I felt confident that finally Neil had found what he had been searching ever since I'd first known him.

I sensed he'd found himself.

Epilogue

Jakarta, March 2008

The ceremony is a simple one with fewer than two-dozen guests. It's performed in the Indonesian equivalent of a registry office at 11am on a weekday, and afterwards, as neither has asked for or been given a full day's leave from their job, they go their separate ways.

Before they part there is time for one brief kiss.

She holds him close and whispers once again: 'I will save you.'

And, again, he believes her.

Discover more books set in Indonesia

FICTION

Cigarette Girl by Ratih Kumala

Island of Demons by Nigel Barley

Island Secrets by Alwin Blum

Rogue Raider by Nigel Barley

Shaman of Bali by John Greet

Snow over Surabaya by Nigel Barley

NONFICTION

Bali Raw by Malcolm Scott

Bali Undercover by Malcolm Scott

In the Footsteps of Stamford Raffles by Nigel Barley

Jakarta Undercover I & II by Moammar Emka

Olivia & Sophia by Rosie Milne

Raffles and the British Invasion of Java by Tim Hannigan

Toraja by Nigel Barley

You'll Die in Singapore by Charles McCormac